凱信企管

用對的方法充實自己，
讓人生變得更美好！

凱信企管

用對的方法充實自己，
讓人生變得更美好！

凱信企管

用對的方法充實自己，
讓人生變得更美好！

凱信企管

用對的方法充實自己，
讓人生變得更美好！

世界好好玩

旅遊英語帶著走

User's guide 使用說明

出國旅行好好用，在家學習也容易的旅遊英語書，
這一本就夠！

11 大主題、140 個情境，常見旅遊實境全收錄

① 從搭機，旅遊中的吃喝玩樂，到購物、入住飯店
以及各種突發狀況，通通以實境對話方式呈現，
對方可能說什麼、你該怎麼回話，都
有相對應的情境讓你放心開口好
好說，溝通無障礙。

📖 實境對話

A: Good day, sir. Do you want to eat here or take away?
日安，先生。你要外帶還是內用？

B: We want to eat here, please. We need a table for three.
我們要在這裡用餐，麻煩給我們三個人的位置。

A: Sorry, sir. It's full now. Can you wait or do you want to take away?
抱歉，今天客滿，你們要稍等一下，或者要外帶呢？

1400句好用句型＋1400組關鍵詞彙，讓你聽懂／口說能更多

② 依不同情境，特別增加你可能必需要聽懂或是臨
時要用的一句話，以及旅遊實用必備的單字及片
語，不論碰到緊
急時刻都能隨找
隨用、自由替換
關鍵字，快速化
險為夷，旅遊更
容易也更安心。

👍 你可以聽懂／口說更多

01. 我只是隨便看看。
I am just browsing around.

02. 請問這件衣服還有別的顏色嗎？
Does this shirt come in of...

03. 尺寸有哪幾種呢？
What are the sizes?

04. 請問女化妝室在哪裡？
Where is the ladies' room...

05. 請幫我包裝成禮物。
Please wrap it as a gift.

06. 我要最小號。
I want a XS.

...y are new arrivals.

🔑 關鍵單字／片語

01. fitting room 試衣...
02. size 尺寸
03. color 顏色
04. try on 試穿
05. wrap 包裝
06. attach a ribbon 綁緞...
07. browse around 隨便...
08. men's room 男...
09. ladies' room
10. new arrival

✈ 140個必備的旅遊情報，同步充實旅遊相關資訊

③ 140個必備的旅遊情報，帶你熟悉旅遊相關資訊及文化訊息，確保旅遊能更省事安全又盡興，也不怕出國踩雷或出遊鬧笑話！

13 用餐禮儀

TRACK 063

西餐禮儀當中，餐巾的用法是必須放在腿上，打開代表要用餐，放在餐盤右邊表示已用完餐。餐具從離自己餐盤最遠的開始用。另外，我們以碗就口的習慣對他們來說反而是不禮貌的表現。為了不鬧笑話，旅遊之前務必先了解清楚。

06 電話訂票

TRACK 106

電話預訂和購票時，要問好時間和場次。可以在網路上先看好座位表，再打電話給票務人員。除了事先匯款的選擇，就是提供信用卡資料扣款。票務人員有時候可以提供一些訊息。讓你可以選擇好位子和比較少人、位置選擇多的場次。

✈ 收錄情境對話中英雙語速MP3，耳聽口說齊訓練

④ 英語部分特別以慢一遍及正常語速一遍的方式錄音，隨時想學習都可以利用音檔，同步訓練道地口說能力及敏銳的英語聽力。

13 要求送貨

TRACK 078

通常買大型的家具或者不能夠在現場……
可以視店家有無提供送貨服務來決定……
送貨的詳情，來決定什麼時間送貨……
訊息和窗下店家付給的收據和號碼……
和抱歉送貨的確切時間，會比較方便……

📖 實境對話

A: I bought furniture in your store today. Can you tell me when I can have it delivered?
我今天在你們店裡買了家具，請告訴我什麼時候可以送貨？

B: The delivery is from 2 p.m. to 6 p.m., Monday to Friday.
送貨時間從禮拜一到禮拜五的下午兩點到六點。

A: May I have it deliver on Tuesday afternoon?
請問我的貨可以在禮拜二下午送到嗎？

B: Yes. May I have your address, please?
可以。請給我你的住址。

A: Yes, here is my address. Is there a delivery charge?
好的，這裡是我的住址。運送費用要多少錢？

B: No. The delivery is free if you purchase more than 3,000 dollars.
不用錢。如果你買超過三千塊錢，是免費。

A: Shall I give you my telephone number?
我要給你我的電話號碼嗎？

B: Yes, please. You can write it here.
好的。你可以寫在這裡。

全書音檔雲端連結

因各家手機系統不同，若無法直接掃描，仍可以至以下電腦雲端連結下載收聽。(https://tinyurl. com/mrt9s56m)

Preface
作者序

　　「行萬里路勝讀萬卷書」，旅遊不僅能增廣見聞，還能讓身心放鬆，同時在愉快的行程裡，培養國際視野，真可說是一舉數得。

　　和跟團被限制的行程相比，自助出遊的人口比例愈來愈多了，不論是近處的東南亞、東北亞日韓國家，甚至連遠一點的美國、歐洲，自由行的更是大有人在，除了是網路的旅遊資訊愈來愈發達之外，旅遊專用語言書的出版品，也更是推波助瀾了一把；而其中，「英語」是最主要也最共通的溝通語言了，只要英語能通，出門就安心，世界就真的任你行了。

　　以往，因擔心語言和文化的差異，怕旅遊時會遇到一些困難，像是到餐廳點餐，想開口詢問菜色卻一句話也想不起來；或到服飾店血拼，看到喜歡的衣服卻不敢開口問尺碼；又或是旅行途中，遇到緊急狀況想要求助時，不知道如何用語言表達……現在一點都不用怕，只要能看懂ABC，再帶著這一本旅遊英語書，不論想去世界各地，都能溝通。

這一本書由於體積尺寸小，最適合讀者隨身攜帶。而且，全書共收錄140個旅遊情境會話和必備資訊，從機場出發到外國當地的食衣住行，所有旅行時可能遇到的問題和大小事，都以實境的對話模式設計，讓讀者可以身歷其境的學習或直接翻開對照使用，更生動有趣，也更容易。另外，每個主題都有收錄「你可以聽懂／口說更多」和「關鍵單字／片語」單元，幫助你在重要時刻用一句話或是一個詞彙，即能表達想法，應對不再驚慌失措；平時在家自學容易，帶出門使用更便利！

　　隨著國門大開，出國旅遊的心情亦更顯興奮，也更值得珍惜。你，準備好了嗎？就讓這一本《世界好好玩，旅遊英語帶著走》帶你壯膽出遊，不論一人自助或三五好友，訂了機票就出發吧！Let's go！

CONTENTS 目錄

➤ Chapter 04 飯店住宿篇

➤ Chapter 05 享受美食篇

➤ Chapter 06 逛街購物篇

✈ Chapter 07 休閒娛樂篇

✈ Chapter 08 打電話篇

✈ Chapter 09 銀行金融篇

✈ Chapter 10 郵務篇

✈ Chapter 11 緊急狀況篇

Chapter

01

搭飛機篇

Chapter 01 音檔雲端連結

因各家手機系統不同，若無法直接掃描，
仍可以至以下電腦雲端連結下載收聽。
（https://tinyurl.com/2b4yr7su）

01 | 買機票

除了找固定旅行社購買機票之外，大部分的遊客也經常透過網路訂購機票，但提醒大家除了比價之外，也要注意應以知名度較高且評價較佳的商家為優先選擇，同時要注意買到的機票使用期限還有多久，以及退換票的規定，才不會發生購票糾紛，壞了出遊興致。

實境對話

A: I want to buy a round-trip ticket from Taipei to LA
我想要買一張台北到洛杉磯的來回機票。.

B: OK. Economy class?
好的，經濟艙嗎？

A: No. I'd like a business class ticket.
不，請給我商務艙的票。

B: No problem, sir. Would you please tell me when you're going to leave?
沒問題。請問您預定的出發日是哪一天？

A: I plan to leave on April sixth.
四月六日。

B: OK. And when are you going to return?
好的，那回程的時間大約是什麼時候？

A: Around May tenth.
五月十日左右！

B: All right. I'll let you know your reservation number in a minute.
好的。我稍後告訴您您的訂位代號。

B: Here, your reservation number is BL8852.
您的訂位代號是 BL8852。

👆你可以聽懂／口說更多

01. 起飛前三天還需要再重新確認機位嗎？
Do I need to reconfirm my flight three days before departure?

02. 如果能訂好機票的話，我就回家。
I will go home if I can book my air ticket.

03. 你如果提前幾個星期買機票會更便宜。
It is cheaper if you buy the ticket a few weeks in advance.

04. 學生買機票可以享受八折優惠。
Students can get a 20% discount on plane tickets.

05. 經濟艙票價要便宜得多。
An economy class air ticket costs much less.

06. 千萬不要拖到最後關頭才預訂機票。
Never wait until the last minute to try to reserve airline tickets.

07. 你買機票了嗎？
Have you bought the tickets yet?

08. 我想預訂一張下星期四去紐約的機票。
I want to book a plane ticket to New York for next Thursday.

09. 我必須在旅行社買機票嗎？
Do I have to buy air tickets at a travel agency?

10. 現在似乎非常難訂到特價機票。
It seems very difficult to book a budget fare now.

✍ 關鍵單字／片語

01. **round-trip ticket**	來回票	
02. **economy class**	經濟艙	
03. **business class**	商務艙	
04. **first class**	頭等艙	
05. **make a reservation**	預訂	
06. **travel agency**	旅行社	
07. **flight**	班機	
08. **departure**	出發	
09. **in advance**	提前、預先	
10. **airline / airlines**	航線／航空公司	

02 | 前往機場

大部分先進國家前往機場的交通方式都很多元，例如：捷運、電車、機場接駁車，或自行開車等，都相當方便。但要注意航空公司所在的航廈，以免在不同航廈之間疲於奔命。如果要租車的話，也別忘了事先向租車公司說清楚時間及接送地點，才不會錯過登機時間喔！

🔊 實境對話

A: Hello. This is National Car Rental. How may I help you?
全國租車公司您好。我可以幫您的忙嗎？

B: I need to rent a car with a driver to the airport.
我需要一台附司機的車子前往機場。

A: When do you need it? And would you please give me your "flight number"?
好的，請問您何時需要？還有，請給我您的航班編號。

B: I need it tomorrow morning at 8:30, and my flight number is BR0068.
我明天早上八點半要，航班編號是 BR0068。

A: You're taking EVA airlines, and that should be at terminal 2.
您搭的是長榮航空，那是在第二航廈。

B: That's right.
是的。

A: Where do you want us to pick you up?
請問要到哪裡接您呢？

B: No. 67, Thatcher Avenue.
柴契爾大道 67 號。

✋ 你可以聽懂／口說更多

01. 開車去機場幾分鐘就到了。
It's only a few minutes' drive to the airport.

02. 可不可以請您告訴我去機場的路怎麼走？
Could you show me the way to the airport?

03. 請帶我去機場，謝謝！
Please take me to the airport. Thanks!

04. 到機場的計程車費多少錢？
How much is the taxi fare to the airport?

05. 您知道如何去機場嗎？
Do you know how to get to the airport?

06. 您想去哪一個機場呢？
Which airport do you want to go?

07. 您能開車送我去機場嗎？
Could you drive me to the airport?

08. 我需要輛計程車去機場。
I need a taxi to the airport.

09. 我們最好早點去機場。
We'd better go to the airport earlier.

10. 不好意思，能不能載我到機場？
Excuse me. Could you take me to the airport?

✍ 關鍵單字／片語

01. **airport**	機場
02. **rent a car**	租車
03. **flight number**	航班編號
04. **terminal**	航廈
05. **pick up**	接送
06. **avenue**	大道
07. **on time**	準時
08. **a few**	一點點
09. **How much...?**	多少……？
10. **taxi fare**	計程車費

03 | 劃位

透過電腦至航空公司或訂票網站完成網路報到／線上劃位的動作，已相當普遍。旅客亦可於班機起飛前2-3小時至受理臨櫃報到及劃位，最遲應於起飛前45-60分鐘（各航空公司規定不同）前完成報到手續及劃位手續。

實境對話

A: May I have my boarding pass now?
我現在可不可以辦理我的登機證？

B: OK, please give me your passport and ticket.
好的，請給我您的護照和機票。

A: I want a window seat, closer to the front.
我想要坐靠窗、前面一點的位置。

B: OK, let me check. How many pieces of luggage do you have?
好，我查詢一下。請問您有幾件行李呢？

A: Only these three.
嗯，就這三件。

B: OK, here is your boarding pass; your boarding gate is C51. The boarding time is nine thirty, and your seat number is 17D. Please check to see whether your name is right, if it's correct, then you are all set.
好的，這是您的登機證，您的登機門是 C51，登機時間是九點半，座位號碼是 17D，請確認您的姓名是否正確，正確無誤的話手續就完成了。

A: Yes, that's right. Thank you!
沒有錯，謝謝！

👆 你可以聽懂／口說更多

01. 請問西北航空的登記櫃檯在哪裡？
Where is the Northwest Air check-in counter?

02. 請問直飛高雄的班機可以辦理登記了嗎？
May I check in for the direct flight to Kaohsiung now?

03. 我想更改我的飛機班次。
I want to change my flight.

04. 這班飛機是全面禁菸的嗎？
Is this a non-smoking flight?

05. 你的行李超重了，必須要付超重的費用。
Your luggage is overweight, you will be charged for overloading.

06. 超重的費用是多少？
How much do I have to pay for overloading?

07. 如果你有易碎物品請在這裡簽名。
If you have anything fragile, please sign here.

08. 請問我要另外付機場稅嗎？
Do I have to pay airport tax separately?

09. 我的手續已經辦好了嗎？
Am I done with all the procedures?

10. 請問這班飛機準時起飛嗎？
Is this plane going to take off on time?

✏️ 關鍵單字／片語

01. **check-in counter**	登記櫃檯
02. **airport tax**	機場稅
03. **window seat**	靠窗座位
04. **aisle seat**	靠走道座位
05. **smoking area**	吸菸區
06. **non-smoking flight**	禁煙班機
07. **departure lobby**	出境大廳
08. **boarding pass**	登機證
09. **passport**	護照
10. **permit**	允許

04 | 行李托運

搭飛機前往不同國家時，最好先確認每位乘客的行李托運重量上限。因為多數國家都有托運行李以及隨身行李的重量與體積限制，一旦超過上限，就會要求旅客另外支付昂貴的超重費用，甚至可能因為單件行李超重太多而被拒絕托運喔。

實境對話

A: Do you have any luggage you'd like to check in?
請問你有行李要托運嗎？

B: Yes, I've got two items to check in.
有的，我要托運兩件行李。

A: Please put them here.
麻煩您直接放上來。

A: Oh. Your bags are overweight.
喔，你的行李超重了。

A: Each passenger can check in two items but not over 20 kilograms for each.
一位旅客可以托運二件行李，且每一件不能超過 20 公斤。

B: Really? OK. I'll come back later.
真的嗎？好吧，那我待會兒再過來。

B: Here. I've tried my best to unload some unnecessary stuff.
這裡。我已經盡量把不需要的東西拿掉了。

B: I have some precious souvenirs inside this one. Could you please take extra care of it?
這件行李裡面有些貴重的紀念品。可以請你們特別小心嗎？

A: Sure. I'll put a "fragile" sticker on it.
好的。我會在上面貼「易碎物品」的貼紙。

👆 你可以聽懂／口說更多

01. 我應該在哪個櫃檯辦理行李托運？
Which counter should I go to have my luggage checked in?

02. 能不能把這個包包也用行李托運？
Can I check this bag too?

03. 免費行李托運限重 20 公斤。
The free baggage allowance is 20 kilograms.

04. 請填寫行李托運單。
Please fill in the luggage consignment notes.

05. 您想把行李托運到哪裡？
Where do you want to send it?

06. 這個箱子不能作為行李托運。
This box can not be checked in.

07. 您有行李托運嗎？
Do you have luggage to check in?

08. 我要把這個手提箱托運到倫敦。
I will check in this suitcase to London.

09. 你們有什麼特殊物品要托運的嗎？
Do you have any special items to check in?

10. 對不起，你托運的行李超重 5 公斤。
Sorry, your checked in luggage is 5 kilos overweight.

✎ 關鍵單字／片語

01. **luggage / baggage**	行李
02. **overweight**	超重
03. **maximum**	最大量
04. **kilogram / kilo**	公斤
05. **try one's best**	盡某人最大之力
06. **unload**	卸下
07. **carryon**	可帶上飛機的小行李
08. **free baggage allowance**	免費行李托運量
09. **"fragile" sticker**	「易碎物品」的貼紙
10. **baggage identification tag**	行李鑑別標籤

05 | 班機延誤

就算在任何先進的國家，搭飛機都有可能碰到班機延誤。建議大家在出發前，可以先撥打電話至航空公司或上網查詢，確定您欲搭乘的航班是否準時起降。尤其當您中途有轉機的安排，更需事前確認，以免到了機場之後才發現班機延誤，而影響後續的行程。

實境對話

A: This is American Airlines. How can I help you?
這是美國航空。請問需要為您服務嗎？

B: I want to check if AA9683 is going to take off on schedule?
我想確認一下編號 AA9683 的飛機是否準時起飛？

A: Hold on a second. AA9683 will be delayed for an hour because the schedule has been changed.
請稍候。AA9683 因班機時間調整，會延遲一個小時起飛。

B: An hour delay? But I need to transfer to Dallas. Will that be OK?
延遲一個小時？可是我必須轉機到達拉斯，會不會有問題？

A: You'll arrive at LA a half hour late. You still have one and a half hours for transferring.
預定抵達洛杉磯的時間大約晚半小時。您大約還有一個半小時的時間轉機。

B: That shouldn't be any problem for me.
那我就放心了。

A: We're so sorry for the inconvenience.
造成您的不便我們非常抱歉。

👆你可以聽懂／口說更多

01. 抱歉，你的班機延誤了。
Sorry, your flight is delayed.

02. 這班機會延誤嗎？
Will the flight be delayed?

03. 班機將延誤多長時間？
How long will the flight delay?

04. 由於天氣惡劣，班機延誤了。
The flight was delayed due to the bad weather.

05. 因為班機延誤，我們恐怕不能準時趕到了。
I am afraid we cannot get there on time due to the flight delay.

06. 很遺憾向您報告 H125 次航班將延誤一小時。
I am sorry to report that flight H125 will be delayed for one hour.

07. 延誤似乎是無法避免的。
The delay seems to be unavoidable.

08. 我的班機延誤了。
My flight has been delayed.

09. 我搭乘的航班會延誤嗎？
Will the flight I take be delayed?

10. 是什麼導致了班機延誤？
What is delaying the flight?

✍ 關鍵單字／片語

01. **take off**	起飛
02. **on schedule**	按照預定時間
03. **delay**	延誤
04. **inconvenience**	不方便
05. **due to**	由於
06. **unavoidable**	不可避免的
07. **bad weather**	天候不佳
08. **hold on a second**	等一下
09. **arrive**	到達
10. **I'm afraid...**	恐怕……

06 | 詢問登機地點

國際機場的航廈通常非常大，登機閘門大都也有數十個之多。通常在出關經過安檢後會先看到各式大型免稅商店，可以逛逛打發時間。但在此要提醒首次在該機場出關的旅客，先行確定登機閘門的方位及距離，以免趕不上飛機起飛時間。

👍 實境對話

A: Excuse me, sir. I guess I'm lost.
先生，不好意思。我想我迷路了。

A: Would you please help me find out where my boarding gate is?
可以幫我看一下，我是在幾號登機門呢？

B: Let me see your boarding pass.
讓我看一下你的登機證。

A: Here it is.
在這裡。

B: You're taking American Airlines and it's at Gate No. 84.
你搭的是美國航空，登機閘門是 84 號。

A: How do I get there?
請問 84 號登機閘門怎麼走？

B: Turn left here and go straight. You'll see Gate No. 80 after the duty-free shops. It will be on your right-hand side.
從這裡左轉直走，經過免稅商店後就是 80 號登機閘門。在你的右手邊你就會看到 84 號登機閘門了。

A: Thanks a lot.
謝謝你。

👆 你可以聽懂／口說更多

01. 請問我怎麼從這裡到 9 號登機門？
How can I get to Gate No. 9 from here?

02. 我們的航班在 4 號門登機。
Our flight is boarding at Gate No. 4.

03. 不好意思，請問 12 號登機門怎麼走？
Excuse me. Can you direct me to Gate No. 12, please?

04. 請告訴我登機門號碼。
Tell me the gate number, please.

05. 您的班機從 7 號登機門起飛。
Your plane leaves from Gate No. 7.

06. 本班機現在在 18 號登機門準備登機。
The flight is now boarding at Gate No. 18.

07. 我的班機從哪個登機門起飛？
From which gate does my flight leave?

08. 可不可以請您告訴我怎樣找到 14 號登機門？
Could you tell me how I can get to Gate No. 14?

09. 去華盛頓的 17 號航班是哪個登機門？
Which boarding gate is flight 17 to Washington?

10. 不好意思，請問 6 號登機門在哪兒呢？
Excuse me. Which way is Gate No. 6?

✍ 關鍵單字／片語

01. **find out**	發現、找出	
02. **boarding gate**	登機門	
03. **turn left**	左轉	
04. **turn right**	右轉	
05. **duty-free shop / DFS**	免稅商店	
06. **left-hand side**	左手邊	
07. **right-hand side**	右手邊	
08. **go straight**	直直走	
09. **direct**	指路、指點	
10. Gate No.	……號登機門	

07 | 登機

好啦！是時間要登機了，相信你的心情是很愉快的，現在你只需要舒舒服服的坐在候機室，等待空服人員的指示就能上飛機，這個時候你可以打個電話或去廁所，甚至做個小體操，保持最佳狀態來享受這段空中之旅吧！

🔊 實境對話

A: Is this the E17 boarding gate?
請問 E17 的登機門是這裡嗎？

B: Yes, are you holding a business or economy class ticket?
是的，請問您是商務艙還是經濟艙呢？

A: Economy.
經濟艙。

B: Then please wait for a moment. We are boarding the business class right now.
那麼請您稍後一會兒，現在是由商務艙開始登機。

A: Excuse me, may I know when we can start boarding?
不好意思，請問一下我們什麼時候可以開始登機。

B: Sorry, due to the bad weather, all planes need to wait for the tower's signal to take off.
真抱歉，因為天候不佳，所有的飛機都必須等待塔台的指示才能起飛。

A: For how long do we have to wait?
那我們必須等多久？

B: Sorry, we are not sure.
抱歉，我們也不確定。

✋ 你可以聽懂╱口說更多

01. 我要去 20 號登機門，請問該怎麼走呢？
I want to go to Gate No. 20. How do I get there?

02. 我必須搭乘機場巴士才能到達 15 號登機門嗎？
Do I have to take airport shuttle bus to Gate No. 15?

03. 我們什麼時候開始登機？
When do we start boarding?

04. 現在請經濟艙的旅客準備登機，謝謝！
Will the passengers in economy class start boarding.

05. 請準備好你的登機證，謝謝。
Please have your boarding pass in hand. Thank you.

06. 這班飛機準時起飛嗎？
Is this plane going to take off on time?

07. 該登機了。
It's time to board the plane.

08. 10 號登機門的大英航空班機延遲 30 分鐘起飛。
Take off for the British Airways flight at Gate No. 10 will be delayed by 30 minutes.

09. 我們將會被耽擱多久呢？
How long will we be delayed?

10. 再不起飛的話，我會趕不上轉機的時間，請問我該怎麼辦？
If we don't take off soon, I will not be able to catch my next plane. What should I do?

✍ 關鍵單字╱片語

01. **flight schedule board**	班次顯示板
02. **flight schedule monitor**	班次顯示螢幕
03. **shuttle bus**	機場（裡面的）接駁車
04. **heavy fog**	濃霧
05. **typhoon**	颱風
06. **torrential rain**	豪雨
07. **wait a moment**	等一下
08. **tower**	塔台
09. **passenger**	旅客
10. **line up / queue up**	排隊

08 | 過境

TRACK
008

當你所搭乘的飛機不是「直飛班機」的時候，就會在途中某些地方或城市降落暫時停留，做補充油料、更換機組人員的動作，而機上乘客也必須一起在當地短暫停留，這樣情況叫做「過境」，你不必換機，也不用再辦登記手續，你將會有一些時間在當地機場，喝杯咖啡、稍作休息等候廣播再上路吧！而如果你搭的是「直達班機」，就不會在途中作任何停留，直接前往目的地。

實境對話

A: How long do I have to wait for my next flight?
過境需要待上多久的時間？

B: About two and a half hours.
需要兩個半鐘頭。

A: Could I browse around since we are waiting for so long?
既然要待上這麼久，我可以隨處逛逛嗎？

B: Of course.
當然可以。

A: Could you tell me where I can dine or shop?
能夠告訴我這裡有什麼飲食或購物的地方嗎？

B: Sure, I can get an airport map for you.
沒問題，我可以拿一份當地機場的地圖給您。

A: When do I have to come back the latest?
我最晚什麼時候要回來呢？

B: You have to be back for boarding 40 minutes before take off.
您必須在出發前 40 分鐘準備登機。

👆 你可以聽懂／口說更多

01. 請問過境室在哪裡？
Where is the transit lounge?

02. 我們要在這裡停留多久？
How long are we staying here?

03. 什麼時候登機呢？
When do we start boarding?

04. 請問哪裡有當地機場的地圖？
Where can I get a local airport map?

05. 我得攜帶所有的隨身行李嗎？
Do I have to carry all my hand luggage?

06. 我的過境卡掉了，怎麼辦？
I lost my transit pass. What should I do?

07. 你們可以休息兩小時。
You can take a 2-hour break.

08. 我們去吃點東西吧！
Let's have something to eat.

09. 要不要去免稅商店逛逛？
How about go shopping at the DFS?

10. 是時候該回去了。
It's about time to go back.

✎ 關鍵單字／片語

01. **direct flight**	直飛班機
02. **straight flight**	直達班機
03. **transit pass**	過境卡
04. **transit lounge**	過境室
05. **transit counter**	過境櫃檯
06. **destination**	目的地
07. **short stay**	短暫停留
08. **break**	休息
09. **transit passenger**	過境旅客
10. **It's about time to...**	是時候該……

09 | 轉機

當你的目的地無法直飛的時候,就必須要轉機了,而「轉機」顧名思義就是要轉搭其他的飛機,要在哪裡轉搭、要坐哪一架飛機、要辦什麼手續,可要問清楚喔!

實境對話

A: May I help you, sir?
先生,需要幫忙嗎?

B: I will be transferring in New York.
我將在紐約轉機。

B: What should I do?
請問我該怎麼做呢?

A: You will have to go to the transit counter.
您要到轉機櫃檯辦理報到。

B: Will I receive a new boarding pass?
我會領到新的登機證嗎?

A: Yes.
會的。

B: What should I do with my baggage?
請問我的行李會怎麼處理?

A: Please take your personal luggage off the plane and the other luggage will be transferred to your next plane.
您隨身的行李請帶下飛機,而其他的行李會轉送到你所搭的班機上。

B: Got it. Thank you.
知道了。謝謝。

👆 你可以聽懂／口說更多

01. 這裡是轉機櫃檯嗎？
Is this the transit counter?

02. 我該到哪個櫃檯？
Which counter should I go to?

03. 我要轉機到東京，該在哪裡搭乘接駁車呢？
I am transferring to Tokyo. Where can I take the shuttle bus?

04. 我要如何轉到洛杉磯呢？
How do I transfer to Los Angeles?

05. 我需要辦什麼手續呢？
What procedures do I have to go through?

06. 請問出發時間和登機門的號碼是多少？
What time are we taking off? And what is our boarding gate number?

07. 確定我的行李都轉送過來了嗎？
Are you sure that all my luggage has been transferred?

08. 轉機櫃檯在哪裡？
Where is the transit counter?

09. 我的行李該怎麼辦？
What should I do with my luggage?

10. 會有新的登機證嗎？
Will I get a new boarding pass?

✍ 關鍵單字／片語

01. **luggage tag**	行李標籤
02. **take-off time**	出發時間
03. **arrival time**	抵達時間
04. **baggage inspection**	行李檢查
05. **transit passengers**	轉機旅客
06. **transit counter**	轉機櫃檯
07. **procedure**	步驟、程序
08. **personal**	私人的
09. **transfer**	轉移
10. **go through**	經歷

10 | 動植物檢驗所

在報到劃位之前，如果你有攜帶當地食品，就必須先去「動植物檢驗所」檢查是否能攜帶出境，如果沒有辦理這項手續，不要說那些不合法的東西，就算是合法的，到了另一個國家被檢查到時，也是會被全數沒收的，那可真是賠了夫人又折兵！

實境對話

A: Do you have anything to declare?
你有什麼要申報的嗎？

B: I have brought some meat and vegetables; do I need to declare animal / plant quarantine?
我帶了一些肉和蔬菜，需要申報檢驗嗎？

A: Yes, please fill out this form, and put them on the scale.
是的，請填這張表格，並把東西放到磅秤上。

B: Will that be all?
這樣就可以了嗎？

A: Yes, I will give you a certificate.
是的，我會開證明給你。

A: When you reach your destination, you will have to take it to the animal / plant quarantine for inspection.
你到了目的地之後，也必須拿去當地機場的動植物檢驗所檢查。

B: OK, thank you.
好的，謝謝！

👆 你可以聽懂／口說更多

01. 我可以帶這些去嗎？
Could I bring these?

02. 這些東西是需要申報檢驗的。
You need these items to be declared for quarantine inspection.

03. 如果有攜帶蔬菜，必須清洗乾淨，根也必須切掉；肉類的話，必須是熟食。
If you brought vegetables, they have to be washed and the roots have to be cut off; Meat has to be cooked.

04. 這些水果是禁止攜帶進入的。
Bringing these fruits into the country is prohibited.

05. 請問去日本有哪些東西是禁止攜帶進入的？
What items are prohibited to bring to Japan?

06. 請問冷凍食品、罐頭需要檢驗嗎？
Do frozen food and canned food need to be inspected?

07. 這樣手續就完成了嗎？
Have I finished all the procedures?

08. 很抱歉，這些要沒收。
I am sorry, they have to be confiscated.

09. 你有什麼需要申報的嗎？
Do you have anything to declare?

10. 不，我沒有什麼要申報的。
No, I have nothing to declare.

✎ 關鍵單字／片語

01. **animal / plant quarantine center**	動植物檢驗所
02. **declaration of quarantine inspection**	申報檢驗
03. **fresh food**	生鮮食品
04. **cooked food**	熟食
05. **frozen food**	冷凍食品
06. **canned food**	罐頭食品
07. **legal / illegal**	合法／不合法
08. **prohibit**	禁止
09. **declare**	申報
10. **confiscate**	沒收、充公

11│免稅商店

當你辦完劃位手續到登機前的剩餘時間，以及當你回國時有多餘的外幣，建議你可以到機場裡的「免稅商店」去走一走，買些自己要的商品或是買些送人的禮物吧！

實境對話

A: How much is this Lancôme toner?
請問這瓶蘭蔻的化妝水多少錢？

B: Eight hundred each.
一瓶 800 元

A: Please give me three, thank you.
那請給我三瓶，謝謝！

B: Would you like me to wrap it up?
你要我把它包裝起來嗎？

A: Yeah, that would be cool.
好啊，那太棒了。

B: Okay, the total is 2400, thank you!
好的，一共 2400 元，謝謝！

A: Can I pay in NT dollars?
我可以用台幣付嗎？

B: Sure, and we also accept credit cards.
當然，我們也接受信用卡。

A: Okay, then I'll give you NT$1200 and pay the rest by credit card.
好，那我會給你 1200 元台幣，剩下的刷卡。

B: Thank you. Have a nice day.
謝謝，祝你有個愉快的一天。

👆 你可以聽懂／口說更多

01. 請問這兩種牌子的香菸，價錢一樣嗎？
   Are these two brands of cigarette the same price?

02. 我買三瓶這種酒有什麼贈品呢？
   Will there be any free gifts if I buy three bottles of this wine?

03. 請問我可以買多少免稅商品？
   How many duty-free goods can I buy?

04. 請問我是先在這裡結帳，再到裡面領取貨品嗎？
   Excuse me, do I pay here first and then get the goods inside?

05. 我只有 20 美元，其餘不夠的我可以刷卡或付台幣嗎？
   I have only 20 US dollars, could I pay the rest by credit card or NT dollars?

06. 你要怎麼付錢？
   How would you like to pay?

07. 我要付現。
   I would like to pay in cash.

08. 我要刷卡。
   I'm going to pay by credit card.

09. 你們接受信用卡嗎？
   Do you accept credit card?

10. 這真划算。
   It's a real bargain.

✎ 關鍵單字／片語

01. **duty-free goods**	免稅商品
02. **free coupon**	免費優惠券／折價券
03. **traveler's check**	旅行支票
04. **liquor / alcohol**	酒類、酒精
05. **cigarette**	香煙
06. **perfume / fragrance**	香水
07. **jewelry**	珠寶
08. **cosmetics**	化妝品
09. **pay in cash**	付現
10. **credit card**	信用卡

12│入境

下了飛機之後，第一個會碰到的就是入境檢查，通常你只要跟著標示走，就可以順利的完成這項手續。但在國外，你要記得自己的身分是「外國人」，當你在排隊時，別忘了看清楚你排的隊伍是不是外國人排的，免得辛苦排到最後又要重來一次！

🔊 實境對話

A: What is your purpose here?
你來這裡的目的是什麼？

B: I am a tourist.
我來這裡觀光。

A: How long will you be staying?
你要在這裡停留多久呢？

B: About a week.
大概一個星期。

A: Where are you staying?
住哪裡呢？

B: I have booked a hotel.
我有預約飯店。

A: Which hotel?
哪一間飯店？

B: The First Hotel.
第一飯店。

A: Do you have any relatives here?
你在這裡有親友嗎？

B: My aunty lives here.
我的阿姨住在這裡。

👆 你可以聽懂／口說更多

01. 請問入境管理處在哪裡？
Where is the immigration?

02. 請到非本國人的地方辦理。
Please line up in front of the foreign passport counter.

03. 請拿出你的護照和簽證以及入境申請表。
Please show me your passport, visa and disembarkation form.

04. 請給我一張申報單（入境申請表），好嗎？
Can you give me a disembarkation form, please?

05. 我和朋友一起跟團旅行。
My friends and I are here with the tour.

06. 我一個人自助旅行。
I am traveling by myself.

07. 你打算去哪些地方遊覽呢？
Where do you plan to visit?

08. 我想去一些美術館和科學館。
I want to go to some science museums and art museums.

09. 你一個人來嗎？
Are you here alone?

10. 你以前有來過歐洲嗎？
Have you been to Europe before?

✍ 關鍵單字／片語

01. **immigration**	入境管理處
02. **foreigner**	非本國人／外國人
03. **citizen**	本國人
04. **study abroad**	留學／遊學
05. **on a business trip**	出差
06. **business visa**	商務簽證
07. **tourist visa**	觀光簽證
08. **student visa**	學生簽證
09. **valid date**	有效日期
10. **invalid**	無效

13 | 領取行李

入境審查完畢之後，就是循著指標到提領行李處的大轉盤等候您的行李，由於行李出來的順序是照頭等艙、商務艙、經濟艙，而經濟艙又照你報到劃位時間的先後，所以如果你是很早劃位的人，就要有耐心，稍等一會囉！另外，萬一你的行李遺失，要盡快通知地勤人員，辦理相關手續。

實境對話

A: My name is Lily Liu. I can't find my luggage.
我的名字叫劉麗麗，我找不到我的行李。

B: How many items of luggage do you have? Could you describe them?
你的行李有幾件？你可以形容一下嗎？

A: There are two, one is an orange hand-baggage, and the other one is a black plastic suitcase with wheels.
有二件，一個是橘色的手提袋，另外一個是黑色、大型塑膠製有輪子的行李箱。

B: What's inside?
裡面有什麼東西？

A: There are some clothes, shoes, personal items and gifts.
裡面有一些衣物、鞋、隨身用品、禮物。

B: Please give me your luggage tag, and fill out this form, I will go check for you right away. Please hold on for a minute.
麻煩您給我您的行李標籤，然後填一下這張表格，我立刻去調查，請稍等一會。

🖐 你可以聽懂／口說更多

01. 請問行李提領處在哪裡？
Excuse me, where is the baggage claim area?

02. 原本在 8 號領取，剛剛臨時更改為 2 號。
It was suppose to be collected at the NO. 8 carousel, but it was changed to NO. 2.

03. 你們會將找回的行李送到我的住處嗎？
Will you deliver my lost baggage to my place once you find it?

04. 我少了一件行李。
One piece of my baggage is missing.

05. 那是我的行李。
That's mine!

06. 行李手推車在哪裡？
Where is the trolley?

07. 我的行李破損的很嚴重，請問你們怎麼處理？
My baggage is seriously damaged, how are you going to deal with it?

08. 我要求行李損壞賠償！
I demand a compensation for my damaged luggage.

09. 我得自己回來領取嗎？
Do I have to come back and claim it myself?

10. 請儘快送回給我。
Please send it back to me as soon as possible.

✍ 關鍵單字／片語

01. **baggage claim area**		領取行李處
02. **baggage turntable indicator**		行李轉盤顯示器
03. **baggage service center**		行李服務處
04. **lost and found**		失物招領處
05. **baggage claim check**		隨身行李領取憑證
06. **trolley**		推車
07. **cart**		手推車
08. **damage compensation**		損害賠償
09. **damage**		損壞
10. **make up**		補償

14 | 海關、出關

當你領完行李，接著就是最後一道手續——出關，記得先準
備好護照和申報書。如果你沒有攜帶特別貴重、需要申報甚
至違法的東西，通常問個一兩句就 OK，但是如果你有需要
申報的東西，就要誠實、乖乖的申報，否則萬一被檢查到可
是會被沒收喔！

🖐 實境對話 —————————

A: Please take out your customs declaration form.
請拿出你的申報表。

A: What's inside this luggage?
這一個行李箱裡面裝的是什麼？

B: Some clothes and personal belongings.
一些衣服和私人用品。

B: And I've got some gifts for my friends.
還有買給朋友的一些禮物。

A: Do you have anything that needs to be declared?
你有東西需要申報嗎？

B: I've got a carton of cigarettes for myself. That
shouldn't need to be declared, should it?
我買了一條香菸，是自己要的，應該不用申報吧？

A: No. It's okay.
不用，那沒有問題。

B: May I leave now?
我可以走了嗎？

A: Yes, you may go now.
是的，你可以走了。

☝ 你可以聽懂／口說更多

01. 請你把行李箱打開。
Please open your baggage.

02. 這些是我的私人用品。
These are my personal items.

03. 你有帶超過一萬元的現金嗎？
Do you have over ten thousand dollars cash with you?

04. 你有帶價值超過兩萬元的東西嗎？
Do you have anything worth more than twenty thousand dollars with you?

05. 酒可以帶幾瓶呢？
How many bottles of wine can I bring?

06. 我必須付稅嗎？
Do I need to pay tax?

07. 你有帶違禁品嗎？
Do you have any contraband goods?

08. 你的健康狀況如何？
How is your health condition?

09. 你有帶什麼貴重物品嗎？
Do you have anything valuable with you?

10. 很抱歉，你不能把這些東西帶進本國，必須要沒收。
I am sorry, but you cannot bring these here. They have to be confiscated.

✎ 關鍵單字／片語

01. **Customs**	海關
02. **currency declaration form**	貨幣申報
03. **customs duties**	關稅
04. **customs inspection**	海關檢查
05. **agricultural products**	農產品
06. **health certificate**	健康證明
07. **tobacco**	菸、菸草
08. **local products**	土產
09. **contraband (goods)**	違禁品、走私貨
10. **smuggle**	走私

15｜機場稅

機場稅的完整名稱是飛機乘客離境稅，為各地機場或政府委託代收的旅客稅捐（例如：安檢稅、導航稅、機場稅、兵險等），通常隨著機票一併繳納。有些國家對於二十四小時之內入境又出境的旅客提供免收機場稅的優惠，但旅客於購票時要事先提出。

🗣 實境對話

A: Could you please tell me if this ticket includes airport tax?
可以請你告訴我這張票是否已付過機場稅了？

B: OK. Please show me your ticket.
好的，請讓我看一下你的機票。

B: According to the O on the ticket, you haven't paid for airport tax yet.
根據您票面上的○號顯示，您尚未付機場稅。

A: Really? Well...how much should I pay for it?
是嗎？那麼請問機場稅多少錢？

B: Ten US dollars.
10 美元。

A: I'm sorry. I don't have enough US dollars with me. Can I pay by NT dollars?
不好意思，我身上的美金不夠，可以付台幣嗎？

B: Sorry. We don't accept NT dollars. Please exchange currency at the counter over there, or we also accept credit cards.
抱歉，我們不收台幣。你可以到那邊的櫃檯兌換貨幣，或是我們也收信用卡。

你可以聽懂／口說更多

01. 我是不是在這裡繳機場稅？
Is this where I pay the airport tax?

02. 我是否要付機場稅？
Do I have to pay for the airport tax?

03. 這班機的機票是 831 元，含機場稅。
The price for that flight will be $831, including airport tax.

04. 請問我要另外付機場稅嗎？
Do I have to pay airport tax separately?

05. 辦理登機手續前你得先付機場稅。
You have to pay the airport tax before you check in.

06. 我們不用先去付機場稅嗎？
Don't we have to go pay the airport tax first?

07. 我需要交多少機場稅？
How much should I pay the airport tax?

08. 那包括機場稅了嗎？
Does that include airport tax?

09. 你們國家要交多少機場稅？
How much is the airport tax in your country?

10. 出入境的旅客必須繳納 15 美元的機場稅。
Passengers must pay the airport tax of 15 US dollars.

關鍵單字／片語

01. **airport tax**	機場稅
02. **sign**	簽名
03. **seperately**	個別地
04. **show me**	給我看
05. **include**	包含
06. **enough**	足夠
07. **country**	國家
08. **How much...?**	……多少錢？
09. **have to**	必須
10. **here it is**	在這裡

Chapter

02

飛機遨遊篇

Chapter 02 音檔雲端連結

因各家手機系統不同，若無法直接掃描，
仍可以至以下電腦雲端連結下載收聽。
（https://tinyurl.com/yj95dfny）

01 | 機艙內

終於，一連串的手續告一段落，現在你可以坐在屬於你的座位上享受空姐、空少完善的服務。儘管説出你的需求，這也是你的權益，只要你能正確地表達所需，相信受過良好訓練的空服員們可以讓你感到賓至如歸。另外，提醒您，上飛機之後請關掉您隨身的電子產品，直到廣播可以使用為止，以確保飛航安全！

📱 實境對話

A: Good morning! Thank you for flying with Japan Air, is there anything I can do for you?
早安！歡迎您搭乘日本航空，有什麼可以為您服務的嗎？

B: I want to change my seat, because my friend is also on this plane. May I change to a seat that's near him?
我想換座位，因為我有一位朋友也在這班飛機上，可以換到他附近嗎？

A: I am sorry, all the seats are full today, but I can ask for you, please wait.
不好意思，今天的機位都滿了，但是我可以幫您詢問一下，請您稍候。

B: Ok, please!
好，麻煩你。

A: I am sorry, I have checked, there isn't any vacant seat.
很抱歉，我查過了，真的沒有空位。

B: Ah, never mind then. Thank you.
呃……沒關係，謝謝你。

🎧 你可以聽懂／口說更多

01. 可以帶我到 17A 的座位嗎？
    Could you take me to seat 17A?

02. 對不起，你好像坐到我的位子了。
    I am sorry, I think you are in my seat.

03. 你可以幫我把行李放到置物箱嗎？
    Could you put my baggage into the luggage compartment?

04. 請給我一副耳機和毛毯。
    Please give me a pair of earphone and a blanket.

05. 我的耳機沒有聲音，請換新的給我。
    My earphone has no sound, please change a new pair for me.

06. 請問洗手間在哪裡？
    Excuse me, where is the lavatory?

07. 我想要一杯威士忌。
    I'd like a glass of Whisky.

08. 我現在不餓，可以晚一點再送餐給我嗎？
    I am not hungry now, could you bring me the meal later?

09. 可以給我一本免稅商品的目錄嗎？
    Can you give me the duty free catalog?

10. 可以給我撲克牌嗎？
    May I have poker cards?

✍ 關鍵單字／片語

01. **captain**	機長	
02. **pilot / co-pilot**	機師／副機師	
03. **steward / stewardess**	男空服員／女空服員	
04. **flight attendant**	空服員	
05. **oxygen mask**	氧氣罩	
06. **disposable bag**	嘔吐袋	
07. **emergency exit**	緊急出口	
08. **landing**	降落	
09. **turbulence**	亂流	
10. **instant noodle**	速食麵	

02 | 尋找座位

國際航線的飛機通常座位都有三、四百個之多。例如：波音
747 有三大排，左右兩大排分別有三個座位，中間那一大排
則有四個座位相連。座位號碼通常包含數字（排）和英文字
母（座位代號），座位代號為面對駕駛艙的左側按照字母順
序由 A 排到 J。

👆 實境對話

A: Excuse me. Where is my seat?
不好意思，請問我的座位在哪？

B: Let me check your boarding pass.
讓我看一下你的登機證。

B: OK. Your seat number is 34D.
好的。你的座位是 34D。

A: 34D? Is it on the 34th row?
34D？是第三十四排嗎？

B: Yes. Please go this way with the numbers on top
you'll see the 34th row.
是的，從這邊跟著上面的號碼一直往後走就可以看到三十四
排。

B: 34D is in the middle by the aisle.
34D 就在中間靠走道的位置。

A: I need to take some medicine before take off.
Could you please give me a cup of water?
我需要在起飛前吃藥。可以麻煩你幫我倒杯水嗎？

B: No problem. I'll bring a cup of water to your seat
right away.
沒問題。我馬上拿杯水到您的座位。

👆 你可以聽懂／口說更多

01. 可以帶我去找 16A 的座位嗎？我找不到在哪裡。
Would you please lead me to seat 16A? I can't find where it is.

02. 空中小姐會幫你找到你的座位。
The stewardess will help you find your seat.

03. 不好意思，請問可否幫我找找座位？
Excuse me. Can you show me my seat?

04. 這個座位號已經開始登機了嗎？
Has this seat number started boarding?

05. 恐怕這個不是我的座位。
I am afraid that it's not my seat.

06. 請等一下，我幫您查詢您的座位狀況。
Please hold on while I check your seat status.

07. 請您帶我們去找座位好嗎？
Could you show us to our seats?

08. 先生，您的座位號碼是多少？
What is your seat number, sir?

09. 我去為您找座位，您等一會好嗎？
Would you please wait a moment before I find your seat?

10. 我的座位號是 23A。
My seat is 23A.

✏️ 關鍵單字／片語

01. **seat**	座位
02. **check**	檢查
03. **row**	排
04. **in the middle**	在中間
05. **status**	狀況、狀態
06. **seat number**	座位號碼
07. **lead**	帶領
08. **go this way**	往這邊走
09. **by the aisle**	靠走道
10. **by window**	靠窗

03│換座位

如果有特殊的座位需求，可以於訂位時提出，以便事先安排。若登機後再提出，難免碰到其他旅客沒有意願交換，或班機客滿無法調整的狀況。例如：有二歲以下嬰兒隨行者，可以坐在可懸掛嬰兒籃的位置，除非繫上安全帶的警示燈亮起，否則都可以讓小朋友躺在嬰兒床內。

🗨 實境對話

A: Excuse me. Can I exchange my seat with you?
請問，我可以跟你換座位嗎？

B: Oh? What's wrong?
喔？怎麼了？

A: My wife's seat is next to you. She gets airsick frequently and hopes I can sit next to her.
我太太的座位在你旁邊。她經常會暈機，希望我可以陪她。

B: No problem.
沒問題。

A: Thank you very much for your kindness. You're such a nice person.
謝謝你。你人真好。

B: Don't mention it. Are you going on a honeymoon?
不用客氣。你們是去度蜜月嗎？

A: That's right. We just got married last week.
是的。我們上星期剛結婚。

B: Congratulations! Have a nice trip.
恭喜！祝你們旅途愉快！

👆 你可以聽懂／口說更多

01. 您介意我換座位嗎？
Do you mind if I change seats?

02. 我們換座位好不好？
Shall we change seats?

03. 請問我可以換座位嗎？
May I change my seat, please?

04. 恐怕您坐到我的位子了。
I am afraid that you are in my seat.

05. 你可以和我更換座位嗎？
Could you change seats with me?

06. 我有沒有可能跟你換座位？
Is there any way I could switch seats with you?

07. 我想換我的座位。
I'd like to change my seat.

08. 不好意思，不知您是否願意和我換座位？
Excuse me. I was wondering if you are willing to switch seats with me.

09. 你的座位在哪？
Where is you seat?

10. 我的座位是 34D，靠走道的位置。
It's 34D,an aisle seat.

✎ 關鍵單字／片語

01. **frequently**	經常
02. **kindness**	善心、好意
03. **mention**	提起
04. **go on a honeymoon**	度蜜月
05. **get married**	結婚
06. **congratulations**	恭喜
07. **switch**	換
08. **Shall we...?**	我們可以……？
09. **be willing to**	願意
10. **Would you mind...?**	你介意……？

04｜找盥洗室

幾乎所有飛機在每個艙段的前後都設有盥洗室。盥洗室面對
乘客座位的上方，會有燈號顯示是否有旅客正在使用。在飛
機上的盥洗室內也備有乳液提供旅客使用，建議大家在使用
盥洗室之後可以抹一些乳液，讓皮膚不會太乾燥。

實境對話

A: Excuse me. Could you please tell me where the lavatories are?
不好意思。請問盥洗室在哪兒？

B: They're right there in front. There are two on each side.
就在走道前方的左右手邊分別有二間。

A: All right. Thank you.
好，謝謝。

B: But the occupied lights are all on which means the lavatories are occupied at the moment.
不過現在燈號都亮著，表示盥洗室目前都在使用中。

A: I see. Are there any other lavatories?
我知道了。那……還有其他的盥洗室嗎？

B: Sure. There are two at the back. I'll go check if they're occupied.
有的，在後方也有二間。我先幫您過去看看有沒有人在使用。

A: OK. I hope this won't bother you too much.
好的，希望不會太麻煩你。

B: Not at all. Please just wait a second.
不會，請麻煩等一下。

👆 你可以聽懂／口說更多

01. 不好意思，請問盥洗室在哪裡？
Excuse me, where is the lavatory?

02. 請告訴我洗手間在哪裡好嗎？
Could you show me the way to the restroom?

03. 您可以去後方的盥洗室，目前都是空的。
You may take the lavatories at the back. They are all empty now.

04. 洗手間在那個門的後面。
The lavatory is behind that door.

05. 我在哪裡可以找到廁所？
Where can I find a lavatory?

06. 廁所現在沒有人在使用。
The lavatory is vacant now.

07. 請問洗手間在哪兒？
Where is the restroom, please?

08. 廁所裡沒有人吧？
Is the lavatory vacant?

09. 請問廁所是在那邊嗎？
Is the lavatory over there?

10. 對不起，請問洗手間在哪兒？
Excuse me, where is the restroom, please?

✎ 關鍵單字／片語

01. **right there**	就在那裡
02. **vacant**	無人使用
03. **occupied**	使用中
04. **bother**	打擾
05. **medication**	藥物
06. **restroom**	廁所
07. **lavatory**	廁所
08. **toilet**	廁所
09. **toilet paper**	衛生紙
10. **behind**	在後面

05 | 暈機

部分乘客在搭乘飛機時會有暈機的症狀,你可以先試著看遠一點的地方,讓視線不要一直固定在近距離的物品上。另外,搭飛機時還常常會感覺耳鳴或內耳疼痛,可以試著捏住鼻子,然後鼓起腮幫子感覺像是要把空氣往耳朵擠出來一樣,重複做幾次耳朵就會舒服一些。

🖐 實境對話

A: I don't feel well.
我有點不太舒服。

A: I feel dizzy.
我覺得頭很暈。

B: You can try to look out of the window. That will make you feel better.
您可以往窗外的地方看,或許會舒服一點。

A: Let me try that. But I still feel uncomfortable.
我試試。可是我還是覺得不太舒服。

B: Don't worry. It sometimes happens to some passengers.
很多旅客搭飛機都會有這種情形。您不要擔心。

A: May I have some medicine for airsickness?
可以給我一些暈機藥嗎?

B: Sure. Let me get some for you.
沒問題,我立刻去拿過來。

B: Here is your pill with a cup of water. Try to get some sleep after you take the medicine.
這是您的暈機藥和一杯水,吃了藥以後試著睡一下。

👆 你可以聽懂／口說更多

01. 我覺得有點暈機。
   I am feeling a bit airsick.

02. 你們有暈機藥嗎？
   Do you have any medicine for airsickness?

03. 我們有暈機藥，我去給您拿來。
   We have the medicine for airsickness. I'll go and get it for you.

04. 您暈機嗎？
   Do you get airsick?

05. 可以給我一些暈機藥嗎？
   May I have some medicine for airsickness?

06. 小姐，恐怕我有點暈機。
   Miss, I am afraid that I feel a bit airsick.

07. 請給我一些暈機藥。
   Please give me some airsick pills.

08. 讓我先把嘔吐袋準備好。
   Let me get the air sick bag ready.

09. 我覺得不舒服，我有一點暈機。
   I am not feeling well. I am a little airsick.

10. 在你前方的座位後面有一個暈機嘔吐袋。
   There is an air sick bag behind the seat in front of you.

✍ 關鍵單字／片語

01. **airsick pill**	暈機藥
02. **dizzy**	頭暈
03. **air sick bag**	嘔吐袋
04. **a bit**	有點
05. **try to**	試著
06. **uncomfortable**	不舒服
07. **a cup of**	一杯
08. **get some sleep**	睡一下
09. **a set**	一份、一組
10. **get ready**	準備好

Chapter

03

交通趴趴
走篇

Chapter 03 音檔雲端連結

因各家手機系統不同，若無法直接掃描，
仍可以至以下電腦雲端連結下載收聽。
（https://tinyurl.com/48k5tjbn）

01 | 問路

只要到了一個我們不熟悉的地方，問路是在所難免的事情，即使你是個認方向的高手，還是不要辛苦拿著地圖找路，只要開口問人，就能既快速又不費力的到達你想去的地方啦！建議您，在問路的時候帶著紙筆，可以寫下怎麼走，就不怕忘記，如果有解釋不清的狀況，還可以請對方畫出來，也是一個好方法喔！

實境對話

A: Excuse me, could you tell me how to get to the closest department store?
不好意思，你能告訴我怎麼去附近的百貨公司嗎？

B: Of course! Are you going to take the subway or walk there?
當然，你想搭乘地鐵或是走路去呢？

A: I will walk, and I can browse around at the same time. Could you tell me how to get there?
我走路好了，順便可以觀光，請你告訴我怎麼走。

B: Ok, turn left at this traffic light and then go straight down to a big television wall. There will be a forked road, take the right, walk past three traffic lights and you will see a big department store.
好，你在這個紅綠燈左轉，然後直走到有一面電視牆的地方，那裡是岔路，你走右邊，一直走過三個紅綠燈就會看到一間很大的百貨公司了。

A: You are very nice, thank you very much!
你真好，謝謝你！

👆 你可以聽懂／口說更多

01. 請問華爾街怎麼走呢？
How could I get to the Wall Street?

02. 路上有什麼醒目的標示嗎？
Is there any clear signs on the way?

03. 你可以幫我畫地圖嗎？
Can you draw a map for me?

04. 從這裡開始走要多久的時間呢？
How long will it take to get there from here?

05. 你如果順路的話，可以帶我一起去嗎？
Could you take me with you if we are going in the same direction?

06. 我迷路了，請告訴我這裡是什麼地方？
I am lost. Could you tell me where I am?

07. 可以告訴我去博物館最近的路嗎？
Could you tell me the nearest route to the museum?

08. 我是觀光客，所以對這裡一點也不熟。
I am a tourist. I am not familiar with here.

09. 我可以走路到中央公園嗎？
Could I walk to the central park?

10. 我要去中國城，是這個方向嗎？
I want to go to China Town, is this the way?

✍ 關鍵單字／片語

01. **exit / entrance**	出口／入口
02. **east / west**	東／西
03. **south / north**	南／北
04. **short cut**	捷徑
05. **landmark**	地標
06. **traffic lights**	紅綠燈
07. **zebra crossing**	斑馬線
08. **road / street**	路／街
09. **alley / boulevard**	巷／大道
10. **cross road**	十字路口

02 | 騎自行車

騎自行車對於暢行樂活主義的先進國家是一個非常夯的休閒
活動，尤其是在背包客盛行的歐美國家，也都非常流行騎自行
車。但是在規劃自行車之旅的同時，要先查清楚是不是只
能騎在自行車專用道上、捷運或地下鐵是否可以攜帶自行
車，以及其他相關規定。

實境對話

A: Do you know any place that I can take a sightseeing bicycle tour?
你知道有什麼地方可以騎腳踏車觀光嗎？

B: Yes. There's a park near the riverside.
有的。有一座公園在河岸附近。

A: How long does it take by bike?
請問騎自行車過去大概要多久？

B: It takes only 5 minutes to get there.
只要五分鐘就到了。

B: In the early morning, people in town like to go jogging or riding a bike there.
清晨時，附近的居民喜歡去那兒慢跑或騎自行車。

A: That sounds great.
聽起來很不賴。

B: By the way, the sunlight gets quite strong at midday. You might need to apply some sunscreen.
對了，中午時候陽光很強，你可能需要擦些防曬。

B: And wear your sunglasses as well.
還有戴著你的墨鏡。

✋ 你可以聽懂／口說更多

01. 你會騎自行車嗎？
Can you ride a bicycle?

02. 騎自行車去怎麼樣？
How about going there by bike?

03. 我們要騎自行車去那裡嗎？
Shall we go there by bike?

04. 騎自行車對我來說太難了。
It is too difficult for me to ride a bicycle.

05. 你喜歡騎自行車旅行嗎？
Do you like traveling by bike?

06. 這坡太陡了，騎自行車可上不去。
This slope is too steep to ride up on a bicycle.

07. 我們是步行去還是騎自行車去那裡呢？
Shall we walk there or ride a bike there?

08. 我和泰德要騎自行車出去玩。
Ted and I will go out for a bike ride.

09. 和開車比，騎自行車不會有環境問題。
Compared with driving, riding a bicycle has no environment problems.

10. 騎自行車去那兒恐怕會花很長時間。
I am afraid that it will take too much time there by bicycle.

✍ 關鍵單字／片語

01. **bicycle / bike**	腳踏車
02. **ride a bicycle / bike**	騎腳踏車
03. **riverside**	河邊、河畔
04. **bike / bicycle lane**	腳踏車道
05. **LOHAS**	樂活
06. **sun / sunlight**	太陽／陽光
07. **midday**	中午、正午
08. **as well**	也、同樣地
09. **apply some sunscreen**	擦防曬
10. **slope**	斜坡

03 | 搭電車

想要在預定時間內或是想用最快速的方式到達目的地，建議
您搭乘電車或是火車，都是最保險的。或許地下鐵路錯綜複
雜，但是只要弄清楚月台方向、轉車地點，相信這是最快速
的交通工具。還有，國外的乘車票券有很多種類，在使用方
法和價錢上也都不同，最好花個時間詢問一下，搞不好會為
你省下一筆不小的費用喔！

實境對話

A: Excuse me, how do I get to the Tokyo station?
不好意思，請問東京車站怎麼去呢？

B: Oh, you can take the Mountain Hand Line from
here.
喔，你可以搭山手線。

B: Get off at the third stop.
在第三站下車。

A: How much is the fare?
那請問車票是多少錢呢？

B: I am not sure.
這個我不清楚。

B: You will have to ask the information center.
你要去問服務台。

A: Where is the information center?
請問服務台在哪裡？

B: Go straight and turn left.
往前走，左轉就是了。

A: Thank you!
謝謝！

☝ 你可以聽懂／口說更多

01. 請問離這裡最近的地下鐵怎麼走？
How do I get to the nearest subway station?

02. 先搭電車，再轉火車。
Take the subway first, then take a train.

03. 我明天想去劍橋，怎麼樣能到達呢？
I want to go to Cambridge tomorrow, how can I get there?

04. 這輛火車有餐車嗎？
Is there a dining car on this train?

05. 請給我兩張去巴黎特快車的票。
Please give me two express tickets to Paris.

06. 一小時內有幾班特快車呢？
How many express trains are there in an hour?

07. 不好意思，售票機故障了，請問服務人員在哪裡呢？
Excuse me. The ticket machine is broken. Where is the service staff?

08. 可以給我一份時刻表嗎？
Could you give me a timetable?

09. 請問有賣一日票嗎？
Do you have one-day pass?

10. 對不起，我買錯票了，可以退錢嗎？
I am sorry, I bought the wrong ticket, could I have a refund?

✎ 關鍵單字／片語

01. **subway**	地下鐵
02. **non-stop bus**	直達車
03. **platform**	月台
04. **get on**	上車
05. **get off**	下車
06. **miss the stop**	坐過站
07. **ticket vending machine**	售票機
08. **track**	軌道
09. **ticket collector**	剪票員
10. **express**	特快車

04 | 看時刻表

由於幅員較廣，外國人大部分都以車代步，而且幾乎都是自行開車。對於喜愛到處觀光的背包客來說，搭公車是非常實惠的，事先查清楚時刻表可以免去久候的時間。站牌上通常都有時刻表，有些地方在公車上都可免費取用，十分方便。

實境對話

A: Any plans today?
你今天有什麼計畫嗎？

B: I'm planning to go downtown by bus and do some window shopping.
我打算搭公車去市區逛逛。

A: Both 402 and 317 go downtown from here.
附近有兩班公車，402 和 317 都可以到市區。

B: Great!
太棒了！

A: I have the timetable for the buses. Let me check it for you first.
我有公車時刻表，我先幫你看一下。

B: That would be nice.
那太好了。

A: There's one coming in 20 minutes. You're about to go. Take this timetable with you for your return trip.
二十分鐘後有一班，你差不多可以出發了。這份時刻表你帶著，回程的時候可以查。

B: You're very thoughtful. Thank you.
你真周到，謝謝。

☝ 你可以聽懂／口說更多

01. 我可以看看時刻表嗎？
    May I see the timetable?

02. 我不太會看這個時刻表。
    I don't know how to read this timetable.

03. 讓我們看看時刻表。
    Let's check the timetable.

04. 能給我一份時刻表嗎？
    Can you give me a timetable?

05. 看看火車時刻表來瞭解一下火車的時間安排。
    Look at the railway timetable to find the schedule of the train.

06. 我能看一下國內航班時刻表嗎？
    Can I see a domestic timetable?

07. 最後一班車十分鐘後到達。
    The last bus will be arriving in ten minutes.

08. 你能在這一時刻表上找到你的火車時刻。
    You can find the times of your trains in this timetable.

09. 從這裡到市區最早的公車是幾點？
    When is earliest bus from here to downtown?

10. 我可以給你一份時刻表，你自己看看。
    I can give you a timetable and you can check by yourself.

✎ 關鍵單字／片語

01. **timetable**	時刻表
02. **window shopping**	櫥窗購物、只看不買
03. **arrive**	到達
04. **come**	來
05. **about to**	即將、正要……
06. **schedule**	時間表
07. **look at**	看
08. **last bus**	末班車
09. **earliest bus**	首班車
10. **downtown / uptown**	市區／住宅區（非市區）

05 | 看交通路線圖

國際大都市通常都有非常便利的捷運或地鐵系統，以紐約為例，它的捷運線就高達二十六條左右，且分別由不同的捷運或地鐵系統經營，但是路線都可以互相銜接。欲搭乘捷運或地鐵則建議事先將交通路線圖研究清楚，才不會在複雜的捷運線中迷失方向。

實境對話

A: How do I get to Queens from Central Park in Manhattan?
請問從曼哈頓中央公園到皇后區該怎麼去？

B: Let's check the MTA New York City Transit.
我們來看一下紐約大眾交通的路線圖。

B: You can take subway line F at Central Park Station from 57th St. to 169th St..
你可以從中央公園第 57 街站搭地鐵 F 線到第 169 街站。

A: And then?
然後呢？

B: And then take the shuttle bus to Homelawn St., Hillside Av. to take bus Q31.
然後搭轉乘車到翠巒大道的鄉林街，改搭 Q31 號公車。

A: Is the bus Q31 going directly to Queens?
轉搭 Q31 就可以到皇后區了嗎？

B: You should get off at 67th Av. and walk to Queens in 8 minutes.
到 67 大道下車後，再步行大約八分鐘就可以到達皇后區了。

B: Call me any time if you can't find your way.
任何時候你找不到路，打電話給我。

你可以聽懂／口說更多

01. 對不起，請給我一份公車路線圖好嗎？
    Excuse me. May I have a bus route map, please?

02. 你有這個城市的交通圖嗎？
    Do you have a transportation map of the city?

03. 請給我一份公車路線圖好嗎？
    May I have a bus route map?

04. 我可以拿一份路線圖嗎？
    Could I have a route map?

05. 請給我一份捷運交通圖。
    May I have a subway route map?

06. 請給我一份巴士和捷運的路線圖。
    I would like a bus and subway route map, please.

07. 要是我看不懂地圖怎麼辦？
    What shall I do if I can't read the map?

08. 我迷路了。我沒能找到路，因為我沒有城市交通圖。
    I got lost. I could not find the way because I didn't have a city map.

09. 你會看這個捷運路線圖嗎？
    Can you read the subway route map?

10. 我們去找份路線圖吧。
    Let's go find a route map.

關鍵單字／片語

01. **bus route map**	公車路線圖
02. **route / line**	路線
03. **transportation map**	大眾運輸地圖
04. **traffic**	交通
05. **walk**	走路
06. **directly**	直接地
07. **cell phone number**	手機號碼
08. **chance**	機會
09. **and then**	然後
10. **Central Park**	中央公園

06 | 搭捷運

搭乘各地的捷運之前,可先了解捷運車票的優惠方式。很多城市為了促進觀光,多會提供套票,通常是以日期來計算,有一日票、三日票,甚至月票等等,而且這些票種還經常提供與其他交通系統通用的功能,例如:公車、火車。

實境對話

A: Hi. I want to buy a MetroCard.
你好,我要買捷運票。

B: Do you need a card with Pay-Per-Ride or 5-Days unlimited ride?
請問你要買單程票,還是五天的無限票?

A: What's the difference between these two cards?
請問這兩種票有何不同?

B: The card with Pay-Per-Ride means you can only use it once. The 5-days unlimited ride means you can use it unlimitedly within 5 days.
單程票限搭一次;五天的無限票可以在五天之內無限次使用。

A: Do you have any other MetroCards?
請問還有其他票種嗎?

B: Yes. We do have a MetroCard with 30-Days unlimited ride.
有的,還有三十天的無限票。

A: I see. I'll get one with 5-Days unlimited ride.
我明白了。我買一張五日票。

B: OK. This is your MetroCard. It's $105.
這是你的捷運票。一共 105 元。

你可以聽懂／口說更多

01. 搭捷運來這裡是最快的方法。
    The subway is the fastest way to come here.

02. 我寧可坐捷運也不開車。
    I'd rather take the subway than drive.

03. 我想搭捷運去那兒。
    I want to get there by subway.

04. 搭捷運去好嗎？
    How about going by subway?

05. 搭捷運可以輕易地到達這個城市的任何地方。
    You can easily go everywhere in the city by subway.

06. 搭捷運去會快些。
    It's faster to go there by subway.

07. 我要一張五日票。
    I need a card with 5-Days unlimited ride.

08. 我通常搭乘捷運上班。
    I usually go to work by subway.

09. 我們走吧，我也要去坐捷運。
    Let's go. I'm going to take the subway, too.

10. 我們是搭捷運還是坐公車呢？
    Shall we go there by subway or bus?

關鍵單字／片語

01. **MRT**	（＝ Mass Rapid Transit）捷運
02. **metro**	地鐵
03. **Pay-Per-Ride**	單程票
04. **unlimited ride**	無限搭乘
05. **one-day pass**	一日票
06. **weekly pass**	週票
07. **regular pass**	一般票
08. **valid day**	有效日期
09. **first station**	起站
10. **terminal station**	終點站

07 | 找出口

許多國際大都市都有便捷的交通運輸系統，通常都會有十數條捷運路線交會，再加上地下街規劃，出口都十分複雜。而這些出口通常會有不同顏色的標示，所以只要根據指示走，通常不會迷路。出口處也常會標示轉乘公車的資訊，以節省轉換交通工具的時間。

實境對話

A: We just got off from the Red Line. We should turn right to the nearest exit.
我們剛剛從紅線下車。我們應該在最近的出口右轉。

B: But we're going to the department store. The bus stop is at the exit of the Blue Line. That means we should take a left turn.
我們要去百貨公司，公車站應該在藍線出口，所以我們得左轉。

A: You're right. We should turn left here.
對！我們得先左轉。

B: Look! The exit is over there.
你看，出口在那裡！

A: Uh? There are two exits. Which one should we pick?
咦？有兩個出口，我們該走哪一個？

B: Let's check the map here.
我們看一下這裡的標示圖。

A: It looks like we should go through the exit at the left side.
看來好像是左邊的出口。

🖐 你可以聽懂／口說更多

01. 不好意思，我找不到出口了。
Excuse me. I can't find the exit.

02. 一直往前走你就會看到了。
Keep straight on and you will find it.

03. 對不起，我也不知道出口在哪裡。
I am sorry. I don't know the exit, either.

04. 打擾了，請問我要怎麼找到出口？
Excuse me. How can I get to the exit?

05. 我找不到出口了，請告訴我在哪裡。
I am lost to the exit. Please tell me where it is.

06. 我正試著找個出口呢。
I am trying to look for an exit.

07. 請告訴我最近的出口在哪兒好嗎？
Would you please tell me the nearest exit?

08. 我現在不知道該如何出去了。
I don't know how to get out now.

09. 看！出口就在那裡，柱子後面。
Look! The exit is right there! Behind the pillar.

10. 我知道了，非常感謝！
I got it. Thank you very much!

✍ 關鍵單字／片語

01. **nearest**	（near 的最高級）最近的
02. **take a left turn**	向左轉
03. **take a right turn**	向右轉
04. **department store**	百貨公司
05. **Which one...?**	哪一個……？
06. **look like...**	看起來像……
07. **be going to**	正要去……
08. **uh**	嗯、啊
09. **pillar**	柱子
10. **keep straight on**	直直往前走

08 | 搭火車

跨都市的旅行，搭火車比較方便。你通常能在旅客服務中心取得火車時刻表，當然火車站也有更詳細的資訊。大都市火車路線很複雜，你得注意搭車的月台。還有，購買來回票通常會有折扣。另外，有的火車站會像搭飛機一樣提供行李托運，你也能在服務台詢問到相關資訊。

🖐 實境對話

A: Is the round-trip ticket cheaper than one-way?
請問買來回票比單程票便宜嗎？

B: Of course. We also have a 30-Days unlimited ticket for tourists. You don't need to pay for each trip. You can take as many rides as you want within 30 days.
當然，我們有提供觀光客旅行月票，三十天之內你可以無限次搭乘，都不用再付費。

A: Oh. Thank you for your recommendation.
喔！謝謝你的推薦，很可惜。

A: Unfortunately, I'm staying only for a week.
我只在這裡待一個星期。

B: That's too bad. This is your ticket and change. Have a nice trip.
那太可惜了，這是你的火車票和找零。祝你旅途愉快。

A: By the way. Can I have my luggage checked in?
對了！我想請問你們有提供行李托運嗎？

B: Yes. You can go to the luggage check-in counter on the left.
有的！你可以到左邊行李托運處托運。

👆 你可以聽懂／口說更多

01. 我們將在歐洲坐火車旅行。
We are going to travel by train in Europe.

02. 你是坐火車去還是坐公車去？
Are you going by train or by bus?

03. 坐火車比坐飛機更節約。
Going by train is more economical than going by plane.

04. 我們打算坐火車去首都。
We are going to take a train to the capital.

05. 到西雅圖還有幾站呢？
How many stops are there until we get to Seattle?

06. 我喜歡坐火車旅行。
I prefer traveling by train.

07. 不好意思，請問在哪裡可以找到列車長？
Excuse me. Can you tell me where I can find the train conductor?

08. 我們可以乘火車去北京旅行。
We can take a train on our trip to Beijing!

09. 我該在哪個月台搭車？
Which platform should I go to?

10. 請到第二月台搭車。
Please go to platform 2.

✍ 關鍵單字／片語

01. **one-way**	單向的、單程的
02. **of course**	當然
03. **tourist**	遊客
04. **too bad**	太可惜了
05. **by the way**	順帶一提
06. **capital**	首都
07. **have a nice trip**	旅途愉快
08. **train conductor**	列車長
09. **miss**	錯過
10. **by train**	坐火車

09 | 乘巴士

巴士，是花費較低的交通工具，但所花的時間相對會比較多，你可以依自己的行程需求、經濟考量來選擇交通工具，反正條條道路通羅馬，只要問清楚搭車地點、所需時間、費用，以及相關事項，就可以整裝上路啦！另外，如果你想做市內觀光的話，搭乘巴士的「市內觀光行程」就是一個很不錯的選擇喔！

實境對話

A: I want to go downtown. Is there any bus that I can take?

我想去市區，請問有巴士可以搭嗎？

B: Yes, there is a bus stop at the next corner. The buses there are heading to the city.

有，下一個路口有巴士站牌，那裡的車都是往市區的。

A: Do you know how long it will take to get there by bus?

你知道坐車過去大概要花多久時間呢？

B: Hum, about an hour and a half.

嗯，大概要一個半鐘頭。

A: Could I also ask, how much is the bus fare?

順便請教，費用大概是多少呢？

B: I am not sure, probably $30.

我不太清楚，大約 30 元吧！

A: I see, thank you!

我知道了，謝謝你！

🔊 你可以聽懂／口說更多

01. 請告訴我最近的巴士站在哪？
Please tell me where the nearest bus stop is?

02. 我在中途需要轉車嗎？
Do I need to transfer?

03. 往美術館的巴士站牌是在這裡嗎？
Is this the stop for buses that are heading to the museum?

04. 有接駁公車嗎？
Is there a shuttle bus?

05. 這輛巴士的班次是多久一班呢？
How frequently does this bus run?

06. 我要預先購票嗎？
Do I need to buy the ticket in advance?

07. 你可以跟我說明一下回數票和優待票的差別嗎？
Could you tell me the difference between transfer ticket and coupon ticket?

08. 請問到拉斯維加斯多少錢？
How much does it cost to Las Vegas?

09. 這輛巴士中途會停在哪裡？
Where will this bus stop during the trip?

10. 要停在這多久呢？
How long are we going to stop here?

✍ 關鍵單字／片語

01. **bus fare**	費用
02. **token**	代幣
03. **round ticket**	來回票
04. **coupon ticket**	優待票
05. **interval**	間隔、距離
06. **bus stop**	巴士站、公車站
07. **switch bus**	換巴士
08. **transfer ticket**	轉乘票
09. **bus driver**	公車司機
10. **head**	出發前往

10 | 計程車

計程車，可説是最方便的交通工具了，隨時只要招招手就停在你面前，不必換車，也不用人擠人，直達目的地，但費用頗高，尤其是國外有些地方沒有用跳表計費，記得在搭乘以前千萬要把價錢談好，免得平白無故被敲詐一筆冤枉錢喔！

實境對話

A: How much is it to London?
請問到倫敦市區多少錢？

B: Fifty pounds.
50 元。

A: I heard that it only costs 30 pounds to go there, £50 is too expensive. Can you lower the price?
我聽別人説這段路只需要 30 元，50 元太貴了，不能算便宜一點嗎？

B: Ok, it will be 30 pounds then.
好吧，那就 30 元。

A: I have a piece of luggage; can you help me put it in the trunk?
我有一件行李，可以請你幫我放到後車箱嗎？

B: Yes, but I need a 10 pounds tip.
可以，但是要小費 10 元。

A: No problem! It's a deal.
沒問題，成交！

A: Here's your tip.
這是給你的小費。

B: Thank you. You're so generous.
謝謝，你真大方。

👆 你可以聽懂／口說更多

01. 請問計程車招呼站在哪裡？
Excuse me, where is the taxi stand?

02. 我想叫一台計程車。
I need a cab.

03. 在哪裡可以叫到計程車？
Where can I get a taxi?

04. 請載我去這個地址。你可以在十分鐘內到達嗎？
Please take me to this address. Can you get there in ten minutes?

05. 請在前面轉角靠邊停。
Please stop at the corner.

06. 對不起，我要在這裡下車。
Excuse me, I want to get off here.

07. 你用跳表計費嗎？
Do you charge by the meter?

08. 我們有五個人，坐得下嗎？
Can we squeeze in five people?

09. 你的價錢太貴了。
Your price is way too expensive.

10. 請不要繞遠路，我趕時間。
Please don't take the long way, I am in a hurry.

✍ 關鍵單字／片語

01. **taxi stand**	計程車招呼站
02. **vacant car**	空車
03. **taxi / cab**	計程車
04. **change**	找零
05. **pullover**	靠邊停
06. **extra charge**	額外費用
07. **meter**	跳表
08. **night fare rate**	夜間加成
09. **squeeze**	擠
10. **trunk**	後車廂

11│轉乘～到目的地

在國際大都市中旅行，有時候轉乘交通工具的時間掌握十分重要，可以盡量選擇固定時間的交通工具，譬如：捷運、火車，才不會耽誤回程時間。但有時候去程可以搭火車，但回程的班次時間卻無法配合，你恐怕就只能選擇長途巴士了。

實境對話

A: How long does it take from here to the train station by subway?
請問從這裡搭地鐵到火車站要花多少時間？

B: About 15 minutes.
大約 15 分鐘。

A: And how long does it take to the village near Lake Tahoe by train?
那麼搭火車到離塔荷湖最近的鄉鎮要多久呢？

B: It's about an hour.
大約一個小時。

A: How about the bus from the village to Lake Tahoe?
那從鄉鎮轉乘巴士到塔荷湖呢？

B: You need one more hour. I suggest you can take the bus back here directly.
還要一個小時，不過我建議你回程不要搭火車，可以從塔荷湖全程搭巴士回來。

B: You don't need to restrict yourself to the schedule of the train. And it's cheaper.
你不需要配合火車時間，而且比較便宜。

🖐 你可以聽懂／口說更多

01. 你得在西雅圖換搭另一班飛機。
    You will have to change plane in Seattle.

02. 我們在倫敦下了火車，轉乘了一輛公共汽車。
    In London, we transferred from the train to a bus.

03. 這就是我們從捷運站換乘巴士的地方。
    This is where we change from subway to bus.

04. 國貿站是換乘車站，下車的乘客請提前做好準備。
    GuoMao is a transformation station; please get ready for
    your arrival.

05. 往台北的旅客請在本站下車。
    All passengers transferring to Taipei please get off the train
    at this stop.

06. 換乘火車多少有些不便。
    Having to change trains is a small inconvenience.

07. 到工廠的路上要換乘巴士。
    I have to change buses on the way to the factory.

08. 帶著行李換乘火車真是件麻煩事。
    Changing trains with the luggage is too much trouble.

09. 我們在哪兒換車？
    Where shall we change?

10. 你必須在中央車站換車。
    You need to transfer at Central Station.

✎ 關鍵單字／片語

01. **village**	村莊、鄉鎮
02. **suggest / suggestion**	建議
03. **restrict**	限制、約束
04. **even better**	更好
05. **transformation station**	轉乘車站
06. **arrival**	到達
07. **convenience**	方便
08. **inconvenience**	不方便
09. **too much trouble**	太麻煩
10. **troublesome**	麻煩的

12 | 租車

國外的土地大多都很寬廣，租車自助旅遊是最方便不過的了，但首先你必須要有合格的國際駕照，所以記得在台灣要先辦好喔！特別注意的是美國有些州並不承認國際駕照，你需要同時擁有美國駕照才能夠租到車以及在該州境內合法開車，這些資訊都要事先查清楚才能省下很多麻煩喔！

👆 實境對話

A: I want to have a look at your pamphlet?
我想看一下你們的手冊。

B: No problem.
沒問題。

A: Is there any promotion that I can benefit from?
有沒有對我有利的優惠方案？

B: Yes, here's a look at this special offer.
有的，請看看這個特價方案。

A: May I see the cars first?
我可以先看車嗎？

A: I'll rent this type of car starting today for 3 days.
我要借這款車，從今天起 3 天時間。

B: May I please have your driver's license, passport, and credis card?
請提供你的駕照、護照和信用卡。

A: Do I have to fill up the gas when I return the car?
如果我要在洛杉磯還車，會有額外的收費嗎？

A: Do I have to fill up the gas when I return the car?
還車以前需要把油加滿嗎？

☝ 你可以聽懂／口說更多

01. 請問你們現在有空餘的車嗎？
Do you have any cars available now?

02. 我想租輛車，一個星期左右。
I'd like to rent a car for about a week.

03. 每天的租金是多少錢？
How much is the per-day rate?

04. 您想要什麼車呢？
What kind of car would you like?

05. 我們的租金是一天五十美元。
Our rent is 50 dollars a day.

06. 請問你們有多少人一起旅行？
Would you please tell me how many people will be traveling together?

07. 您這有什麼種類的車呢？
What type of car do you have?

08. 或許您可以選擇寶馬或者奧迪。
Perhaps you could choose a BMW or Audi car.

09. 我們要先收取訂金。
We have to ask for a deposit first.

10. 您介意我們檢驗一下汽車來確保一切正常嗎？
Do you mind if we check the car to make sure it has good running?

✎ 關鍵單字／片語

01. **sedan**	轎車
02. **recreation vehicle**	（=RV）休旅車
03. **convertible**	敞篷車
04. **sports car**	跑車
05. **wagon**	旅行車
06. **limo**	（=limousine）豪華大禮車
07. **international driver's license**	國際駕照
08. **automatic**	自排
09. **clutch**	離合器
10. **car rental**	租車

13│搭船

在國外，有一些景色是需要搭船才能欣賞得到，雖然費用不低，但是既然出國了，就要玩個盡興，相信國外的美景一定會讓你值回票價，不虛此行！

🗨 實境對話

A: How much does it cost to tour Tokyo Bay?
請問坐船遊覽東京灣一趟要多少錢呢？

B: 3000 dollars.
3000 元。

A: How long is the tour?
請問航程是多久呢？

B: About an hour and a half.
大約一個半小時。

A: Will we make any stops during the trip?
中途有停靠站嗎？

B: No.
沒有。

A: Is there a restaurant on the ship?
船上有餐廳嗎？

B: Yes, and there are vending machines too.
有，也有自動販賣機。

A: I got it, then give me four tickets please.
我知道了，那給我四張票，謝謝！

A: I am seasick.
我暈船了。

B: So am I.
我也是。

👆 你可以聽懂／口說更多

01. 我好像暈船了。
    I think I am seasick.

02. 你要吃點藥嗎？
    Do you need to take some pills?

03. 我想吐。
    I feel like puking.

04. 請問一天有幾班航次？
    How many voyages are there in a day?

05. 明天會到哪一個港口？
    Which harbor are we going to reach tomorrow?

06. 有單程票嗎？
    Is there a one-way ticket?

07. 我可以在途中下船嗎？
    Could I get off the ship in the middle of the trip?

08. 船上的遊樂設施太令我驚訝了。那些設施真的棒極了！
    Those entertainment facilities on board amazed me. They are fantastic!

09. 請問可以上去甲板嗎？
    Could I get on the deck?

10. 當然，但請小心點。
    Sure, please be careful.

✍ 關鍵單字／片語

01. **cruise ship**	遊輪、遊艇、渡輪
02. **lifeboat**	救生艇
03. **set sail**	出航
04. **captain**	船長
05. **yacht**	遊艇
06. **upper deck**	上甲板
07. **harbor / port**	港口
08. **anchor**	停泊、錨
09. **cabin for one**	一人艙
10. **cabin for two**	二人艙

14│坐飛機

有些國家比較大，轉乘搭飛機會比較省時間，還有些風景區也非得搭飛機遊覽不可，譬如：大峽谷。除了注意票價和時間之外，天氣和安全也是要注意的重點，如果是風景區的小飛機，你更要注意購買保險。小飛機通常比較顛簸，身體狀況不好，最好不要勉強自己。

🔈 實境對話

A: Excuse me. How can I get to the Grand Canyon?
請問一下該怎麼去大峽谷？

B: You can take a plane there. And take a helicopter to enjoy the Grand Canyon.
你可以先搭國內線飛機到大峽谷，再搭直升機欣賞大峽谷。

A: Should I take a bus there if I arrive by train?
如果我想搭火車去，是不是還得換巴士？

B: Yes. It's cheaper but it takes more time.
是的，費用雖然便宜，但是會花比較多的時間。

A: I think I'll go by plane then.
那我想還是搭飛機去好了。

B: By the way, are you in a good health condition?
對了，你的身體狀況還好嗎？

A: I'm OK. Why?
我還不錯呀。怎麼了？

B: Helicopters are not as stable as planes. If you don't feel well then you'd better not take them.
大峽谷的直升機不像一般飛機這麼平穩，如果你身體狀況不好，最好不要搭乘直升機。

👆 你可以聽懂／口說更多

01. 現在坐飛機是平常事。
Air travel is a commonplace nowadays.

02. 你坐飛機去那兒嗎？我可以和你一起去嗎？
Do you go there by plane? Can I go with you?

03. 坐飛機去倫敦需要多長時間？
How long does it take to fly to London?

04. 坐飛機回家太貴了。
It is too expensive going home by air.

05. 你是坐船還是坐飛機去？
Are you going there by boat or by plane?

06. 坐飛機比坐火車更快，所以我會選擇搭飛機。
Going by plane is faster than going by train. So I would choose to take a plane.

07. 你最好搭飛機去巴黎。
You'd better go to Paris by air.

08. 與其坐火車不如乘飛機。
I would rather go by air than by train.

09. 這是我第一次坐飛機。
This is my first flight.

10. 祝您旅途愉快！
Have a nice flight!

✍ 關鍵單字／片語

01. **Grand Canyon**	（美國）大峽谷
02. **take a plane / airplane**	搭飛機
03. **helicopter**	直升機
04. **condition**	情況、狀況
05. **stable / unstable**	穩定／不穩定
06. **commonplace**	司空見慣的事
07. **fly**	飛
08. **expensive / cheap**	昂貴／便宜
09. **go home**	回家
10. **would rather**	寧願

15｜坐空中纜車

有些國際級的山區遊覽景點會提供空中纜車服務，滑雪勝地更會提供小型雙人座纜車，由空中飽覽美景。不過，要注意纜車開放時間，除了營業時間外，要注意是否會因為天候因素而停駛。你可以透過導覽手冊或服務台獲得相關資訊。

實境對話

A: Do you think the cable cars will run today?
你覺得今天纜車會開放嗎？

B: I have no idea. I don't think they would run if it is too windy.
我不知道。我覺得如果風太大，纜車不會開放載客。

A: Where can I buy the ticket?
要去哪裡買票呢？

B: You can use the vending machine.
你可以用自動售票機買票。

A: But I don't know how it works.
可是我不知道怎麼操作。

B: Don't worry. You can ask the ticket officer. And don't forget to ask them whether the cable cars will operate today.
沒關係，那兒有票務人員協助。別忘了順便問他們今天纜車是否開放。

A: Guess what? The lady told me the wind force is still within safety range. The cable cars will be operating in fifteen minutes.
你猜怎麼了？票務人員說，今天的風力還在安全範圍內，纜車十五分鐘內會開始運作。

👆 你可以聽懂／口說更多

01. 咱們坐纜車上去怎麼樣？
How about riding up in the cable car?

02. 為什麼不坐纜車到滑雪場呢？
Why not ride the cable car to get to the ski resort?

03. 好多人在排隊。
So many people are lining up.

04. 纜車馬上就要出發了。
The cable car is leaving soon.

05. 歡迎您乘坐纜車！
Welcome to the cable car!

06. 上纜車，它可以帶你上山。
Get into the cable car, it can get you up to the top.

07. 我們可以坐纜車到山頂。
We can take the cable car to the top of the hills.

08. 你坐過空中纜車嗎？
Have you ever ridden a cable car?

09. 坐纜車上山，整個城市就能盡收眼底。
When the cable car goes up the hills, you can look down over the city.

10. 我差點錯過了最後一班纜車。
I nearly missed the last cable car.

✍ 關鍵單字／片語

01. **cable car**	空中纜車
02. **sky line**	空中纜車
03. **ticket booth**	售票亭
04. **line up**	排隊
05. **operate**	運行、運作
06. **guess what**	猜猜看、你猜怎麼了
07. **wind force**	風力
08. **follow me**	跟我來
09. **ski resort**	滑雪場
10. **top of hill**	山頂

Chapter

04

飯店住宿篇

Chapter 04 音檔雲端連結

因各家手機系統不同，若無法直接掃描，仍可以至以下電腦雲端連結下載收聽。
（https://tinyurl.com/24ddrrxe）

01 | 預訂飯店

國際連鎖飯店的品質都有一定的水準，通常可以從飯店名稱看出它的類型。例如：「hotel」一般就是整棟高樓的建築物；「inn」則規模小一點；有時你也會看到「resort」（度假村）這個字，通常會有比較大的戶外場地或設施。

實境對話

A: Good morning. This is Holiday Inn Santa Barbara.
早安，這裡是聖塔芭芭拉假日飯店。

B: I want to book two rooms for March 14th.
我要預定三月十四日，兩間房。

A: What kind of rooms would you like?
請問要什麼房型？

B: A single room and a double room.
一間單人房，一間雙人房。

A: No problem.
沒問題。

B: When is your check-in time?
請問你們幾點可以登記入住呢？

A: Our regular check-in time is 3 p.m..
一般入住的時間是下午三點。

B: We will probably arrive around lunch time, and we plan to have lunch in the hotel. Is it possible for us to check-in earlier?
我們可能午餐時間就會到了，而且我們計畫要在旅館用餐。請問我們可以早點入住嗎？

A: Let me see. Yes, that should be fine.
我看一下。好的，應該可以。

🖐 你可以聽懂／口說更多

01. 這裡是客房預訂部，能為您效勞嗎？
This is Reservations, may I help you?

02. 我想訂一個房間，要住五天。
I want to book a room for five days.

03. 我們還有一間單人房。
We still have a single room available.

04. 我想預定一間雙人房。你們還有空房嗎？
I'd like to book a double room, please. Do you have any vacancies?

05. 先生，您是要單人房還是雙人房？
Would you like a single room or a double room, sir?

06. 你們提供的這間單人房有沒有浴室？
Is the single room you offer with or without a bathroom?

07. 你能幫我保留這間雙人房嗎？
Could you reserve the double room for me?

08. 您什麼時候到達？
When will you arrive?

09. 我已經幫你訂了一間帶有浴室的單人房。
I have booked a single room with a bathroom for you.

10. 可以留下您的聯絡方式嗎？
May I have your contact info?

✏️ 關鍵單字／片語

01. **Room Reservations**	訂房部
02. **hotel**	旅館、飯店、酒店
03. **inn**	（規模較小的）旅館、飯店
04. **resort**	渡假村、渡假中心
05. **suite**	套房
06. **check-in time**	登記入住時間
07. **check-out time**	退房時間
08. **fully booked**	客滿
09. **villa**	別墅飯店
10. **five-star hotel**	五星級飯店

02 | 詢問房價

世界各國對於學生都是非常友善的，經常在很多需要購買票券的機構提供學生優惠的折扣。建議大家在出國前可以先申辦國際學生證或上網瞭解各種優惠方式，不管是機票、船票、火車票，甚至是電影票、美術館與博物館門票，皆可節省不少旅費開支。

實境對話

A: This is Sheraton Vancouver Wall Centre. Good day, sir.
這裡是溫哥華喜來登酒店。您好，先生。

B: May I know how much your prices are?
我想請教一下，你們的定價是多少？

A: Are you asking a standard room, a deluxe room or an executive suite?
你要詢問的是標準房、豪華房還是商務套房？

B: How much for each of them?
請問房價分別是多少？

A: $135 for standard room; $180 for deluxe room and $250 for executive suite.
標準房一個晚上 135 元、豪華房 180 元、商務套房則是 250 元。

B: I see. Is there any discount during weekdays?
我了解了。請問平日有折扣嗎？

A: Yes. You'll get 30% off during weekdays. And you can get another 15% off for student visa.
有，打七折。學生簽證可以再打 85 折。

☝ 你可以聽懂／口說更多

01. 你們的房價是多少？
    What is your room rate?

02. 我們的房價從 20 美元到 70 美元不等。
    Our room rates range from $20 to $70.

03. 您能報一下貴酒店的房價嗎？
    Could you tell me the prices at your hotel?

04. 旅館房價較高是因為現在是旅遊旺季。
    Hotels cost more because it's the peak tourist season.

05. 這家旅館一間房間開價多少？
    How much does the hotel charge for a room?

06. 這裡的房價是每天一百美金。
    The room rate is 100 dollars per day here.

07. 您想要什麼價位的房間？
    How much do you want to pay for the room?

08. 住三天要多少錢？
    How much will it cost for three days?

09. 我們酒店的房價要加收 4% 稅金。
    Our hotel rates are subject to 4% tax.

10. 您想預定什麼類型的房間？單人房還是雙人房？
    What kind of room would you like to order? A single room or a double room?

✎ 關鍵單字／片語

01. **standard room**	標準房
02. **single room**	單人房
03. **double room**	雙人房
04. **twim room**	一間房有兩張床
06. **deluxe room**	豪華房
07. **executive suite**	商務套房
08. **ocean (view) suite**	海景套房
08. **penthouse**	頂樓套房
09. **president suite**	總統套房
10. **room rate**	房價

03 | 詢問飯店設備

國際級的飯店通常都有許多休閒設施，游泳池、健身房、三溫暖和兒童遊憩室，但是是否要另外付費，可能得問清楚。如果你不是休閒旅遊而是洽公商旅，那麼你可能更關心房間裡是否有網路設備，或者在大廳是否有準備商務中心。這是在前往飯店前要先確認的。

實境對話

A: May I know what recreation facilties you offer?
請問飯店裡面有什麼休閒設施？

B: We have a swimming pool, a gym and a sauna by the swimming pool. We also have a 24-hour massage service.
我們有游泳池和健身房，游泳池旁附設三溫暖，還有提供按摩服務。

A: Do I need to pay for them?
要另外付費嗎？

B: They're all free for our guests except for the massage. It costs $20 each time.
設施對房客都免費提供，但是按摩服務每次加收 20 美金。

A: Do you have free Wi-Fi here?
你們這裡有免費的Wi-Fi 嗎？

A: Can you tell me the Wi-Fi password?
可以告訴我Wi-Fi密碼嗎？

👆 你可以聽懂／口說更多

01. 你們有游泳池嗎？
Do you have swimming pool?

02. 我們酒店擁有各種現代化的設施。
Our hotel is fitted up with every kind of modern facilities.

03. 飯店有空調設備嗎？
Is there any air-conditioning in this hotel?

04. 我們飯店設備齊全。
Our hotel is well-appointed.

05. 我們飯店擁有中西餐廳、卡拉 OK 等。
Our hotel has Chinese and Western restaurants, karaoke, and etc.

06. 我們為客人提供幽雅溫馨的環境。
We offer guests an environment of elegance and warmth.

07. 我們是一家有新式設備的旅館。
Our hotel is one with modern facilities.

08. 哪些飯店設施對您是必要的？
Which facilities are essential to you?

09. 您有什麼特殊要求嗎？
Do you have any special requirements?

10. 我想瞭解一下你們酒店的設備狀況。
I would like to know the equipment status of your hotel.

✍ 關鍵單字／片語

01. **recreation**	娛樂、遊戲
02. **mahjong room**	麻將室
03. **gym**	健身房
04. **massage**	按摩
05. **sauna (bath)**	三溫暖、桑拿
06. **facility**	設備
07. **wireless Internet**	無線網路
08. **wired Internet**	有線網路
09. **karaoke**	卡拉 OK
10. **Jacuzzi**	按摩浴缸

04 | 櫃檯報到

國際級的飯店在報到時通常會要求出示護照，而且會要求以信用卡預刷完成入住報到的手續。飯店報到的時間在下午兩點或三點，如果有需要提早入住，也可以在訂房時詢問，若不是太熱門的日子，飯店多半會給予通融。

實境對話

A: Good afternoon, sir. May I have your name?
午安，先生。請問貴姓大名？

B: My name is Jett Wu.
我是吳傑特。

A: Let me check, Mr. Wu. You're going to stay in our deluxe suite for two nights.
我查一下，吳先生。你訂的是我們的豪華套房兩晚。

B: Yes, I do.
是的。

A: May I have your passport please, Mr. Wu?
吳先生，請讓我看一下你的護照。

B: Sure. Here it is. I need a morning call at 7:20 tomorrow.
當然，在這兒。明天早上七點二十分打電話叫我起床。

A: No problem. Here is your key card and all the coupons of our facilities.
沒問題。這是您的房卡和所有我們飯店設施的招待券。

B: OK. I need New York Daily, please.
好的。我想要一份紐約日報。

A: Of course. It'll be ready in your room shortly.
好的。待會兒就會送到您的房間。

👆 你可以聽懂／口說更多

01. 我想確認一下我預訂的房間。我上禮拜三有訂房。
I'd like to confirm my reservation. I made a reservation last Wednesday.

02. 早上好，能為您效勞嗎？
Good morning, how may I help you?

03. 能告訴我您的全名嗎？
May I have your full name, please?

04. 您預定的是雙人房對嗎？
You booked a double room, right?

05. 請問飯店櫃檯在哪裡？
Could you tell me where the front desk is?

06. 長城飯店，我能為您服務嗎？
Great Wall Hotel, how may I help you?

07. 請到這個櫃檯來。
Please come over to this counter.

08. 非常感謝您的服務。
Thank you very much for your service.

09. 我可以延長到四天嗎？
Could I extend my stay to four days?

10. 我們期待為您服務。
We look forward to serving you.

✍ 關鍵單字／片語

01. **key card**	房門卡
02. **morning call service**	叫醒服務
03. **daily**	日報
04. **confirm / reconfirm**	確認／再次確認
05. **full name**	全名
06. **come over**	過來
07. **room number**	房間號碼
08. **serve**	服務
09. **look forward to(+Ving)**	期待
10. **extend**	延長

05 | 登記住宿

TRACK
040

如果你已預訂好飯店,只需拿出你的預約憑證;如果要當場登記,備妥你的護照和相關證件即可。

👆 實境對話

A: I have reserved a room.
我有預定房間。

B: No problem, sir. Your name is on our list.
沒有問題,您的大名在我們的住宿名單上。

A: I booked for four nights, but I have changed my plan, I want to extend two more nights, is it ok for you?
我改變行程,原本預定的是五天四夜,現在要多加兩晚,可以嗎?

B: Yes, but you will need to change to another room. Will that be ok?
可以,但是您要換房間才行,您願意嗎?

A: Well, sure, will the price be the same?
這樣啊!好吧,但換的房間價格一樣嗎?

B: Don't worry, we will move you to a room with the same rate.
您不用擔心,我們會幫您換同等價位的房間。

A: Ok, then.
那就這樣吧!

B: Ok, here is you key card. Please take the elevator on the left, thank you.
好,這裡是您房間的鑰匙卡,請搭左邊電梯上去,謝謝!

👉 你可以聽懂／口說更多

01. 請問有空房嗎？
Is there any room available?

02. 請問從今天起五天有空房嗎？
Do you have any room available for five days?

03. 給我一間面海的房間。
I want a room with an ocean view.

04. 這個價錢包括早餐嗎？
Does this price include breakfast?

05. 有沒有便宜一點的？
Do you have any cheaper rooms?

06. 浴室內是淋浴或是浴缸？
Does the bathroom come with a tub or a shower?

07. 加一張床多少錢？
How much do you charge for an extra bed?

08. 有小孩子價錢怎麼算？
What's the price if I'm taking a kid with me?

09. 我想要延長幾天的住宿。
I'd like to extend my stay for a few days.

10. 我應該什麼時候退房？
When should I check out the room?

✍ 關鍵單字／片語

01. **hotel accommodation**	飯店住宿
02. **motel**	汽車旅館
03. **reception desk**	接待櫃檯
04. **guard**	警衛
05. **lobby**	飯店大廳
06. **take the elevator**	搭電梯
07. **manager on duty**	值班經理
08. **on the list**	在名單上
09. **vacancy**	空房
10. **stairs**	樓梯

06 | 客房服務

飯店的客房服務除了提供餐點之外，也包含衣物送洗或者房間打掃甚至備品提供等。另外，如果你是非常重視隱私的人，你也可以在門把掛上「請勿打擾」的牌子。有些不錯的飯店對於消耗性的房間備品可重複提供，如果有需要的話，也不用客氣喔。

🎧 實境對話

A: Room Service. How may I help you?
客房服務部，你好。需要什麼服務嗎？

B: I want to order a set meal A.
我想點一份 A 餐。

A: OK. Anything else?
好的，還需要什麼嗎？

B: Yes. A fresh juice, please.
我還要一杯現打果汁。

A: OK. They'll be ready for you in 15 minutes.
好的。十五分鐘後會幫你送過去。

B: Would you please bring me some more sugar and iced water?
可以麻煩你幫我送一些糖還有冰水嗎？

A: Sure. Do you need any other services?
當然。還需要其他服務嗎？

B: Could you please also give us some extra shampoo and conditioner?
可以麻煩你多給我一些洗髮精和潤髮乳嗎？

A: That won't be a problem.
沒問題。

☝ 你可以聽懂／口說更多

01. 這是客房服務部，需要我幫忙嗎？
Room Service. May I help you?

02. 現在可以過來收拾房間嗎？
Will it be OK to clean the room now?

03. 請明天早上六點半叫醒我好嗎？
Would you please give me a wake up call at half past six tomorrow?

04. 您可以用內部電話叫客房服務。
You can call room service on the house phone.

05. 先生。客房服務員馬上就到。
Sir, the housemaid will be there shortly.

06. 如果您有任何需要，就打電話通知客房服務部。
Anything you need, just dial room service.

07. 能再給我一條毛毯嗎？
Could you give me one more blanket?

08. 您還有什麼其他的吩咐嗎？
Anything else we can do for you?

09. 客房服務嗎？我想要一些礦泉水。
Room Service? I want some mineral water, please.

10. 懷特夫人，您需要醒床服務嗎？
Do you need a morning call, Mrs. White?

✎ 關鍵單字／片語

01. **room service**	客房服務
02. **order**	點餐
03. **shampoo / conditioner**	洗髮精／潤絲精
04. **safe**	保險箱
05. **air-conditioning**	空調
06. **bed sheet**	床單
07. **pillow case**	枕頭套
08. **switch on / off**	打開／關掉
09. **shower gel / soap**	沐浴乳／肥皂
10. **hair dryer**	吹風機

07 | 餐廳

通常飯店裡都會附設餐廳，除了提供早、午、晚餐的自助餐廳之外，還會有很多其它的特色餐廳，例如：牛排屋、咖啡廳提供午茶甜點，有的餐廳還會附設酒吧，甚至提供樂團演奏或現場演唱。若是週末假期入住，也建議特別注意各餐廳是否提供特別的優惠或服務項目。

實境對話

A: Excuse me. How should I use this voucher?
抱歉，請問這張兌換券要怎麼使用？

B: You can use it in our night club. And you'll get a free soft drink with it.
你可以在我們的夜總會裡使用。你可以換一杯無酒精飲料。

A: That's wonderful. I really like to try it.
太好了。我很想試試看。

B: By the way, we have special guests tonight in the club.
順帶一提，今天夜總會有特別來賓。

A: I shouldn't miss it then.
那表示我不應該錯過囉。

B: Definitely not. It's a famous band with a lovely singer.
完全正確。他們是一個很有名的樂團，而且主唱非常漂亮。

A: When is the show going to start?
他們的表演什麼時候開始？

B: Nine thirty tonight.
晚上九點半開始。

☝ 你可以聽懂／口說更多

01. 您今天想吃點什麼呢？
What would you like to eat today?

02. 現在可以幫您點餐嗎？
May I take your order now?

03. 我期待在你們飯店的餐廳嚐正宗的法國料理。
I expect to taste authentic French cuisine at your hotel restaurant.

04. 我想吃清淡一點的。
I would like to eat something light.

05. 您要點餐了嗎？
Are you ready to order?

06. 您為什麼喜歡飯店裡的餐廳？
Why do you favor hotel restaurants?

07. 飯前您想喝點什麼嗎？
Would you like something to drink before your meal?

08. 你們飯店的餐廳幾點停止營業？
What time does the restaurant of your hotel close?

09. 這個飯店的餐廳非常整潔優雅。
The hotel restaurant is very tidy and elegant.

10. 今天的午餐有什麼特別菜色啊？
What is your special for lunch today?

✎ 關鍵單字／片語

01. **restaurant**	餐廳
02. **cuisine**	菜餚
03. **special**	特餐
04. **special guest**	特別來賓
05. **live show**	現場演奏
06. **breakfast**	早餐
07. **brunch**	早午餐
08. **lunch / luncheon**	午餐
09. **tea time**	下午茶時間
10. **dinner / supper**	晚餐

08│健身房

飯店的健身房通常都只有簡單的設施，而且數量也不會太多，一旦旺季房客太多，可能得預約，所以要使用健身房得盡量利用離峰時間，或者問清楚預約辦法。大部分的飯店健身房都會要求更換運動服裝和運動鞋才能進入，而且裡面通常不會有淋浴設施。

實境對話

A: When does the health club open?
請問健身房開放時間是什麼時候？

B: It opens at six o'clock in the morning and closes at eleven o'clock at night.
早上六點到晚上十一點。

A: What kind of facilities are there in the health club?
有什麼設施呢？

B: There're treadmills, biking machines and weight lifting machines.
有跑步車、腳踏車，和舉重設備。

B: Be sure to go there during daytime so that you don't need to wait for long.
請你盡量白天使用，才不會等太久。

A: Do you have shower rooms there, and do I need to bring towels?
那麼有淋浴設備或提供毛巾嗎？

B: Sorry, there's no shower room. And you may need to bring a towel from your room.
抱歉，那裡沒有淋浴間。恐怕得請你從房間帶毛巾。

☝ 你可以聽懂／口說更多

01. 如何使用這些健身器材呢？
How to use the fitness equipment?

02. 你最好穿運動鞋及運動服以避免傷害。
You'd better wear sneakers and fitness outfits in case of injuries.

03. 請問這個飯店的健身房在哪裡？
Where is the health club in the hotel?

04. 請你告訴我們怎麼使用健身房裡的跑步機？
Can you tell us how to use the treadmills in the gym?

05. 為什麼不改去健身房呢？
Why not go to the gym instead?

06. 你想要和我一起去健身房運動嗎？
Would you like to come with me to exercise in the gym?

07. 我們的健身房有很多器材。
There are many facilities in our gym.

08. 你們飯店有健身房嗎？
Do you have a gym in your hotel?

09. 你能告訴我飯店的健身房在什麼地方嗎？
Can you tell me where the gym is in the hotel?

10. 你們有專業的健身房指導員嗎？
Do you have any professional gym instructor?

✍ 關鍵單字／片語

01. **gymnasium / gym**	健身房
02. **health club**	健身房
03. **instructor**	指導員
04. **fitness equipment**	健身器材
05. **treadmill**	跑步機
06. **weight lifting**	舉重
07. **punch-bags**	沙包
08. **upright bike**	立式腳踏車
09. **recumbent bike**	臥式腳踏車
10. **stepper / climber**	踏步機

09 | 游泳池

休閒渡假飯店通常會有不錯的游泳池設施,不過如果是位於市中心的飯店,通常都是位於天台或屋頂,這類游泳池都會偏向親子戲水,因此往往也會附帶兒童池。游泳池還是會有更衣和淋浴設備,所以為了禮貌,請不要直接著泳裝在飯店裡走來走去。

實境對話

A: Do you have a swimming pool? I'd like to go swimming every morning.
請問貴飯店有游泳池嗎?我有晨泳的習慣。

B: Yes, we have a standard one on the top floor.
有的,我們有一個標準池,位於頂樓天台。

A: Is it an outdoor swimming pool?
是露天的嗎?

B: Yes. So it would be closed for rainy days.
是的,所以雨天不開放。

A: Is the changing room included?
那裡有更衣室嗎?

B: Yes, but you may need to bring towels and toiletries.
有的,但需自備毛巾和盥洗用具。

A: I'm going to take my son there. Is there a lifeguard?
我會帶小孩一起去游泳。請問有救生員嗎?

B: Yes, there is. We do have a little pool for children. Your son is going to love it.
有救生員。我們還有個兒童池,你的孩子一定會喜歡。

👆 你可以聽懂／口說更多

01. 你想跟我一起去游泳池嗎？
Would you like to go to the swimming pool with me?

02. 你們的酒店連游泳池都沒有嘛！
You don't even have a pool in the hotel!

03. 我們要不要一個小時左右在游泳池見？
Shall we meet by the pool in about an hour?

04. 你們飯店有游泳池嗎？
Do you have swimming pool in your hotel?

05. 我在哪裡買得到泳裝和蛙鏡？
Where can I buy swimming suit and goggles?

06. 我們飯店有一個很大的游泳池。
There is a very large swimming pool in our hotel.

07. 我喜歡你們的運動設施，尤其是游泳池。
I like your sports facilities, especially the swimming pool.

08. 如果你下午沒事，我們去游泳吧。
Let's go swimming if you are free this afternoon.

09. 順便問下游泳池在哪裡？
Where is the swimming pool, by the way?

10. 我們飯店有一個保齡球館和一個室內游泳池。
There are a bowling center and an indoor swimming pool in our hotel.

✍ 關鍵單字／片語

01. **swimming pool**	游泳池
02. **lifeguard**	救生員
03. **swimming suit / trunks**	（女生的）泳衣／泳褲
04. **goggles**	蛙鏡
05. **swimming cap**	泳帽
06. **bikini**	比基尼
07. **swimming ring**	泳圈
08. **outdoor**	室外
09. **indoor**	室內
10. **steam room**	蒸氣室

10 | 房內設備

飯店房間裡面主要電器設備除了電燈，就是電視、音響和電冰箱，一到房間最好把全部電器包含電燈都打開，檢查是否故障，其次就是檢查衛浴設備。最後再看看寢具是否有短少，毛巾是否乾淨。都檢查好，才會住得安心、舒服。

👉 實境對話

A: The toilet is leaking. I can't sleep with the noise.
我房間的馬桶在漏水，那噪音吵得我不能入睡。

B: Sorry, sir. I'll have someone fix it up for you immediately.
先生，真是不好意思。我會立刻派人過去修理。

A: All right. Oh, I almost forgot. I need a roll of toilet paper and two disposable cups.
好呀。喔，差點忘了，我需要一卷衛生紙和二個免洗杯。

B: Sure. Is there anything more you need?
當然。請問還需要其他東西嗎？

A: Yes, could you have someone come to my room and do something about the air conditioner?
有，可否麻煩你派人上來處理一下空調呢？

B: Yes, sir. May I ask what's the problem with the air conditioner?
好的。可以請問空調有什麼問題嗎？

A: It's not cold enough.
不夠冷。

B: I'll report it to the maintenance right away. We apologize for the inconvenience.
我馬上請維修人員過去看。很抱歉造成您的不便。

🖐 你可以聽懂／口說更多

01. 這是一間有浴室的房間。
This is a room with a bath.

02. 房間裡有洗滌設施嗎？
Does the room have any washing facilities?

03. 我們飯店提供一流的房間設施。
Our hotel offers high-class accommodation.

04. 我們要一間帶洗手間的房間。
We want a room with a bathroom.

05. 房間裡可以上網嗎？
Is there an internet connection in the room?

06. 我們飯店的房間設施完備、裝飾典雅。
Our room facilities are complete and elegant.

07. 房間裡的床非常柔軟舒適。
The bed in the room is very soft and comfortable.

08. 這個房間設施不全，而且裝飾粗糙。
The room was poorly appointed and badly decorated.

09. 房間裡有電視和空調。
There is a TV set and an air conditioner in the room.

10. 房間裡有暖氣設施嗎？
Is there any heating facilities in the room?

✍ 關鍵單字／片語

01. **air-conditioner**	空調、冷氣
02. **pay channel**	付費頻道
03. **refrigerator**	冰箱
04. **coffer / safe**	保險箱
05. **razor**	刮鬍刀
06. **shaving cream / foam**	刮鬍膏、刮鬍泡沫
07. **tea bag**	茶包
08. **drinking fountain**	飲水機
09. **toothbrush / toothpaste**	牙刷／牙膏
10. **bathrobe**	浴衣、浴袍

11 | 衣物送洗

一般飯店都有提供衣物送洗的服務，只要將欲送洗的衣物放在客房內的洗衣袋內，並附上洗衣單及需求的時間、是否熨燙……隔日早上客房清掃時就會被收走。若有緊急狀況（如衣服沾到醬汁或油墨）需要處理時，可立即連絡客房服務前來將衣物收走處理。

實境對話

A: I have some laundry that needs to be done. Is there a valet service in this hotel?
我有些衣物需要清洗，請問旅館裡有清洗服務嗎？

B: Certainly. Please fill out the laundry form and put the laundry in the laundry bag. When do you need it back?
當然。請填寫洗衣單，並將衣物放在洗衣袋內就行了。您什麼時候需要衣物呢？

A: I need the dress for a party tonight. Do you think it could be done before 4 p.m.?
我今晚需要那件洋裝來參加派對。你覺得四點以前可以洗好嗎？

B: We charge an extra 50% more for an express service; and it will take three hours.
快洗服務需加收百分之五十的服務費，需要三小時的時間。

A: That would be fine, as long as it's done.
沒關係，只要衣服洗好就好。

B: Great. I'll send someone up to collect the laundry bag in ten minutes.
好。約十分鐘後我請人上去收衣服。

你可以聽懂／口說更多

01. 我想洗這些衣服。
I'd like to have this laundry done, please.

02. 請您填寫一下這張洗衣單好嗎？
Would you please fill out the laundry list?

03. 洗衣服務，可以幫您嗎？
Laundry Service. May I help you?

04. 您有衣服要洗嗎？
Do you have any laundry?

05. 請問你們能派人來收我要洗的衣服嗎？
Could you send someone up for my laundry, please?

06. 我有一些衣物要送洗。
I would like to have some clothes cleaned.

07. 我要乾洗這套西裝。可以也幫我把西裝燙好嗎？
I want this suit dry-cleaned. Would you have the suit ironed as well?

08. 我們有快速洗衣服務。
We have express laundry service.

09. 請告訴我洗衣服的時間好嗎？
Could you tell me your laundry service hours?

10. 我什麼時候能夠取回洗的衣服呢？
When can I get my laundry back?

關鍵單字／片語

01. **laundry**	送洗的衣物
02. **laundry / valet service**	清洗服務
03. **laundry basket**	洗衣籃
04. **iron**	熨燙、熨斗
05. **dry-clean**	乾洗
06. **stain**	污漬
07. **suit**	西裝
08. **clothing / clothes**	衣服
09. **laundry service**	洗衣服務
10. **express**	快速

12 | 換房間

有時候房間隔壁住了喜歡開派對的房客，或者隔壁房有小孩哭鬧時，我們可以向櫃檯反應，如果仍然沒有改善，可以要求更換房間。一般來說，如果有空房的話，飯店通常會安排更換，如果沒有空房的話，也可以加價更換到好一點的房間，才不會因此影響旅行的心情。

實境對話

A: Good evening, sir. This is the front desk.
晚安，先生。這裡是櫃檯。

B: I'm in room 304. I can hear a baby crying out loud next door. Could you please tell them to lower down that noise?
我住 304 房。我不斷聽到隔壁房有嬰兒哭鬧聲。可以請他們小聲一點嗎？

A: We'll inform them right away.
我會立刻去通知他們。

B: That's from their newborn baby. It seems that they don't know how to keep the baby quiet. I'd like to know if it's possible to change my room.
隔壁夫婦的新生兒在哭鬧。他們看起來應該不知道怎麼安撫嬰兒。我想知道我是否可以換一間房間。

A: We're fully booked today; let me see what I can do. We have room 728 unoccupied. Please give me a call when you're ready to move, and I'll send a luggage man to help you.
今天的住房率很滿，我來看看可以怎麼辦。728 號房是空房。您準備好後請給我一通電話，我請行李員上去協助您。

👆 你可以聽懂／口說更多

01. 假如有必要的話，我可以換房間。
   I can change rooms if necessary.

02. 我是住在 401 房間的大衛。你可以為我換個房間嗎？
   I'm David in Room 401. Can you change a room for me?

03. 我恐怕沒辦法為您更換房間。
   I am afraid that I can't change a room for you.

04. 我想換房間，因為隔壁太吵了！
   I want to have my room changed because it's too noisy next door.

05. 我的房間太靠近電梯了，能換房間嗎？
   My room is too close to the elevator. Can I change it?

06. 您可以多住幾天，也可以調換房間。
   You can stay longer, and you can also change your room.

07. 如果隔壁房仍有噪音，請你給我換房間好嗎？
   If it is still noisy next door, could you give me a different room, please?

08. 您什麼時間換房間最方便？
   When is it convenient for you to change rooms, sir?

09. 很抱歉，我們馬上給您換房間。
   I am sorry. We will switch rooms for you right away.

10. 無論如何，我們都要換房間。
   Anyhow, I'd like to change our room.

✎ 關鍵單字／片語

01. **front desk**	櫃檯
02. **newborn baby**	新生兒
03. **unoccupied**	沒人住的
04. **change room**	換房間
05. **next door**	隔壁房
06. **noisy**	吵鬧的
07. **right away**	馬上
08. **if necessary**	如果需要的話
09. **inform**	通知
10. **be quiet**	安靜

13 | 遺忘東西

住房期間，我們最容易把鑰匙遺忘在房內。這時候可以請櫃台提供備用鑰匙，櫃台通常會要求預付押金，所以，一定要記得歸還。其次就是在使用其他休閒設施時，也常常把手機或皮包遺忘。除非被有心人士帶走，否則通常你會在櫃檯找到你遺失的物品。

實境對話

A: I lost my key.
我的鑰匙好像弄丟了。

B: Is it in your room? Which room are you staying at?
是放在房間裡嗎？請問你住幾號房？

A: Room 8113. I'm not sure where I lost it. I just had dinner at the restaurant. Maybe I lost it with my purse.
8113 號房。但我也不清楚，我剛剛在餐廳用餐，我不確定是否和皮包一起遺失了。

B: You lost your purse, too?
你也遺失了皮包嗎？

A: I don't know. That's why I'm going back to my room to check if I left both of them in my room.
我不知道。我想回房間去確認，我是不是都沒帶出來。

B: Here's the spare key that you can use.
沒問題，我可以給您備用鑰匙。

B: Wait a minute, Miss. Is your purse black?
等一下，小姐。請問您的皮包是黑色的嗎？

A: Yes. Oh, this is my purse. And... my key is inside the purse. Thank you very much.
是的，哦！這就是我的皮包，鑰匙也在裡面，謝謝。

👆 你可以聽懂／口說更多

01. 請您別遺忘東西。
    Please don't leave anything behind.
02. 今天早上我找不到我的手錶了。
    I couldn't find my watch this morning.
03. 您確定它沒在房間裡嗎？
    Are you sure it is not in your room?
04. 請填寫這份財產遺失單好嗎？
    Could you fill out the Lost Property Form, please?
05. 能描述一下您錢包的特徵嗎？
    Can you describe the features of your wallet?
06. 你沒遺忘什麼東西吧？
    Are you sure you haven't left anything behind?
07. 我記起我的眼鏡遺忘在房間書桌上了。
    I just remembered that my glasses were left on the desk in my room.
08. 別著急，我們馬上就去找。
    Don't worry. We will look for it for you right now.
09. 您最後一次看到它是什麼時候？
    When was the last time you saw it?
10. 我想我可能把它丟在什麼地方了。
    I think I might have left it somewhere.

✍ 關鍵單字／片語

01. **lose**	遺失
02. **spare key**	備用鑰匙
03. **remember**	記住、想起
04. **fill out**	填寫
05. **Lost Property Form**	財物遺失表
06. **feature**	特徵、特色
07. **leave behind**	忘了帶、留下
08. **somewhere**	某個地方
09. **purse**	皮包
10. **watch**	手錶

14│退房

退房通常是中午的十二點鐘,在退房之前,最重要的就是整理好你的行李,是否有東西遺留在衣櫥?還是被棉被蓋住了?千萬要再巡視整個房間一次,當然護照、機票也不要忘了,然後拿著鑰匙到櫃檯辦理退房結帳,記得要檢查帳單上的金額是否正確!

🗨 實境對話

A: I want to check out.
我要退房。

B: Ok, please return your keys. Did you drink any beverages in the refrigerator?
好的,請把鑰匙給我,您有使用冰箱的飲料嗎?

A: Yes, I had a coke and a bottle of mineral water.
有,我喝了一瓶可樂還有礦泉水。

B: The water is free, the coke is 1.5 dollars, plus, you have made an international call, the charge will be 30 dollars.
礦泉水是飯店贈送,可樂一瓶是 1.5 元,另外您有打國際電話,費用是 30 元。

B: The sum is 300 dollars; will you pay in cash or credit card?
總共是 300 元,請問要刷卡還是付現呢?

A: By credit card.
刷卡。

B: Please check your receipt and sign your name here, thank you.
請核對一下你的帳單並在這裡簽名,謝謝!

👆 你可以聽懂／口說更多

01. 我想在 10 點退房，請先幫我把帳單準備好。
    I want to check out at 10, please have the bill ready.

02. 逾時退房費用怎麼算？
    How do you charge for delayed checkout?

03. 總共是多少？
    What's the grand total?

04. 你們收支票嗎？
    Do you take checks?

05. 帳單金額有錯誤。
    The amount is wrong.

06. 我沒有要求客房點餐服務。
    I didn't order any room service.

07. 我沒有看付費頻道。
    I didn't watch the pay-per-view TV.

08. 可以幫我把行李拿下來嗎？
    Could you bring my luggage down?

09. 請幫我叫一台計程車。
    Please get a cab for me.

10. 我可以暫時把行李寄放在這裡嗎？我想去喝杯咖啡。
    Could I leave my baggage here for a while? I want to go
    have a cup of coffee.

✍️ 關鍵單字／片語

01. **check-out counter**	結帳櫃檯
02. **procedure**	手續
03. **bill**	帳單
04. **beverage**	飲料
05. **mineral water**	礦泉水
06. **supplementary fee**	追加費用
07. **extend my stay**	延長住宿時間
08. **get a cab**	叫一台計程車
09. **bellboy**	旅館大廳的服務生
10. **grand total**	（最後加起來的）總和

15 | 青年之家

如果你的住宿預算不多，可以選擇物美價廉的青年之家，但是你必須持有國際青年之家住宿會員卡才能登記住宿，只是有些地區的青年之家不會比小旅館方便，所以你還是依自己的需要，尋找最適合的住宿地點吧！

實境對話

A: How many I help you?
有什麼可以為您服務的嗎？

B: I would like to check in.
我想辦理登記住宿。

A: Do you have a YH card?
你有青年旅館卡嗎？

B: Yes, how much do I need to pay?
有，請問我要付多少費用呢？

A: You will have to pay for the bed sheet if you don't bring your own.
如果你沒有自備床單的話，就要額外付費。

B: Oh, may I cook there?
喔，那我可以自己炊煮嗎？

A: Of course. You could use the kitchen.
當然，你可以用廚房。

A: There is one on every floor.
每一樓層都有一間。

B: That would be great!
那實在太棒了！

☝ 你可以聽懂／口說更多

01. 你們有哪些種類的房間呢？
    What kind of room do you have?

02. 請問幾個人住一間房呢？
    How many people share a room?

03. 請問熱水供應到幾點？
    Excuse me, when will you stop supplying hot water?

04. 請問要付押金嗎？
    Do I need to pay a deposit?

05. 請問住兩個星期有優惠嗎？
    Is there any discount if I stay for two weeks?

06. 請問有空調設備的房間嗎？
    Do you have any room that is air-conditioned?

07. 這裡有蚊子，請問有蚊香嗎？
    There are mosquitoes here. Do you have any mosquito coil incense?

08. 這是我的青年旅館卡。
    Here's my YH card.

09. 兩個人一間房。
    Two people share a room.

10. 是的，你可以開伙。
    Yes, you can cook here.

✎ 關鍵單字／片語

01. **kitchen**	廚房
02. **YH card**	青年旅館卡
03. **pan**	平底鍋
04. **kettle**	茶壺
05. **hot water bottle**	熱水壺
06. **bathroom**	浴室
07. **blanket**	毛毯
08. **sleeping bag**	睡袋
09. **mosquito**	蚊子
10. **incense**	線香

Chapter

05

享受美食篇

Chapter 05 音檔雲端連結

因各家手機系統不同，若無法直接掃描，
仍可以至以下電腦雲端連結下載收聽。
（https://tinyurl.com/3nx8vb6h）

01 | 蒐羅美食

到任何一個國家都一樣，當地著名的美食是不容錯過的旅遊體驗。建議大家可以在出發前先蒐集資料，不管是利用網路，或者是曾經去過的朋友，當然最好的是能找到當地的朋友當嚮導，絕對可以吃到道地卻不一定貴的平民美食喔。

實境對話

A: I know some good food in New York. Do you want to try some?
我知道紐約一些好吃的東西。你要嚐嚐看嗎？

B: I do. Are they expensive?
我真的很想試試。很貴嗎？

A: Not exactly. First of all, you shouldn't miss the cinnamon rolls and hotdogs.
不盡然。首先，你不該錯過肉桂捲和熱狗。

B: I've heard that fast food here is very delicious.
我聽說紐約的速食很好吃。

A: Those are in fast food restaurants. What I mentioned were the food stands.
那是在速食店裡，我剛講的是路邊小吃攤。

B: Food stands? I thought they were only famous in Taiwan.
路邊小吃攤？我以為那只有在台灣才出名。

A: Let's go get some cinnamon rolls around the corner first.
我們現在就先去轉角買一些肉桂捲吃。

B: Yum! I love the frosting on the top. It's delicious.
好吃耶！我喜歡上面的糖霜，太好吃了。

👆 你可以聽懂／口說更多

01. 你能推薦個好餐館嗎？
    Can you recommend a good restaurant?

02. 我真的抗拒不了那些美食的誘惑。
    I really can't resist all the delicious food.

03. 今天菜單上有什麼好吃的呢？
    What is good on menu today?

04. 你知道有什麼好地方去吃飯嗎？
    Do you know any good place to eat?

05. 涮羊肉是我們最好的特色菜之一。
    Instant-boiled mutton is one of our best specialties.

06. 我可以吃一鍋那麼好吃的燉肉。
    I could eat a whole pot of that yummy stew.

07. 這是這個鎮最好的餐廳了。
    This is the best restaurant in the town.

08. 這裡有什麼好吃的可以用來搭配蕃茄醬？
    Do they serve anything good here to go with ketchup?

09. 對我們大家來説那是一個很棒的餐廳。
    It's a good restaurant for all of us.

10. 要説當地的特色美食，當然少不了海鮮。
    Speaking of local delicacies, one can't ignore seafood.

✎ 關鍵單字／片語

01. **first of all**	首先
02. **delicious**	美味的
03. **food stand**	路邊小攤子
04. **cinnamon roll**	肉桂捲
05. **get rid of**	擺脫
06. **calorie**	卡路里
07. **local**	當地的
08. **taste**	嚐起來
09. **yammy / yum**	好吃
10. **yucky**	難吃、噁心

02 | 訂位

大部分著名的美食餐廳都必須事先訂位，某些高級餐廳甚至會要求你穿著正式服裝進入，因此務必在訂位的時候詢問清楚。另外，訂位的時候，也必須確認清楚座位可以保留多久時間，以免路上因事耽擱或遇到塞車而白跑一趟了。

實境對話

A: Good afternoon, New York Restaurant.
午安，紐約餐廳。

B: Good afternoon. I want to make a reservation at eight tonight.
午安，我要訂今天晚上八點鐘的位置。

A: I'm sorry, but we are fully-booked tonight. I can put you on the waiting list if you want to.
很抱歉，今晚的位置已經全部客滿了。如果您需要的話我可以將您列在等候名單。

B: How about Friday night?
那星期五晚上呢？

A: Friday night is also full. We have plenty of seats available next week.
星期五晚上也客滿了。我們下星期有許多位置。

B: Please make it next Tuesday night then.
那請安排在週二晚上吧。

A: May I know how many people?
請問有幾位？

B: We're four with a child under two. We want a non-smoking table by the window.
我們有四個人還帶著二歲以下的小孩。我們想要非吸菸區靠窗的位置。

☝ 你可以聽懂／口說更多

01. 我需要提前訂位嗎？
Do I need to make a reservation in advance?

02. 很抱歉，我在訂位名單中找不到您的名字。
I am sorry that I can't find your name on the reservation list.

03. 我們會不會錯過晚餐訂位時間？
Are we too late for dinner reservation?

04. 我想預訂兩個人的餐位，晚上七點鐘的。
I want to make a reservation for two at 7:00 p.m..

05. 您要不要訂本飯店另一家餐廳的餐位？
Would you like to make a reservation for another restaurant in the hotel?

06. 晚上好，先生，請問訂位了嗎？
Good evening, sir. Do you have a reservation?

07. 今晚的餐位恐怕已經訂滿了。
I'm afraid we are fully booked for tonight.

08. 請問你們晚餐預訂座位了嗎？
Do you have a reservation for dinner?

09. 我想預訂明天晚上的餐位。
I'd like to reserve a table for tomorrow evening, please.

10. 歡迎光臨本餐廳，請問您訂位了嗎？
Welcome to our restaurant. Do you have a reservation?

✍ 關鍵單字／片語

01. **reserve a table**	訂桌
02. **waiting list**	等候清單
03. **full**	客滿
04. **highchair**	兒童進食用高腳椅
05. **I'd like to**	我想要
06. **welcome to**	歡迎光臨……
07. **taken**	被佔走了、有人坐
08. **tonight**	今晚
09. **plenty of**	足夠
10. **How about...?**	……如何？

03 | 內用／外帶

有些餐廳會提供外送服務，但是大部分都只提供內用和外帶。因此進入餐廳的時候，服務生會問你要內用還是外帶。另外，如果用完餐還有剩下的食物，可以請服務生打包。他們會很樂意為你服務，因為這表示你很滿意他們的食物。

👆 實境對話

A: Good day, sir. Do you want to eat here or take away?
日安，先生。你要外帶還是內用？

B: We want to eat here, please. We need a table for three.
我們要在這裡用餐，麻煩給我們三個人的位置。

A: Sorry, sir. It's full now. Can you wait or do you want to take away?
抱歉，今天客滿，你們要稍等一下，或者要外帶呢？

B: We can wait. How long do you think we'll have to wait?
我們可以等。大概需要等多久呢？

A: About fifteen minutes.
可能要十五分鐘。

B: That's quite a long time.
這樣太久了。

A: We do have a table for three in the smoking area. I'm wondering if it is ok for you.
目前吸菸區有一個三人的位置，不知道你們要不要？

B: Yes, we'll take it.
好的，我們要。

👆 你可以聽懂／口說更多

01. 先生，您是內用還是外帶？
Will that be eat in or take away, sir?

02. 我可以在這兒點外帶食物嗎？
Can I order take-out here?

03. 您要帶走還是在店裡吃？
Is this for here or to go?

04. 你們有餃子可以外帶嗎？
Do you have dumplings to take away?

05. 我可以在這吃嗎？
Can I eat my meal here?

06. 請給我外帶一份中薯條和一杯大可樂。
I'd like a medium fries and a large coke to go, please.

07. 我要內用一個熱狗。
I'd like a hot dog to eat here.

08. 我要外帶。
I'd like to take away.

09. 我想在這吃咖哩飯。
I want to have curry and rice here.

10. 今天我們的外帶食物只有春捲。
We only have spring rolls today for take-out.

✏ 關鍵單字／片語

01. **to go**	外帶
02. **take away**	外帶
03. **eat here**	內用
04. **eat in**	內用
05. **for here**	內用
06. **takeout**	外賣
07. **leftovers**	剩菜
08. **I'd (=I would) say**	我想……
09. **shortly**	立刻、馬上
10. **smoking area**	吸菸區

04 | 點餐

一套正式的西式餐點通常包含開胃菜、湯品、主食、甜點與飲料。所以，點餐時，侍者會逐一詢問您想點用的食物。如果，不太確定怎麼點或是拿不定主意的時候，還可以請侍者推薦菜色，餐廳內通常會有一些主廚特餐，常讓人驚喜。

🐟 實境對話

A: What do you like to order?
請問您要點什麼？

B: I want a rib-eye steak. This lady wants a fish fillet.
我要一份肋眼牛排，這位小姐要一份魚排。

A: Do you need some appetizer? Like Buffalo wings or onion rings?
需要來點開胃菜嗎？像水牛城雞翅或是洋蔥圈？

B: Some onion rings, please.
請給我們一些洋蔥圈。

A: Anything for dessert?
需要任何甜點嗎？

B: No, thanks. But please bring us some wine.
不用了，謝謝你。但請給我們葡萄酒。

A: Do you have a particular choice for wine?
請問酒類您有特殊的偏好嗎？

B: Any recommendation?
有什麼建議嗎？

A: I would suggest Merlot to go with the steak, and white wine with the fish fillet.
我建議牛排搭配梅洛紅酒，魚排搭配白酒。

👆 你可以聽懂／口說更多

01. 我可以幫您點餐了嗎？
   May I take your order now?

02. 我想要一個漢堡和一杯可樂。
   I want a hamburger and a coke.

03. 我馬上回來為您點餐。
   I will come back later to take your order.

04. 我想嚐嚐當地出產的酒。
   I'd like to have some local wine.

05. 晚飯您想吃點什麼？蔬菜還是肉？
   What would you like for dinner, vegetables or meat?

06. 您要現在點餐還是稍後再點？
   Would you like to order now or a moment later?

07. 您想吃點什麼？中餐還是西餐？
   What kind of food do you like, Chinese food or Western food?

08. 您現在準備點餐嗎，小姐？
   Are you ready to order now, Miss?

09. 我想點義大利麵。
   I'm going to order a spaghetti.

10. 要不要喝些湯？
   How about having some soup?

✎ 關鍵單字／片語

01. **recommend**	推薦
02. **hungry / starving**	飢餓的
03. **thirsty**	渴
04. **steak**	牛排
05. **fish fillet**	魚排
06. **red wine / white wine**	紅酒／白酒
07. **champagne**	香檳
08. **meat**	肉
09. **vegetarian / veggie**	素食者
10. **take one's order**	為……點餐

05 上錯餐

有些餐廳因為生意太好，有時難免會上錯餐點。為了避免結帳時產生糾紛，你可以在第一時間請服務生弄清楚。有的時候可能只是送錯桌，當然也有可能點餐的時候就錯了。大部份的餐廳都很注重誠信，所以，如果確定是他們搞錯了，一定會盡快補上一份餐點給你的。

🗣 實境對話

A: Hi, here's your roast chicken.
嗨，這是您點的烤雞。

B: I didn't order roast chicken. My order is fried chicken.
我點的不是烤雞，是炸雞。

A: Oh, sorry, sir. I will go to check with the kitchen. Wait a second, please.
喔，不好意思，我去跟廚師確認，請稍等一下。

A: Sir, here is your fried chicken and a soda.
先生，這是您點的炸雞還有汽水。

B: Well... I thought I ordered a cola not a soda.
嗯……我以為我點的是可樂不是汽水。

A: Oh, the soda will be my treat. I will go get a cola for you.
喔，這杯汽水我請客。我現在就去拿可樂給您。

B: You seem to be new here. I can't quite stand all the mistakes you've made.
你看起來像新來的。我不太能忍受這種種的錯誤。

A: I'm terribly sorry, sir.
真的非常抱歉。

👆 你可以聽懂／口說更多

01. 這不是我點的菜。
   It's not what I ordered.

02. 我剛才並沒有點龍蝦啊。
   I didn't order lobster just now.

03. 我們馬上為您換菜。
   We will change it for you right away.

04. 非常抱歉我們弄錯了。
   We are terribly sorry for the mistake.

05. 給您上錯了菜真的很抱歉。
   I am so sorry for giving you the wrong dish.

06. 我馬上把您點的菜端來。
   I'll bring your dish right away.

07. 真對不起，我似乎犯了個錯誤。
   I'm really sorry. It seems that I've made a mistake.

08. 那麼這次為什麼不嚐嚐這道菜呢？
   So why not try the dish this time?

09. 我們一定會在帳單上減掉這道菜的費用。
   We will be sure to cross out the dish in the bill.

10. 我們保證這樣的事不會再發生了！
   We promise such thing will never happen again!

✏️ 關鍵單字／片語

01. **roast**	烤
02. **smoked**	煙燻
03. **fried**	炸
04. **stand / bear**	忍受
05. **make a mistake**	犯錯
06. **try harder**	更盡力
07. **at once**	馬上、立刻
08. **cross out**	刪掉
09. **my treat**	我請客
10. **dish**	一盤菜、菜餚、盤子

06 | 野餐

常去國外旅行就會發現，野餐也是一種西方人很喜歡的用餐方式。除了一般家庭會選擇郊外或公園野餐之外，一些渡假村式的飯店也會提供野餐的服務，除了麵包、水果和乳酪之外，有時候也會準備烤肉，甚至像正式餐點一樣，提供前菜、餐前酒、主食和甜點。

🗨 實境對話

A: Today, we'll serve you dinner in the garden. Right there under the white camp.
今天的晚餐安排在花園用餐，就在那邊的白色帳篷下。

B: That means we're going to have sandwiches and fruits for dinner, right?
意思是我們今天晚上要吃三明治和水果，是嗎？

A: No, sir. We prepared different kinds of bread with cheese which is very famous locally.
不，我們準備了不同口味的麵包搭配本地相當有名的乳酪。

B: That sounds delicious.
聽起來好美味喔。

A: And, we'll serve roast steak or lamb for your choice. And fresh green salad.
另外我們還準備了現烤牛排和羊排，以及新鮮的蔬菜沙拉。

B: How about beverage? Are beers available?
那麼飲料呢？會有啤酒嗎？

A: Yes. We also provide red wine.
有的，除了啤酒之外，還有佐餐的紅酒供您選擇。

B: That's sumptuous.
真的太豐盛了。

🎧 你可以聽懂／口說更多

01. 天氣多好啊！為什麼不去野餐呢？
What a nice day! Why not go for a picnic?

02. 我們正準備去山上野餐。
We are preparing for a picnic on the hill.

03. 你願意和我們一起去野餐嗎？
Would you like to go on a picnic with us?

04. 我們現在來決定一下野餐的時間吧。
Let's fix the time for the picnic now.

05. 可以在這兒野餐嗎？
Is it OK to picnic here?

06. 為什麼不邀請我們的鄰居一起野餐呢？
Why not invite our neighbors to the picnic together?

07. 如果明天天氣晴朗，我們就出去野餐。
We will go out for a picnic if it is sunny tomorrow.

08. 明天野餐你帶什麼好吃的？
What would you like to bring for tomorrow's picnic?

09. 我為野餐準備了水果和香腸。
I've prepared fruit and sausage for the picnic.

10. 到這裡來野餐可真奇怪！
Coming here to have a picnic can be so strange!

✍ 關鍵單字／片語

01. **go on a picnic**	去野餐	
02. **prepare**	準備	
03. **sandwich**	三明治	
04. **beer**	啤酒	
05. **sumptuous**	豪華的、豐盛	
06. **nice weather**	天氣不錯	
07. **picnic area**	野餐區	
08. **picnic mat**	野餐墊	
09. **sunny**	晴朗	
10. **on the hill**	在小山上	

07 | 吃到飽餐廳

和台灣一樣，國外也有很多家庭式的吃到飽餐廳。有的食物很多元，像是飯店的歐式自助餐；也有的餐廳只提供某種食物和飲料吃到飽，譬如：披薩和飲料，或烤雞和飲料。有的吃到飽餐廳是自助式的，需要自己去拿菜；有的則是直接跟服務生點菜，由他們服務。

實境對話 ────────

A: Is this an all-you-can-eat restaurant?
你們餐廳是全面吃到飽嗎？

B: Yes, the salad bar and dessert are all-you-can-eat. You will have to order a main dish with it.
是的，沙拉吧和甜點是吃到飽的，但我們的主食必須單點。

A: All right. We'd like a table for two.
好的，我們要兩個人的位置。

B: This way, please. This is your table. What do you want for the main dish?
請跟我來。這是你們的位置。請問兩位主餐要點什麼？

A: We'd like a seafood pasta and a roast chicken with seasoned rice.
我們要一份海鮮義大利麵和一份烤雞加香料飯。

B: Got it. Now you can go for the salad bar.
好的，你們可以先去取用沙拉吧了。

A: Do we need to order beverages?
飲料要另外點嗎？

B: Yes. And refills are free.
要，但是可以免費續杯。

你可以聽懂／口說更多

01. 明天晚上去吃自助餐怎麼樣？
How about having a buffet dinner tomorrow?

02. 這是我第一次在自助餐廳裡吃飯。
This is the first time for me to eat in a buffet restaurant.

03. 要不要試試我們的自助餐呢？
Why not try our buffet dinner?

04. 自助餐在那邊，請隨便用。
The buffet is over there. Please help yourself.

05. 聽說他們有很棒的自助餐。
It is said that they have wonderful buffet.

06. 你覺得這家自助餐廳怎麼樣？
How do you think of the food in this cafeteria?

07. 只要十美元就可以吃到飽。
Only pay $10, then you can have all you want.

08. 請告訴我你們自助餐的供餐時間是幾點？
Could you tell me what your buffet's serving hour is?

09. 聽說附近有家很棒的自助餐廳。
I heard that there was a good cafeteria nearby.

10. 你想不想跟我們去吃到飽餐廳？
Would you like to go to the buffet restaurant with us?

關鍵單字／片語

01. **all-you-can-eat**	吃到飽
02. **salad bar**	沙拉吧
03. **refill**	續杯
04. **sip**	一小口、啜飲
05. **pasta / spaghetti**	麵／義大利麵
06. **buffet**	自助餐
07. **help yourself**	自己來
08. **think of**	認為
09. **cafeteria**	自助餐廳
10. **serving hour**	供應時間

08 | 咖啡店

逛街逛累了，口也渴了，想找個地方歇腳嗎？在國外，到處都有著裝潢優雅、咖啡香味四溢的咖啡店，不妨點杯香濃滑順的卡布其諾，再來塊新鮮味美的乳酪蛋糕，找個靠窗的位子，享受一個充滿異國風情的下午茶吧！

實境對話

A: Excuse me, I want a latte.
麻煩你，我想要一杯拿鐵咖啡。

B: Do you want it iced or hot?
請問要冰的還是熱的？

A: Iced.
冰的。

B: Ok, and do you want some fresh baked bread? It's very good.
好的，要不要來一個我們剛出爐的麵包呢？很好吃喔！

A: No, thanks.
不了，謝謝。

B: How about cake?
還是想要蛋糕呢？

A: Umm... a cheese cake, please.
嗯……請給我一個乳酪蛋糕。

B: Ok, thank you! It's 5 dollars.
好的，謝謝！一共是 5 元。

B: Please wait for a moment. It will be served right away.
請稍等，馬上就好。

👆 你可以聽懂／口說更多

01. 請給我一杯義大利咖啡。
Please give me a cup of Italian coffee.

02. 請問可以續杯嗎？
Could I refill?

03. 請再給我一杯。
Please give me one more cup.

04. 請再給我一個奶精。
Please give me one more cream.

05. 我喜歡牛奶比較多的咖啡。
I like coffee with a lot of milk.

06. 這咖啡太濃了！
This coffee is too strong.

07. 請換一杯給我。
Please change another one for me.

08. 我的咖啡不要加糖。
I don't want sugar in my coffee.

09. 你們這裡有什麼蛋糕嗎？
Do you serve cakes?

10. 我要一個提拉米蘇蛋糕。
I would like a tiramisu.

✏️ 關鍵單字／片語

01. **ice coffee**	冰咖啡
02. **Mocha coffee**	摩卡咖啡
03. **black coffee**	黑咖啡
04. **espresso**	濃縮咖啡
05. **cappuccino**	卡布其諾
06. **latte**	拿鐵
07. **coffee bean grinder**	咖啡研磨機
08. **cream**	奶油球、奶精
09. **decaf coffee**	無咖啡因咖啡
10. **hot chocolate**	熱可可

09｜酒吧

如果你不想靜靜的坐在路邊啜飲咖啡，你還可以去一個地方，就是「酒吧」。在那裡可以喝到各種類的酒，還放著節奏性強的音樂，喜歡熱鬧氣氛的你，邀幾個好友到酒吧去瘋狂一番吧！

實境對話

A: Sorry miss, you have to be 20 to enter.
對不起，小姐，要滿 20 歲才能進入本店。

B: I am over 20!
我已經超過 20 歲了！

A: Please show me your ID.
請給我看你的證件。

B: Here.
在這裡。

A: Ok, thank you.
好了，謝謝。

A: You may go in now.
你可以進去了。

A: Hey, I'm so bored. Let's go for a drink.
嘿，我好無聊。出去喝一杯吧！

B: How about going to the bar around the corner?
不如去轉角那間酒吧？

B: Tonight's lady's night. Free entrance for we girls.
今晚是淑女之夜，我們女生進去不用錢。

A: Good idea. Let's rock the night!
好主意！今晚一起瘋狂吧！

👉 你可以聽懂／口說更多

01. 請給我一杯威士忌，加冰塊。
Please give me a whisky on rocks.

02. 這裡有東西可以吃嗎？
Do you serve food here?

03. 可以推薦我一杯雞尾酒嗎？
Can you recommend me a cocktail?

04. 給我一杯啤酒和一些炸薯條。
Please give me a beer and some fries.

05. 這啤酒已經沒有氣了，請換一杯給我。
This beer is flat, please change it for me.

06. 請再給我一杯相同的。
Please give me another one.

07. 你們有哪些種類的酒？
What kind of wine do you have?

08. 是幾年份的？
What year is this?

09. 請給我看酒單。
Please give me a wine list.

10. 請幫我把軟木塞拿掉。
Please take out the cork for me.

✍ 關鍵單字／片語

01. **bartender**	酒保
02. **night club**	夜店
03. **lady's night**	淑女之夜
04. **mix drink**	調酒
05. **Vodka**	伏特加
06. **Whisky**	威士忌
07. **Cognac**	干邑白蘭地
08. **Martini**	馬丁尼酒
09. **Tequila shot**	龍舌蘭
10. **alcohol-free beer**	無酒精啤酒

10｜速食店

速食店，是一種既省時又經濟實惠的餐點，如果你不知道要吃什麼，這可以讓你輕鬆地解決一餐喔！

實境對話

A: Welcome sir, do you want a special combo?
歡迎光臨，先生您好，要不要來份超值全餐呢？

B: Yes, I want two #3 combos, for here.
好，我要兩份三號餐，內用。

A: Do you want an apple pie or sundae?
要不要來份蘋果派或是聖代呢？

B: Yes! I want two chocolate sundaes.
好啊！我要兩個巧克力聖代。

A: What drinks do you want?
您要什麼飲料呢？

B: Two cokes.
兩杯可樂。

A: Let me repeat your order: two #3 combos and two chocolate sundaes, the drinks will be coke. The total is 38 dollars.
重複一次您點的餐點：兩份三號餐和兩個巧克力聖代，附餐飲料是可樂。總共是 38 元。

B: Ok, and please give me three packs of ketchup.
好的！請給我三包蕃茄醬。

A: No problem!
沒問題

A: Enjoy your meal!
祝您用餐愉快。

👆 你可以聽懂／口說更多

01. 請問要外帶還是內用？
    For here or to go?

02. 我要單點一份雙層吉事牛肉漢堡，不要加洋蔥。
    I want a double cheese burger, no onions.

03. 附餐薯條我要換成大薯。
    I want to change the fries to large.

04. 請問有烤洋芋嗎？
    Do you have baked potatoes?

05. 現在還可以點早餐嗎？
    Could I still order breakfast now?

06. 兒童餐有附贈玩具嗎？
    Is there any free toy in the kid's meal?

07. 附餐的飲料有哪些選擇？
    What choices do I have when ordering the combo?

08. 可以給我一些餐巾紙嗎？
    Could you give me some napkins?

09. 我要三號餐。
    I want meal #3.

10. 我的可樂不要加冰塊。
    I want my coke with no ice.

✍ 關鍵單字／片語

01. **napkin**	餐巾紙
02. **straw**	吸管
03. **tray**	餐盤
04. **large / regular / small**	大份／中份／小份
05. **corn soup**	玉米湯
06. **drive-thru**	得來速
07. **fried chicken nuggets**	炸雞塊
08. **Combo**	全餐
09. **Happy Meal**	快樂兒童餐
10. **diet coke**	健怡可樂

11 | 西餐廳

正統的西餐廳非常注重用餐氣氛與用餐禮儀。以服裝方面來說，男生必須穿西裝打領帶，女生則必須穿洋裝搭配高跟鞋。用餐的順序也很講究，通常一套完整的餐食，至少包含前菜、沙拉、湯品、主食、甜點和餐後咖啡或紅茶。

實境對話

A: I really like the appetizers here. Especially the French escargot and smoked salmon.
我很喜歡這家餐廳的開胃菜，尤其是焗田螺和燻鮭魚。

B: Sounds great. What about soup? What do you recommend?
嗯，聽起來很不賴。那湯呢？你推薦哪一道？

A: I like onion soup.
我喜歡他們的洋蔥湯。

B: I like clam chowder more.
我比較喜歡蛤蠣濃湯。

A: Caesar's salad is one of the best choices.
凱薩沙拉是我每次必點的美食。

B: Their rice pudding is the most delicious dessert I've ever had.
他們的米布丁是我吃過最好吃的甜點。

A: What do you want for your main course?
那你的主餐要什麼？

B: I think I'll have the T-bone. How about you?
我要丁骨牛排。你呢？

A: I want baked salmon.
我要烤鮭魚。

👉 你可以聽懂／口說更多

01. 小姐，有什麼可以為您效勞？
What can I do for you, miss?

02. 先生，您還要些什麼東西嗎？
Would you like anything else, sir?

03. 我想來一瓶紅葡萄酒。
I would like to order a bottle of red wine.

04. 我已經很久沒有吃西餐了。
I haven't had western food for a long time.

05. 這間飯店裡有西餐廳嗎？
Is there a western restaurant here in this hotel?

06. 您想要點一份今日特餐嗎？
Would you like an order of today's special?

07. 您要不要嚐嚐牛排？
Would you like to try some beef steak?

08. 妳喜歡吃中餐或西餐？
Which kind of food do you prefer, Chinese or Western?

09. 我們今晚去吃西餐怎麼樣？
What about having some western food tonight?

10. 我們去吃西餐吧。你覺得怎麼樣？
Let's go to a western restaurant. What do you think of that?

✍ 關鍵單字／片語

01. **rare**	三分熟
02. **medium**	五分熟
03. **medium-well**	七分熟
04. **well-done**	全熟
05. **aperitif**	開胃酒
06. **appetizer / starter**	開胃菜
07. **main dish**	主菜
08. **dessert**	甜點
09. **soup**	湯
10. **drink**	飲料

12 | 烤肉店

在國外的烤肉店有不同的類型，有美式燒烤 BBQ、希臘烤肉 Greek BBQ，和巴西窯烤 Churrascaria。以及近期美國流行的由日裔或韓裔經營的日式烤肉 Japanese BBQ 和韓式燒肉 Korean BBQ，如果吃不慣美式食物，可以試試看。

👉 實境對話

A: I'd like to have BBQ today.
今天我想吃烤肉！

B: Should we have American style? Or try a different one?
那你覺得我們是吃道地美國風味，還是要來點異國風情？

A: What kind of choices do we have?
有什麼選擇？

B: The guide book recommends the Churrascaria near the department store. Are you interested?
旅遊指南推薦一家靠近百貨公司的巴西窯烤，你有興趣嗎？

A: Any other suggestions?
還有其他的嗎？

B: How about Greek BBQ?
希臘烤肉，好嗎？

A: I'd like the oriental style.
我想吃東方口味的。

B: We can have Japanese or Korean BBQ.
那麼有日式和韓式烤肉可以選擇。

A: I'll choose the Korean style then.
那我選韓式烤肉。

👆 你可以聽懂／口說更多

01. 想跟我們一起去烤肉嗎？
Do you want to join us for a barbecue?

02. 我們正打算辦一個燒烤晚會。
We are planning to have a barbecue party.

03. 我再把你的雞翅多烤會兒吧。
Let me roast your chicken wing longer.

04. 我能邀請你這週六來燒烤嗎？
Could I invite you for a barbecue this Saturday?

05. 這肉烤得恰到好處。
The meat is roasted just enough.

06. 我真的很喜歡蒙古烤肉。
I really love Mongolian barbecue.

07. 這星期日我們要烤肉。
We'll have a barbecue this Sunday.

08. 你喜歡吃烤雞肉嗎？
Do you like roasted chicken ?

09. 烤翅為什麼要塗蜂蜜？
Why do you put honey on chicken wings?

10. 我們星期天晚上好好吃一頓烤肉吧。
Let's have a nice barbecue for Sunday dinner.

✍ 關鍵單字／片語

01. **BBQ / barbecue**	烤肉	
02. **Churrascaria**	巴西窯烤	
03. **oriental**	東方的	
04. **tofu**	豆腐	
05. **chicken wing**	雞翅	
06. **Mongolian barbecue**	蒙古烤肉	
07. **hot pot**	火鍋	
08. **style**	類型	
09. **join**	加入	
10. **choose**	選擇	

13│用餐禮儀

西餐禮儀當中，餐巾的用法是必須放在腿上，打開代表要用餐，放在餐盤右邊表示已用完餐。餐具從離自己餐盤最遠的開始用。另外，我們以碗就口的習慣對他們來說反而是不禮貌的表現。為了不鬧笑話，旅遊之前務必先了解清楚。

🔊 實境對話

A: Don't put the napkin on your neck.
你不能把餐巾圍在胸前。

B: I'm afraid that my shirt will get the sauce on it.
我怕沾到醬汁。

A: As long as you eat slower, it won't happen.
你只要慢慢吃，就不會沾到。

A: Take the knife with your right hand and the fork with your left hand. Stick the food on the plate by fork and cut it by knife. Then use the fork to eat. And never put the knife into your mouth.
右手拿刀、左手拿叉，用叉子把食物固定在盤中，然後用刀子切，最後再用叉子吃。刀子永遠不可以放進嘴裡。

B: How should I eat with these utensils?
那麼多餐具怎麼用啊？

A: Always use the farthest one first.
永遠從離自己最遠的開始用。

B: I got it. (Aachoo!)
我知道了。（哈啾！）

A: Hey, you should cover your mouth when sneezing and say "Excuse me".
嘿，打噴嚏的時候應該要把嘴巴遮住，然後說「很抱歉」。

👆 你可以聽懂／口說更多

01. 吃飯的時候要在椅子上坐直。
Sit up straight on the chair while you are having meal.

02. 我們應該有良好的餐桌禮儀。
We should have good table manners.

03. 你了解法國人吃飯的禮節嗎？
Do you know about the French table manners?

04. 你最好閉著嘴巴咀嚼東西。
You'd better chew with your mouth closed.

05. 我來給您夾點肉吧。
Let me help you with some meat.

06. 每個人應該從小學習餐桌禮儀。
Everybody should learn table manners when they are young.

07. 您喜歡用刀叉還是筷子？
Would you like to use the fork and knife or the chopsticks?

08. 這是我們傳統的貴賓席。
This is our traditional seat for the guest of honor.

09. 外國友人正在學習餐桌禮儀呢。
The foreign friends are learning table manners.

10. 根據餐桌禮儀的書，這應該是爸爸的位置。
It's Dad's seat, according to the book about table manners.

✍ 關鍵單字／片語

01. **knife and fork**	刀叉
02. **chopsticks**	筷子
03. **utensil**	餐具
04. **dining etiquette**	餐桌禮儀
05. **table manners**	餐桌禮儀
06. **chew**	咀嚼
07. **You'd better...**	你最好……
08. **picky**	挑剔
09. **in that case**	那樣的話
10. **the guest of honor**	主客、貴賓

14│食物合不合胃口

食物合不合胃口，是國外很多餐廳服務生在用餐完畢會問的問題，因為這關於你給小費的多寡。有時候會是廚師出來問，因為他們很在乎顧客對他們廚藝的評價。有些廚師甚至很在乎你多放了其他調味料在他精心烹調的食物上呢。

實境對話

A: How do you feel about the food today?
今天的食物還合口味嗎？

B: The beef is a little bit too salty.
牛肉有點太鹹了。

A: I saw you put some more salt on it.
我剛剛看你加了很多鹽。

B: I thought that was pepper
我還以為那是胡椒罐。.

A: The one with one hole is salt. And the other with three holes is pepper.
鹽罐只有一個孔，胡椒罐有三個孔。

B: Ah! I made a mistake.
喔！我弄錯了。

A: You should try the original flavor next time.
你應該先嚐嚐原味。

B: I see. I'll do that next time. By the way, I like the spice you used on the steak.
好的，以後我會注意。對了，我喜歡你加在牛排上的香料。

A: I'm glad you like the flavor. It's a secret recipe from my grandmother.
我很高興你喜歡那個味道，那是我祖母的獨家秘方。

👆 你可以聽懂／口說更多

01. 這道菜，你覺得合胃口嗎？
Is this dish cooked to your taste?

02. 請隨便挑合胃口的吃吧。
Please help yourself to suit your own taste.

03. 這飯菜正合我的口味。
The food is pleasing to my taste.

04. 這雞肉不合我的胃口。
This chicken is not quite to my taste.

05. 我現在已經沒有胃口了。
I have lost my appetite now.

06. 總的來說，它符合我的胃口。
Generally speaking, it's to my appetite.

07. 我真的覺得中國菜更合我的口味。
I really find Chinese dish more to my taste.

08. 這個湯很合我胃口。
This soup is my favorite.

09. 這道菜的香味引起了我的食欲。
The smell of the dish appeals to my appetite.

10. 我討厭吃魚，它不符合我的口味。
I hate to eat fish because it doesn't suit my taste.

✍ 關鍵單字／片語

01. **salty**	鹹的
02. **bitter**	苦的
03. **pepper**	胡椒
04. **flavor**	口味
05. **by the way**	順帶一提
06. **spicy**	辣
07. **recipe**	食譜
08. **generally speaking**	總括來説
09. **appetite**	胃口
10. **taste**	口味

15│給小費

許多國家必須給小費,包括飯店、餐廳、搭車都得給小費,除了用餐大約一成之外,其他大多是一、二美元即可。因此每到一處觀光或旅遊,你必須先問一下導遊或者當地人,行情是多少。避免給少了失禮,給多了吃虧。

👆 實境對話

A: May I ask how much tips should I pay?
請問小費通常要給多少?

B: What kind of tips are you talking about?
你是說什麼的小費?

A: Are there any differences among them?
有什麼不一樣嗎?

B: Yes. One dollar for the doorman. One dollar for the parking boy. But 10% for the restaurant.
有,旅館門僮是給一元美金,下車開門的泊車小弟也是給一元,但是餐廳就要給餐費的一成。

A: What if I didn't pay it?
如果我少給了,會怎麼樣呢?

B: They'll think that they didn't do their job well. You wouldn't give them less if they're good.
那麼他們會認為是他們服務不佳,如果服務不錯,你不會給太少。

A: That means I should prepare some more coins.
那麼我得準備很多零錢嗎?

B: Yes. And you can change the bills into coins at the front desk.
是啊!你可以到櫃台換。

👆 你可以聽懂／口說更多

01. 謝謝了，這是給你的小費。
Thank you, this is your tip.

02. 恐怕我們不能收小費。
I am afraid that we can't accept tips.

03. 你知道什麼時候該給小費，該給多少嗎？
Do you know when to tip and how much to tip?

04. 這裡是五十美元，不用找零了。
Here's fifty dollars. Keep the change.

05. 在中國我們沒有給小費的文化。
We don't have a tip culture in China.

06. 記得要給服務員小費。
Remember to give a tip to the waiter.

07. 你有沒有小額的鈔票可以給小費？
Do you have any small bills for the tip?

08. 我們應該給多少小費？
How much tip should we give?

09. 我忘記給小費了。你有沒有給？
I forgot to leave a tip. Did you leave one?

10. 千萬不要忘了給服務生小費哦。
Don't forget to give the waiter tips.

✎ 關鍵單字／片語

01. **tip**	小費
02. **difference**	差別
03. **doorman**	門僮
04. **parking boy**	泊車小弟
05. **coin**	硬幣
06. **bill / note**	鈔票
07. **keep the change**	不用找零
08. **accept**	接受
09. **dollar**	元、美元
10. **pay**	付

Chapter

06

逛街購物篇

Chapter 06 音檔雲端連結

因各家手機系統不同，若無法直接掃描，
仍可以至以下電腦雲端連結下載收聽。
（https://tinyurl.com/yc2w6vy5）

01 | **百貨公司**

「百貨」公司，顧名思義就是備齊了各種各樣東西販售的地方，如果你想買東西，對當地又不熟悉的話，去百貨公司就是最好的選擇了。

👉 **實境對話**

A: Welcome! May I help you?
歡迎光臨，請問有什麼能替您服務的嗎？

B: I want to buy a couple of ties, one for myself and one as a present. Do you have any recommendation?
我想要買領帶，一條自用、一條送人，你可以替我介紹嗎？

A: Would you like to check these out? They are this month's newest style, especially made for successful people. They look mature and classy.
建議您可以看看這幾款，都是這個月的新款式，專門設計給成功人士用的，看起來十分成熟穩重又有品味。

B: Hum, it is rather good. I want the one with the squares.
嗯，的確是不錯，那我要這一條有方格的。

A: You really have a good taste.
您真是有眼光。

A: What about another one?
那另外一條呢？

B: The other one is for my brother, I want something young.
另外一條是要送給我弟弟的，想替他選一條看起來富有年輕氣息的。

☝ 你可以聽懂／口說更多

01. 我只是隨便看看。
    I am just browsing around.

02. 請問這件衣服還有別的顏色嗎？
    Does this shirt come in other colors?

03. 尺寸有哪幾種呢？
    What are the sizes?

04. 請問女化妝室在哪裡？
    Where is the ladies' room?

05. 請幫我包裝成禮物。
    Please wrap it as a gift.

06. 我要最小號。
    I want a XS.

07. 我可以試穿嗎？
    Can I try it on?

08. 試衣間在哪裡？
    Where's the fitting room?

09. 我要這兩件。
    I'll take these two.

10. 這些是新到的。
    They are new arrivals.

✎ 關鍵單字／片語

01. **fitting room**	試衣間
02. **size**	尺寸
03. **color**	顏色
04. **try on**	試穿
05. **wrap**	包裝
06. **attach a ribbon**	綁緞帶
07. **browse around**	隨便瀏覽
08. **men's room**	男廁
09. **ladies' room**	女廁
10. **new arrival**	新貨

02｜超級市場

如果要買一些食品或是生活日用品，您可以去超級市場，那裡的商品種類豐富、齊全，應有盡有，而且價格合理，如果運氣好遇到特價的話，可以省下更多喔！

👈 實境對話

A: Do you have anything on sale?
請問你們有拍賣活動嗎？

B: Yes, every Friday all the dairy goods, vegetables and fruits are on sale.
有，每個星期五是所有的乳製品和蔬果類的拍賣。

A: I meant a big sale, when everything in the store is on sale.
我指的是那種全店所有商品的大型拍賣。

B: Oh! We have that twice a year, during Easter and Christmas.
喔，那一年兩次，分別在復活節和耶誕節期間。

A: Oh, that's ok. Thank you.
真不巧，沒關係，謝謝！

B: No problem.
不客氣。

B: Thanks for coming.
謝謝你的光臨。

A: I can't find pet food. Can you tell me where it is?
我找不到寵物食品，你可以告訴我在哪裡嗎？

B: It's on isle B.
在 B 區。

你可以聽懂／口說更多

01. 請問一次就要買半打嗎？
    Do I have to buy all six?

02. 請問這個產品現在有拍賣嗎？
    Is this product on sale now?

03. 是打幾折呢？
    What's the discount?

04. 請問宣傳單上面的特賣商品還有嗎？
    Do you still have the product that is on sale on your fliers?

05. 我想要買女性衛生用品，可以告訴我在哪裡嗎？
    I want to buy sanitary towels. Could you tell me where I can find them?

06. 請問今天營業到幾點？
    What is your opening hours?

07. 明天是假日，請問有營業嗎？
    Tomorrow is a holiday, are you open?

08. 我買的東西太多，可以幫我送回旅館嗎？
    I bought too many things, could you help me take them back to the hotel?

09. 這個東西可以離開冷凍多久呢？
    How long can this stay out of the freezer?

10. 可以刷卡嗎？
    Could I use my credit card?

關鍵單字／片語

01. **on sale**	拍賣
02. **food**	食品
03. **daily necessities**	日常用品
04. **tampon**	衛生棉條
05. **pad**	衛生棉
06. **household goods**	家庭用品
07. **a dozen**	一打
08. **vegetables**	蔬菜
09. **pound**	磅
10. **bakery**	麵包類

03│跳蚤市場

如果你想買一些中古商品，建議可以去跳蚤市場，在那裡，商品可以有比較大議價空間，能夠以低於原價許多的價格買到你想要的東西。對了！因為要現金交易，別忘了也要帶夠現金，但是也要看緊荷包，以防小偷的覬覦喔！

實境對話

A: How much is this record player?
請問這個舊式唱片機多少錢？

B: Oh, this is very rare, it is 1000 dollars.
喔，這個很稀有，一台要 1000 元。

A: That's expensive!
這麼貴！

A: Could you lower the price? I am taking this back to Taiwan.
不能算便宜一點嗎？我要拿回台灣。

B: Well. Ok then, 800 flat! It is already very cheap.
這樣啊……好吧，一口價 800 元，已經非常便宜了。

A: 500, then I will buy it right away.
500 元吧，可以的話我馬上就買。

B: No! That's way off!
不行啦，差太多了。

A: Then forget it! I don't really need it anyway.
那就算了，反正我也不是很需要。

B: Ok, what about 600? I will sell it for 600!
好吧，600 元怎麼樣？600 元賣你好了。

A: Let me think about it... ok, I will buy it!
我考慮一下，好吧，我買了。

👍 你可以聽懂／口說更多

01. 這三樣我全買的話，你算我多少？
   If I buy all three of them, how much will you charge me?

02. 這樣東西這麼破舊，你賣太貴了！
   This item is so old and shabby. The price is too expensive!

03. 我可以用我的手錶跟你換那個花瓶嗎？
   Could I exchange my watch with that vase of yours?

04. 這裡可以「以物易物」嗎？
   Could I exchange goods with you?

05. 請問這個跳蚤市場是每天都有嗎？
   Is this flea market here everyday?

06. 你有賣手工藝品嗎？
   Do you have any hand-made craft?

07. 我要這個銀戒指，可以幫我擦亮一點嗎？
   I want this silver ring, could you polish it for me?

08. 我怎麼知道這台吹風機不是壞的呢？
   How do I know this hair dryer is not broken?

09. 這一個皮夾是真皮的嗎？
   Is this wallet made of genuine leather?

10. 這件毛衣掉了一個釦子，可以算我便宜一點嗎？
   There is a button missing on this sweater, could you make it cheaper?

✏️ 關鍵單字／片語

01. **antique**	古董
02. **used-clothes**	舊衣服
03. **electronic appliance**	電器用品
04. **musical instrument**	樂器
05. **art work**	藝術品
06. **flea market**	跳蚤市場
07. **leather products**	皮件
08. **books and newspaper**	書報雜誌
09. **record**	唱片
10. **ornament**	裝飾品

04 | 買化妝品

在購買化妝品時，都會對產品想要有更深入的了解。在買到適合自己的化妝品前，可以到專櫃試試各種產品。專櫃小姐會仔細和你討論你的需求和量身訂做適合你膚質的各項商品，以免你買回去之後，感到不適合或者是可能會發生過敏。

🗨 實境對話

A: I want to buy cosmetics. Can you help me please?
我想買化妝品。可以幫我忙嗎？

B: Sure. Would you like lipstick, perfume or something for your skin?
當然。你想要買口紅、香水或者皮膚方面的產品嗎？

A: I would like to try lipstick.
我想要試試口紅。

B: What color or shade would you like?
你喜歡什麼顏色或色彩濃度？

A: Can you recommend one for me?
你可以推薦給我嗎？

B: Well, you need one to suit your eyes, hair and complexion.
嗯，你必須選擇適合你的眼睛、頭髮和膚色的產品。

A: Ok, I will take your advice.
好，我會接受你的意見。

B: You have dark hair and eyes. So a bright lipstick would suit you the best.
你有深色的頭髮和眼睛，所以亮一點的口紅是最適合你的。

☝ 你可以聽懂／口說更多

01. 我想買支淺色的口紅。
I'd like to buy a lipstick in a bright shade.

02. 這款橄欖滋養霜是專門針對混合型肌膚的。
This Cream of Olive is for combination skin.

03. 您知道您是哪一類肌膚嗎？
Do you know your skin type?

04. 你能再推薦些其他的給我嗎？
Can you recommend anything else for me?

05. 您可以在手上試一下。
You can try some on your hand first.

06. 我的 T 字區域容易出油。
My T-zone gets oily easily.

07. 它可以幫助滋潤您的皮膚。
It will help moisturize your skin.

08. 我想買瓶香水。
I am thinking of buying a bottle of perfume.

09. 我的兩頰冬天總是很乾。
My cheeks are always dry in the winter.

10. 你最好首先使用潔面乳。
You'd better use cleansing cream first.

✍ 關鍵單字／片語

01. **lipstick**	唇膏
02. **lip gloss**	唇蜜
03. **make-up**	化妝
04. **lotion**	乳液
05. **light color**	淺色
06. **dark color**	深色
07. **perfume**	香水
08. **skin**	皮膚
09. **mascara**	睫毛膏
10. **eye liner**	眼線筆

05 | 買帽子

選帽子時，每個人都有不同的喜好。想要找個適合自己的帽子，有時常常要逛過很多家店，才會找到心目中理想的一頂。花點時間到店裡試試看每一個可能會適合你的帽子吧。

👆 實境對話

A: How much is this hat?
這頂帽子要多少錢？

B: It's 150 dollars. Would you like to try it on?
它是一百五十塊錢。你想要試戴嗎？

A: Yes, please. Do you have it in different colors and without the rose?
好的。你這頂有不同的顏色而且不要有玫瑰花點綴的嗎？

B: Yes, madam. Try this one.
有的，小姐。試試這頂。

A: I like this one. Do you think it suits me?
我喜歡這頂。你覺得它適合我嗎？

B: Yes. It makes you look special.
是的，它使你看起來很特別。

A: I like feathers on a hat. Can you show me others?
我喜歡有羽毛的帽子。可以給我看看其他頂嗎？

B: Yes, of course. Look here on the middle shelf.
好的，當然。看這邊中間架子上。

A: Ok. I think I prefer this one. How much does this cost?
好的，我想我比較喜歡這一頂。這頂要多少錢？

B: It's 200 dollars.
它是兩百元。

👉 你可以聽懂/口說更多

01. 哇，這頂帽子好大啊！
Wow, it's such a big hat!

02. 你覺得我的新帽子怎麼樣？
How do you think of my new hat?

03. 我們出售各種款式各種尺寸的帽子。
We sell hats in all sizes and styles.

04. 您想要哪種顏色的呢？
Which color do you want?

05. 這頂帽子和你的上衣很相配。
This hat matches your coat.

06. 我更適合戴什麼款式呢？
What style suits me better?

07. 我想要一頂黑色的帽子。
I would like a black hat.

08. 恐怕這頂帽子已經是最大的了。
I am afraid that this hat is the biggest one.

09. 您想要什麼款式的？
What style do you want?

10. 多漂亮的一頂小帽子啊！
What a pretty little hat!

✎ 關鍵單字/片語

01. **hat**	帽子
02. **cap**	棒球帽
03. **peaked cap**	鴨舌帽
04. **suit**	適合
05. **look good**	看起來適合
06. **hand-made**	手工
07. **feather**	羽毛
08. **pattern**	樣式、花樣
09. **biggest**	（big 的最高級）最大的
10. **pretty**	漂亮

06 | 買衣服

買衣服常常要花很多時間試穿，常常在更衣室和衣服展示櫃來回跑了很多趟，才能夠決定最後要買哪幾件。銷售員有時候也尾隨著，要完全滿足你對衣服挑三揀四的情況，讓每一件都能夠令消費者滿意，後來還會再次光臨。

🗣 實境對話

A: I want to buy Levi's Jeans. Do you have the jeans in different colors?
我想要買 Levi's 牛仔褲，請問有不同顏色的嗎？

B: Yes, we have black, gray, blue and white.
有的，我們有黑色、灰色、藍色和白色。

A: Have you got the black pair of jeans in my size?
請問黑色有我的尺寸嗎？

B: Yes, I think so. Just let me check.
是的，我想是有的。讓我查一下。

A: The waist is too tight. Can it be adjusted?
這件腰太緊了，這可以修改嗎？

B: Yes, we have a tailor here at the store.
可以，我們店裡有裁縫師。

A: That's great. I would like to buy these jeans. When the alteration on my jeans would be done?
太好了，我要買這件牛仔褲。什麼時候可以修改好？

B: In 24 hours, madam. Please telephone us before you come in to make sure they are ready for you.
24 小時以內，小姐。妳來拿之前，麻煩妳打電話給我們確認一下是否為你準備好了。

👆 你可以聽懂／口說更多

01. 這件套裝穿在妳身上一定很漂亮。
This suit must look very nice on you.

02. 妳花這麼多錢買衣服啊！
You spent so much money on clothes!

03. 你能不能幫我挑一件漂亮的禮服？
Could you help me choose a beautiful dress?

04. 我買衣服主要看合身與否。
I only buy clothes that fit me.

05. 這件低胸晚裝怎麼樣？
What about this low-cut evening gown?

06. 我不願花這麼多錢買衣服。
I don't like to spend so much money on clothes.

07. 我想給自己買條褲子。
I want to buy a pair of jeans for myself.

08. 你平時在哪裡買衣服？
Where do you usually buy clothes?

09. 外套在那兒呢。這邊請。
The coats are over there. This way, please.

10. 那件黑色外套看起來不錯。
The black coat looks good.

✍ 關鍵單字／片語

01. **dress**	洋裝
02. **(blue) jeans**	（藍色）牛仔褲
03. **trousers**	長褲
04. **T-shirt**	T恤
05. **coat**	外套
06. **(leather) jacket**	（皮）夾克
07. **cut**	剪裁
08. **underwear**	內衣褲
09. **(mini) skirt**	（迷你）裙
10. **shorts / pants**	短褲／長褲

07 | 挑鞋子

在鞋店試穿鞋子時，可以詢問服務人員有什麼樣式和尺寸。通常架上擺的鞋子只是展示用，想找到適合你穿的鞋子，若是自助式鞋店，需要自己從架上庫存尋找；有些店可詢問跟隨在旁的貼心的服務員，直到幫你找到適合的鞋子為止。

實境對話

A: May I try some shoes on, please?
我想試穿鞋子。

B: What style are you interested in?
你喜歡什麼樣的款式。

A: Black with low heels. May I try these on?
黑色低跟的。我可以試試這雙嗎？

B: Sure. Would you like both shoes or just the one?
當然。你想要試穿一隻鞋還是一雙？

A: I would like to try both shoes on to see if they are comfortable.
我想穿一雙來看是否舒服。

B: Ok, here are the shoes.
好的，鞋子在這裡。

A: Do you have a mirror so I can look at the shoes to see if they suit me?
你有鏡子讓我看鞋子適不適合我嗎？

B: Yes, there is a mirror over there and you can check to see how they look.
有的，鏡子在那裡。你可以看看它們看起來如何。

👂 你可以聽懂╱口說更多

01. 我想要一雙穿著舒適的鞋。
I want to buy a pair of comfortable shoes.

02. 您要什麼樣的鞋？什麼牌子的？
What kind of shoes do you want? And which brand?

03. 我想買一雙鞋，36 號的。
I need a pair of shoes, size 36.

04. 它們有點緊。有沒有再大點兒的？
They are a little tight. Have you got a bigger size?

05. 你最好在買鞋前試穿一下。
You'd better try the shoes on before you buy them.

06. 這雙鞋怎麼樣？
What about this pair of shoes?

07. 這雙鞋子有真皮的鞋面以及橡膠鞋底。
These shoes have leather uppers and a rubber sole.

08. 這雙鞋正合我的腳。
This pair of shoes fits me well.

09. 我要怎麼照顧這雙鞋呢？
How do I take care of these shoes?

10. 你必須使用皮革清潔劑。
You must use leather cleaner.

✏ 關鍵單字╱片語

01. **shoes**	鞋子
02. **sneakers**	運動鞋
03. **sport shoes**	運動鞋
04. **sandals**	涼鞋
05. **high heels**	高跟鞋
06. **flip flop**	夾腳拖、人字拖
07. **slippers**	拖鞋
08. **leather shoes**	皮鞋
09. **boots**	靴子
10. **a pair of**	一雙

08 | 買首飾

在選擇首飾時，通常都要請銷售員從櫥窗裡或展示櫃裡把首飾拿出來，才能配戴。所以在看到喜歡的首飾時，可以跟在旁的服務員要求試戴，看看是否適合自己的臉型或者膚色。多試幾種款式，應該就可以找到滿意的首飾了。

🎧 實境對話

A: Can I try both, please?
我可以都試戴嗎？

B: Yes, here are the diamond earrings. You can try the ones with the blue stone later.
可以，鑽石的先拿給你戴。你可以等下再試戴藍色寶石的。

A: I like the diamond earrings. Do you have a necklace to match?
我喜歡鑽石耳環。你有可以搭配的項鍊嗎？

B: Not exactly the same design but very similar.
沒有一模一樣的，但是有類似的。

A: Can I try the necklace too, please?
我也可以試戴項鍊嗎？

B: Yes, the necklace is in a different showcase. Please follow me.
可以，項鍊在另外一個櫥窗裡。請跟我來。

A: Do you have any discount if I buy the necklace and the earrings?
如果我一起買項鍊和耳環，你會給我折扣嗎？

B: Yes, there is a 10% discount if you purchase both items.
有的，如果你買兩項，可以打九折。

👆 你可以聽懂／口說更多

01. 我們這裡有很漂亮的首飾。
    We've got beautiful jewelry here.

02. 請給我看看這枚戒指好嗎？
    May I see this ring, please?

03. 我正為我媽媽選一條珍珠項鏈。
    I am looking for a pearl necklace for my mother.

04. 我怎麼知道鑽石是不是真的？
    How do I know if the diamond is real or not?

05. 它是純金製的嗎？
    Is it made of pure gold?

06. 它是鍍金的，不過非常精美。
    It is gold-plated but quite delicate.

07. 您能給我看看那個手鐲嗎？
    Can you show me that bracelet?

08. 請幫我把它們包起來。
    Please wrap them up for me.

09. 與黃金相比我更喜歡白金。
    I prefer platinum to gold.

10. 我能看看那條手鏈嗎？
    May I have a look at that hand chain?

✍ 關鍵單字／片語

01. **pearl necklace**	珍珠項鍊
02. **bracelet**	手鐲
03. **earrings**	耳環
04. **platinum**	白金
05. **gold**	純金
06. **hand chain**	手鍊
07. **jewel / jewelry**	珠寶
08. **diamond ring**	鑽石戒指
09. **sapphire**	藍寶石
10. **silver**	純銀

09 | 詢問尺寸

到衣服店買衣服時，常常會找不到適合自己的尺寸，這時可詢問服務員有無庫存的衣物，能改成適合你的尺寸，甚至有些店可以要求訂製。在有些店裡也有幫忙調貨的服務，有可能就可以找到適合你尺寸的衣物。

🐾 實境對話

A: Can you tell me the sizes of the clothes that the display model has on?
可以告訴我展示模特兒身上穿的衣服尺寸是多少？

B: Yes, the suit jacket is size 44. The trousers are 36 waist and 32 leg.
好的。西裝外套是尺寸 44，褲子腰身是 36，腿長是 32。

A: What size are the shoes?
鞋子是幾號？

B: Size 8.
是 8 號。

A: Do you have the shoes in my size? My size is 9.
你有我尺寸的鞋子嗎？我是穿 9 號。

B: Sorry, we don't have size 9 but we can order them for you.
抱歉，我們沒有 9 號。但我們可以幫你訂購。

A: Can the suit be altered to fit me?
西裝可以修改成我的尺寸嗎？

B: I would need to take your measurements.
我需要幫你量一下尺寸。

👆你可以聽懂／口說更多

01. 你穿多大尺寸的衣服？
What size do you wear?

02. 我可以量一下您的尺寸嗎？
Can I take your measurements?

03. 這條裙子還有別的尺寸嗎？
Do you have this dress in another size?

04. 你要多大尺寸的？
What size do you want?

05. 你們有大一號的嗎？
Do you have a bigger size?

06. 我幫你量一下尺寸吧。
Let me measure you up.

07. 我的腰圍是 19 寸。
I measure 19 inches round the waist.

08. 你怎麼知道要買什麼尺寸？
How did you know what size to buy?

09. 這種款式還有其他小點的尺寸嗎？
Do you have any smaller sizes of this type?

10. 我不確定我是什麼尺寸。
I'm not sure what size I am.

✍ 關鍵單字／片語

01. **window**	櫥窗
02. **display model**	人型展示模特兒
03. **waist**	腰
04. **leg**	腿
05. **fit**	適合
06. **inch**	寸
07. **measure**	測量
08. **smaller**	（small 的比較級）更小
09. **larger**	（large 的比較級）更大
10. **type**	種類

10 | 試穿

買衣服時，可以要求試穿。有時候各家衣服店裡賣的尺寸大小不太一樣，需要試穿之後，才能了解該買哪一件，穿起來才會合身。找個賣場裡面有空的服務員，可以詢問你找不到的尺寸，他們對於存貨比較了解，也會幫你找到適合你身材的衣服。

👉 實境對話

A: I would like to try on this sweater, please.
我想要試穿這件毛衣。

B: You can choose from these sweaters here. What is your size?
你可以在這邊挑選毛衣。你的尺寸幾號？

A: Medium, please. Do you have fitting rooms where I can try some sweaters?
中號。哪裡有試衣間可以讓我試穿這些毛衣呢？

B: Yes, the fitting rooms are on the left-hand side as you pass the cash desk.
試衣間在你經過收銀台後的左手邊。

A: Can I try a bigger size?
我可以試更大的尺寸嗎？

B: Yes, what size would you like?
有的，你想要多大的尺寸呢？

A: I would like to try a bigger one.
我想要試穿再大一號的尺寸。

B: I will get you one and two sizes bigger to see which one fits.
我會拿大一號和大兩號的尺寸來讓你決定比較喜歡哪一件。

你可以聽懂／口說更多

01. 您要不要試穿一下這件夾克？
Would you like to try this jacket on?

02. 把這兩件外套都試穿看看，比較一下。
Try on both coats and compare them.

03. 請問試衣間在哪兒？
Can you tell me where the fitting room is?

04. 我覺得這件襯衫好像有點小。
I think the shirt is a little small.

05. 有沒有衣架可以讓我在試穿時掛我的衣物？
Do you have hangers so I can hang my clothes as I try the sweaters on?

06. 你能拿那件洋裝讓我看一下嗎？
Could you show me the dress in the window?

07. 試衣間就在那邊。
The fitting room is over there.

08. 我能試穿這件毛衣嗎？
May I try on this woolen sweater?

09. 這件外套看起來不錯。我可以試穿一下嗎？
This coat looks good. May I try it on?

10. 如果您喜歡的話可以試一下。
You can try it on if you like.

關鍵單字／片語

01. **sweater**	毛衣
02. **tight**	緊
03. **choose from**	選擇
04. **hang**	掛
05. **seem**	似乎
06. **compare**	比較
07. **a little**	有一點
08. **loose**	寬鬆的
09. **hanger**	衣架
10. **prefer**	較喜歡

11 | 討價還價

買東西時，有時候可以討價還價，得到比較優惠的價錢。例如：跟小販或者銷售員可以先詢問價錢，買多一點得到優惠。有些店常是不能講價的，通常要到人潮散去之後才能可以撿到便宜。

實境對話

A: How much are the oranges?
橘子要多少錢？

B: 10 cents each or 12 for a dollar.
每一個 10 分或者 12 個一塊錢。

A: Can I just buy 6 and can you give me a discount?
我可以只買六個算折扣價嗎？

B: No, you must buy 12 for the discount.
不行，你必須買 12 個才能算折扣價。

A: Ok, I will take 12. Do you have any special discount on other fruits?
好的，我要買 12 個。其他水果有沒有特別折扣呢？

B: Yes, a bag of apples containing 15 also costs 1 dollar.
有的，一袋 15 顆蘋果也是只賣一塊錢。

A: Ok, I will take some apples too. If I buy a fruit basket, will that be better value?
好的，我也買一些蘋果。如果我買水果籃的話，是不是更划算呢？

B: Yes, the fruit basket is very good value.
是的，水果籃也非常划算。

👆 你可以聽懂／口說更多

01. 這個你要賣多少錢？
    How much is this?

02. 把價格壓一半，包你不會被人騙。
    Just lower the price by half and you will be fine.

03. 您願意出多少錢呢？
    What price are you willing to pay?

04. 你是不是逛許多商店來討價還價？
    Do you shop around a lot for bargains?

05. 這個價格似乎有點高。
    The price seems to be a little high.

06. 這樣的折扣我們沒有利潤了。
    I don't know how we can make a profit at those numbers.

07. 恐怕沒有討價還價的餘地。
    I am afraid there is no room for bargaining.

08. 你能給我特別優惠嗎？
    Could you give me a special offer?

09. 可以給我便宜一點嗎？
    Could I have a lower price?

10. 我不會給你超過五十美元。
    I won't pay you more than 50 dollars.

✏️ 關鍵單字／片語

01. **discount**	折扣
02. **best offer**	最好、最低的價格
03. **lower the price**	降低價格
04. **buy one get one free**	買一送一
05. **half**	一半
06. **bargain**	便宜貨、討價還價
07. **profit**	利潤
08. **special offer**	特別優惠
09. **high**	高
10. **be willing to**	願意

12 | 結帳

買好東西之後，會來到櫃檯結帳。除了現金付款之外，有時候還有很多付款選擇，看店家和你當時的需求可以配合。東西買很多時，現場有時會準備箱子。有時可找人幫忙，讓你購物時流程可以非常順利，還會想要繼續回店光臨。

🔊 實境對話

A: Do you have some boxes as I have a lot of stuff?
因為我有很多東西，請問你有盒子可以裝嗎？

B: Yes, my assistant will get you some boxes. Do you have a discount card?
有的，我的助手會幫你拿盒子。你有折扣卡嗎？

A: Yes, here is my discount card.
有的，這是我的折扣卡。

B: Do you want to pay by cash or credit card?
你要付現金還是刷卡？

A: I would like to pay by credit card, please.
我想要刷卡。

B: Ok, the total is 300 dollars. Sign here, please.
好的，全部是 300 塊錢。請在這簽名。

A: Can I have my free parking token?
我可以索取免費停車代幣嗎？

B: Yes, it's on your receipt. Just print the number in at the exit of the car park and there would be no charge.
可以，它印在你的收據上。只要在停車場出口輸入這個號碼，就是免費。

👆你可以聽懂／口說更多

01. 請你給我們分別結帳好嗎？
Will you give us separate bills?

02. 請幫我買單。
I would like the check, please.

03. 您現在要結帳嗎？
Do you want to settle the bill now?

04. 我能用信用卡結帳嗎？
Can I pay by credit card?

05. 您要用什麼方式買單呢？用現金還是刷卡？
How would you like to pay? Cash or credit card?

06. 請您把帳單準備好可以嗎？
Will you please have the bill ready for me?

07. 麻煩你把帳單拿過來好嗎？
Can I have the bill, please?

08. 我很抱歉，你現在是在只收現金的結帳道上。
I am sorry you are on the "cash only" lane.

09. 你想分開單獨結帳嗎？
Do you want separate bills?

10. 請給我們買單好嗎？
Could you please get us the check?

✍ 關鍵單字／片語

01. **discount card**		折扣卡
02. **total**		總共
03. **assistant**		助手
04. **no charge**		不收費、免費
05. **separate**		分開的
06. **bill**		帳單
07. **pay a bill**		付帳
08. **stuff**		東西
09. **VIP card**		貴賓卡
10. **receipt**		收據

13｜要求送貨

通常買大型的家具或者不能夠在購買時當場帶走的東西，都可以視店家有無提供送貨服務來要求送貨。可以跟店家要求送貨的詳情，來決定什麼時間送貨會適合你。給予店家詳盡訊息和留下店家付給你的收據和號碼，以便讓你在事後等候和追蹤送貨的確切時間，會比較方便。

實境對話

A: I bought furniture in your store today. Can you tell me when I can have it delivered?
我今天在你們店裡買了家具。請告訴我什麼時候可以送貨？

B: The delivery is from 2 p.m. to 6 p.m., Monday to Friday.
送貨時間從禮拜一到禮拜五的下午兩點到六點。

A: May I have it deliver on Tuesday afternoon?
請問我的貨可以在禮拜二下午送到嗎？

B: Yes. May I have your address, please?
可以。請給我你的住址。

A: Yes, here is my address. Is there a delivery charge?
好的，這裡是我的住址。運送費用要多少錢？

B: No. The delivery is free if you purchase more than 3,000 dollars.
不用錢。如果你買超過三千塊錢，是免運。

A: Shall I give you my telephone number?
我要給你的電話號碼嗎？

B: Yes, please. You can write it here.
好的。你可以寫在這裡。

👆 你可以聽懂／口說更多

01. 先生，需要我們送貨嗎？
Shall we deliver it, sir?

02. 請問你們送貨是免費的嗎？
Is your delivery free of charge?

03. 我們明天就給您送貨。
We will deliver the goods to you tomorrow.

04. 我們什麼時候可以送貨？送到哪裡？
When and where can I deliver the goods?

05. 我們能不能把送貨日期延遲一點？
Can we postpone the delivery date a bit?

06. 送貨要收費嗎？
Do you charge for delivery?

07. 我們將在您方便時送貨。
We will deliver at your convenience.

08. 對不起，我們不提供送貨服務。
Sorry, but we don't offer delivery service.

09. 請告知我們送貨地點及時間。
Please inform us your designated place and time.

10. 大概會在送貨時間的前後十分鐘內送達。
The delivery would be close to the time maybe 10 minutes either side.

✍ 關鍵單字／片語

01. **furniture**	家具
02. **deliver**	運送
03. **address**	住址
04. **purchase**	購買
05. **free of charge**	免費
06. **delivery service**	送貨服務
07. **designated place and time**	指定地點和時間
08. **either side**	任一邊
09. **home / house**	家
10. **offer**	提供

14 | 退換

當買到不合意的東西，就可能會換貨或者要求退錢。在換貨時，服務人員都會詢問我們對他們的產品有什麼不滿意。如有合理的不適合理由，也會很誠懇的退換來滿足消費者的需求。當任何款式都不讓你滿意時，相信退錢是最好的方法。

實境對話

A: I would like to exchange these headphones or get a refund.
我想要換這個耳機或退錢。

B: Yes, sir. Is there a problem with the headphones?
好的，先生。耳機有什麼問題嗎？

A: Yes, the quality is not good and they hurt my ears.
有的。這個品質不太好，也會傷我的耳朵。

B: Would you like to try a different brand?
你想要試試不同的牌子嗎？

A: Yes, if you have something better fitting and good quality.
好的。如果你有更好且更適合我的牌子和好的品質。

B: For extra 15 dollars you may exchange for these ones.
再加 15 塊錢你可以換到這一個。

A: No. Is it possible I can just get a refund?
那不用了。退錢給我可以嗎？

B: Yes. If you sign the receipt, the cashier will refund your money.
可以。如果你在這收據簽名，收銀員將會退你錢。

👆 你可以聽懂／口說更多

01. 如果這件襯衫不合身，我可以拿回來退貨嗎？
If this shirt doesn't fit, may I bring it back later?

02. 您是在打折的時候買的，所以不能退貨。
You can't return it because you bought it on sale.

03. 你的退貨政策是什麼？
What is your return policy?

04. 假如你想退貨，應當保留發票。
If you wish to return your purchase, you should keep the receipt.

05. 大部分商品在送貨後 30 天內可以退貨。
You can return most of the items within 30 days of delivery.

06. 我能知道您為什麼退貨嗎？
May I know why you want to return it?

07. 您沒有發票恐怕不能退貨。
I am afraid that you can't return it without the receipt.

08. 我們提供 90 天的退貨保證。
We offer a 90-day return policy.

09. 除非你們在一星期內退貨，否則我們不退還訂金。
We cannot refund your deposit unless you return the goods within a week.

10. 如果可以退貨，馬上去退吧。
If it can be sent back, do it at once.

✍ 關鍵單字／片語

01. **exchange**	交換
02. **refund**	退貨、退費
03. **quality**	品質
04. **brand**	品牌
05. **warranty**	保固
06. **return policy**	退貨政策
07. **cashier**	收銀員
08. **extra**	額外的、多餘的
09. **deposit**	訂金
10. **unless**	除非

15│買紀念品

到一個地方就想買當地的產品來當作紀念品，不論是買回去
自己做紀念或送給朋友，都蠻適合的。在買東西時也要注意
紀念品的大小是否適合你攜帶回家，太大的話反而會造成太
多不便與困擾了！

實境對話

A: I am leaving this country in 4 days and I would
like to buy a souvenir for my family.
我四天後就要離開這個國家，我想要買紀念品給我的家人。

B: We have a selection of souvenirs on the top shelf.
我們在架子的最上層有多樣紀念品的選擇。

A: Do you have anything smaller because it needs to
fit in my suitcase.
你們有任何比較小一點的嗎？因為要能夠裝進我的行李箱。

B: Yes. We have badges, postcards and novelty sets.
有的，我們有紀念章、明信片和新奇小物組合。

A: I would like to see the novelty sets.
我想要看看新奇小物組合。

B: We have a choice of 4.
有四種選擇。

A: May I open the box, please?
我可以打開盒子看嗎？

B: Yes, of course.
當然可以。

A: Can you gift wrap this one for me, please?
可以幫我包裝這一個嗎？

👆 你可以聽懂／口說更多

01. 您想買什麼紀念品呢？
What kind of souvenir do you want to buy?

02. 我可以在哪兒買些紀念品呢？
Where can I buy some souvenirs?

03. 我正在找紀念品部。
I am looking for the souvenir shop.

04. 我想買一點紀念品回去。
I want to buy some souvenirs.

05. 我想買東西給我的老師當紀念品。
I want to buy something for my teacher as a souvenir.

06. 您想不想買些手工藝品呢？
Would you like to buy some handicrafts?

07. 你可以在那裡買到很多紀念品。
You can buy many souvenirs there.

08. 您能為我推薦一些紀念品嗎？
Could you recommend some souvenirs for me?

09. 這些紀念品是中國風格的。
These souvenirs are in Chinese style.

10. 您可以在那個商店找到各種各樣的紀念品。
You can find different kinds of souvenirs at that store.

✍ 關鍵單字／片語

01. **souvenir**	紀念品
02. **selection**	選擇
03. **top shelf**	最上層的架子
04. **badge**	徽章
05. **postcard**	明信片
06. **handicraft**	手工藝品
07. **novelty set**	新奇小物組合
08. **wrap up**	包裝
09. **key chain**	鑰匙圈
10. **choice**	選擇

Chapter

07

休閒娛樂篇

Chapter 07 音檔雲端連結

因各家手機系統不同，若無法直接掃描，
仍可以至以下電腦雲端連結下載收聽。
（https://tinyurl.com/yf4rr3xt）

01 | 美術館

到任何國家都一樣，當地著名的美術館是不容錯過的旅遊體驗。建議大家可以在出發前先蒐集資料，不管是利用網路，或者是曾經去過的朋友，當然最好的是能找到當地的朋友當嚮導，絕對可以看到令人驚豔的藝術作品喔！

實境對話

A: Would you like to rent an audio guide today?
你今天想要租個語音導覽嗎？

B: Yes. How much is that?
是的，請問要多少錢呢？

A: It's 5 dollars per person per day.
一天每個人五塊錢。

B: Ok, I need one and can you please tell me how to use it?
好。那我要租一個，請問怎麼使用它呢？

A: When you see a label with the headphone symbol, enter the number on the label on the audio guide player keypad and press "Play".
當你看到有個耳機符號的標籤時，在語音導覽鍵盤上輸入標籤寫的號碼再按「播放」。

A: You will hear the commentary about the art work. It's easy to use. We also have multiple languages to choose from the programs.
你將會聽到有關於藝術品的講評。操作很簡單，我們也有多國語言可供選擇。

B: That sounds great. Here is 5 dollars.
聽起來還不錯。這裡是五塊錢。

你可以聽懂／口說更多

01. 可不可以陪我去趟美術館？
Would you like to go to the gallery with me?

02. 這幅畫是什麼時期的作品？
When was the painting done?

03. 這個畫廊是中世紀藝術的寶庫。
The gallery is a treasure house of medieval art.

04. 請問今天這兒有什麼展覽嗎？
Is there any exhibition here today?

05. 這家美術館是免費開放的。
This gallery is free entry.

06. 你覺得這幅畫怎麼樣？
What do you think of this painting?

07. 幾號公車可以去美術館？
Which bus goes to the art gallery?

08. 我們去畫廊看畢卡索的畫展吧。
Let's go to the art gallery to see the Picasso Exhibition.

09. 那個畫廊什麼時候開放？
What time does the gallery open?

10. 看畫展是陶冶情操的好方法。
Seeing art exhibition is a good way to cultivate the mind.

關鍵單字／片語

01. **paintings**	繪畫
02. **oil painting**	油畫
03. **water-based paint**	水彩畫
04. **the Renaissance**	文藝復興時期
05. **the Baroque**	巴洛克時期
06. **sculpture**	雕塑
07. **genuine**	真品
08. **imitation**	仿製品
09. **Realism**	寫實派
10. **Impressionism**	印象派

02 | 博物館

有些博物館裡館藏豐富，在參觀時可能會搞不清楚方向而迷路。手上有個館內地圖，可以引導你找到想要觀看的文物。在館內工作人員的指引下，可以對館內的動向有更清楚的瞭解，且能夠在有限的時間內好好的欣賞館內的所有展覽。

實境對話

A: Excuse me. I want to see the painting "Sunflowers" by Vincent Van Gogh, but I can't find it. Can you tell me where it is located?

抱歉，我想要看梵谷的畫「向日葵」，但是我找不到。請問它是放在哪裡呢？

B: Yes. Let's see the museum map here. We are now at the modern art section at the ground floor. That painting is on the second floor at the European painting section. You can use the stairs to get to the second floor.

好的。一起來看博物館的地圖吧。我們現在在一樓的現代藝術區。那一幅畫是在二樓的歐洲畫作區。你可以走那邊的樓梯到二樓。

A: I see. Can you tell me where the European painting section is located?

我知道了。所以當我到二樓時，歐洲畫作區是位於哪裡呢？

B: It's in the main hall between the Islamic art section and Chinese art. You will see the painting on the left-hand side of the exhibition.

它是位於伊斯蘭藝術區和中國藝術區中間的主廳。你會在展覽的左邊看到那幅畫。

👆你可以聽懂／口說更多

01. 您想去參觀哪一個博物館？
Which museum would you like to visit?

02. 打擾了，我在找國家博物館。
Excuse me. I am looking for the National Museum.

03. 去博物館是走這條路嗎？
Is it the right way to the museum?

04. 博物館每天開放八個小時。
The museum is open for eight hours each day.

05. 需要購票入場嗎？
Do I need to buy a ticket to get in?

06. 據說那個博物館很有名。
It's said that the museum is very famous.

07. 你去過那個博物館嗎？
Have you ever been to that museum?

08. 博物館真的是一個有趣的地方。
Museum is really an interesting place to go.

09. 到底是什麼使這座博物館如此受推崇呢？
What makes this museum so worthy of that honor?

10. 我們想要參觀那個博物館。
We would like to visit that museum.

✏️ 關鍵單字／片語

01. **museum**	博物館
02. **modern art**	現代藝術
03. **exhibition**	展覽
04. **brochure**	小冊子
05. **information center**	諮詢中心、服務台
06. **second floor**	二樓
07. **ground floor**	一樓
08. **get in**	進入
09. **famous**	有名
10. **worthy**	值得

03 | 歌劇院

在進入歌劇院裡，第一件事就是找到你的位子。找到位子坐定之後，就可以開始等候將要欣賞的歌劇作品。到歌劇開演前，都可以稍微和隔壁坐位的寒喧一下心裡對此歌劇的想法，了解大家對來看歌劇的目的與動機。在歌劇開演前都能夠開開心心的等候布幕掀起的那一刻。

實境對話

A: Can you tell me how long the opera will take?
這齣歌劇會表演多久呢？

B: One hour and 40 minutes approximately.
大概一小時又四十分鐘。

A: Have you seen this show before?
你以前曾經看過這齣歌劇嗎？

B: Yes, this is my second time. I think it is a masterpiece.
是的，這是我第二次來看。我覺得這齣歌劇是個傑作。

A: Where can I get a program?
請問哪裡有節目手冊呢？

B: You can buy one at the information desk. It's US$10 each.
你可以在服務台買，每份十美元。

A: Could you please tell me where the information desk is?
你可以告訴我服務台在哪裡嗎？

B: It's on the left-hand side of the entrance. If you go out this way, it will be on your right.
在入口的左手邊。如果從這邊出去的話，就是在右手邊。

👆 你可以聽懂／口說更多

01. 你聽過這場歌劇用德語唱嗎？
Have you heard the opera sung in German?

02. 我一直都想去看看雪梨歌劇院。
I have always wanted to visit Sydney Opera House.

03. 我可以到哪裡看歌劇呢？
Where can I see an opera?

04. 你們到歌劇院一定要盛裝打扮嗎？
Do you have to dress up for the opera?

05. 這跟義大利歌劇很不一樣啊。
It's quite different from Italian opera.

06. 我們計畫這個星期六去看歌劇演出。
We are planning to go to the opera this Saturday.

07. 她曾是巴黎歌劇院最好的歌唱家。
She was once the best singer at the Paris Opera.

08. 你最好先去它的網站上看看演出安排。
You'd better check the program schedule on its website first.

09. 有人說：只有在歌劇中，人們才會為愛而死。
Someone says only in opera do people die for love.

10. 這部歌劇在美國的首演是在 1926 年。
The first American performance of this opera was in 1926.

✏️ 關鍵單字／片語

01. **opera**	歌劇	
02. **musical**	音樂劇	
03. **approximately**	大約、大概	
04. **masterpiece**	傑作	
05. **program**	節目單	
06. **dress up**	盛裝打扮	
07. **die for love**	為愛而死	
08. **performance**	表演	
09. **last**	持續	
10. **singer**	歌手	

04 | 音樂廳

如果你想做比較靜態的活動，不妨就去音樂廳讓耳根子「清靜」一下吧，例如：欣賞鋼琴演奏、管絃樂隊演奏等，建議您花個時間充實一下這方面的知識，相信當您在聆聽大師的傑作時，能更深入體會曲中的意思喔！

👊 實境對話

A: I want two tickets for YoYo Ma's concert the day after tomorrow.
我要買兩張後天晚上馬友友大提琴獨奏會的票。

B: OK. Which section do you want?
好，請問你要買多少錢的票呢？

A: What are the choices?
有哪些選擇呢？

B: 30, 40, 50 and 100 dollars.
30 元、40 元、50 元和 100 元

A: I want a 50-dollar ticket.
我要 50 元的。

B: Ok, you can choose where you want to sit from the red area on the computer screen.
好，您可以在電腦螢幕上紅色區域選擇您的座位。

A: I want seats 24E and 26E.
我要 24E 和 26E 的座位。

B: Ok, no problem! Here are your tickets.
沒問題，這是您的票。

A: Thank you.
謝謝！

👆你可以聽懂／口說更多

01. 我想索取本月的節目簡介。
I want this month's program list.

02. 需要購票入場嗎？
Do I need to buy a ticket to get in?

03. 你們有販賣紀念品的地方嗎？
Where do you sell souvenirs?

04. 我想坐高一點的位置。
I want to sit in a higher position.

05. 距離開演還有一點時間。
We still have some time before the performance starts.

06. 請把手機關機。
Please switch off your cell phone.

07. 中場休息時我要去廁所。
I will go to the ladies' room during the intermission.

08. 我們付不起包廂。
We can't afford a box seat.

09. 這場表演超乎我們預期的精采。
The performance is beyond our expectations.

10. 這場表演會在歐洲巡迴演出。
The show will tour Europe.

✍ 關鍵單字／片語

01. **concert**	演奏會
02. **solo**	獨奏
03. **switch off**	關掉
04. **cello**	大提琴
05. **orchestra**	管絃樂隊
06. **conductor**	指揮
07. **beyond expectation**	超乎預期
08. **intermission**	中場休息
09. **tour**	巡迴演出
10. **box seat**	包廂座位

05 | 電影院

看電影前,可以選擇當天上映的一些電影。賣票的服務人員會提供你所想了解的資訊。在購票之後,要好好的搞清楚放映電影的所在和各個符合你需求的地方。在進入電影廳之前準備好各項需要的東西,就可以安安心心的看場電影了。

實境對話

A: Can you tell me what movies are showing today?
請問今天有上映什麼電影呢?

B: Yes, there is a list of the movies showing today over there on the wall.
在那邊牆上有今天上映電影的列表。

A: Can I have one ticket for "Alice in Wonderland"?
我要買一張愛莉絲夢遊仙境的票。

B: Yes, that will be 20 dollars. The number of the seat is on your ticket. It starts in 20 minutes.
好的,這樣是二十塊錢。票上有寫你的座位號碼,二十分鐘後就開演了。

A: Ok, thank you. Can you please tell me where I can get some popcorn and a drink?
好的,謝謝。請問在哪裡可以買到爆米花和飲料呢?

B: Yes, you can buy some on the second floor near the entrance to the movie you will be watching.
在二樓靠近你將要看的電影廳入口的地方可以購買。

A: Ok, thank you. I will buy them before I enter the cinema.
好的,謝謝。我會在進入電影廳前購買。

☝ 你可以聽懂／口說更多

01. 你平時都喜歡看什麼電影？
What kind of movies do you like?

02. 你今晚想看電影嗎？
Do you feel like seeing a movie tonight?

03. 最近有沒有好電影呢？
Is there any good movie recently?

04. 明天將要上映一部非常好的電影。
There will be a very good movie on tomorrow.

05. 電影的名字是什麼？
What is the name of the movie?

06. 那部電影是最近才上映的。
The film was released recently.

07. 我想下周去看《阿凡達》！
I want to see Avatar next week!

08. 我特別喜歡邊看電影邊吃爆米花。
I love to eat popcorn at the movies.

09. 我不喜歡動作片。
I don't like action movies.

10. 想和我一起去看電影嗎？
Do you want to see a movie with me?

✎ 關鍵單字／片語

01. **see a movie**	看電影
02. **go to a movie**	看電影
03. **horror / scary movie**	恐怖片
04. comedy	喜劇片
05. **action movie**	動作片
06. romance	愛情片
07. drama	劇情片
08. documentary	紀錄片
09. **science fiction**	科幻片
10. cinema / theater	電影院

06 | 溫泉泡湯

所謂的「湯」就是溫泉，溫泉的種類有很多，而且根據地質的不同，溫泉的酸鹼度及療效也不一樣。溫泉的主要效能可以幫助恢復疲勞，有些溫泉還有美容的效果呢！所以到了國外，不妨放鬆身心，好好的泡個湯吧！

實境對話

A: Is the hot spring here indoors or outdoors?
這裡的溫泉是室內的還是露天的？

B: We have both. The indoor spring is connected to the outdoor spring. You can stay in the indoor spring before you go outdoors and enjoy the view.
我們兩種都有，而且是從室內溫泉連接到室外的露天溫泉，你可以在室內溫泉泡完後，再到露天溫泉邊泡邊欣賞風景。

A: What kind of hot springs do you have?
那溫泉的種類有幾種呢？

B: We have the ordinary one, electrotherapy hot spring and the milk bath that can brighten your skin.
我們有普通溫泉、電療溫泉，還有養顏美容的牛奶溫泉呢！

A: Are they all public pools? How much do you charge?
請問都是大眾浴池嗎？那收費是多少？

B: Yes, we charge each person 400 dollars, and the towel and shampoo for each person is 100 dollars.
對，我們的收費是每位 400 元，一人份的毛巾和洗髮精是 100 元。

你可以聽懂／口說更多

01. 請問沒有個人或家族自己一間的溫泉嗎？
    Is there a hot spring that is only for individuals or the family?

02. 我想多要一份毛巾。
    I want one more towel.

03. 泡溫泉時我想來杯啤酒。
    I want some beer when I am in the hot spring.

04. 我可以看一下價目表嗎？
    May I take a look at the price list?

05. 要裸體嗎？
    Do I have to be naked?

06. 可以穿泳衣嗎？
    Can I wear my swimsuit?

07. 我要用一條小毛巾遮一下隱私部位。
    I'll cover my privacy parts with a towel.

08. 溫泉通常有高礦物含量。
    Hot springs often contain high mineral content.

09. 不要把毛巾放入水裡。
    Make sure you keep the towel out of water.

10. 有一間新開的溫泉會館。
    There is a newly opened hot spring spa.

關鍵單字／片語

01. **public bathing house**	大眾浴池
02. **mixed bath**	男女混浴
03. **hot spring**	溫泉
04. **relaxing**	令人放鬆的
05. **naked**	裸身的
06. **outdoor spring**	露天溫泉
07. **indoor spring**	室內溫泉
08. **mineral content**	礦物含量
09. **individual**	個人的
10. **newly opened**	新開幕的

07 | SPA

在享受 SPA 之前，需要詢問一些沐浴相關的問題。櫃檯人員會給你詳盡的資訊和 SPA 會館的使用時間，搞清楚一些資訊，沐浴時就可以盡情享受 SPA 消除整天的疲憊，讓你可以感受身心舒暢的放鬆感。下次再有機會繼續光臨享受 SPA 氛圍。

👉 實境對話

A: Can you tell me what time it is open today to the public?
請問今天幾點對外開放？

B: Yes, 10 a.m. to 5 p.m.. And we close for lunch 1 p.m. to 2:15 p.m..
早上十點到下午五點。我們在一點到兩點十五分時，是午餐時間會休館。

A: I would also like to have a pedicure and a foot massage. Do you think those could be managed?
我還想要做足部美容及腳底按摩。請問可以安排嗎？

B: Sure. We have various courses to help you revitalize.
當然，我們有很多課程來幫助你恢復元氣。

A: That would be great. Please arrange it for me. By the way, is there a locker where I can store my clothes when I am in the spa?
那太好了，請幫我安排。對了，在溫泉浴場裡有沒有置物櫃可以放我的衣服呢？

B: Yes, here is the key.
有的，鑰匙在這裡。

🔊 你可以聽懂／口說更多

01. 你有聽說過牛奶浴和巧克力浴嗎？
Have you ever heard about milk SPA and chocolate SPA?

02. 請問您這裡 SPA 的設備有什麼？
What kind of SPA facilities do you have?

03. 我想做臉部緊縮療程。
I want to do the facial toning therapy.

04. 我想做全身美容保養。
I want a whole body beauty treatment.

05. 想不想跟我去做個 SPA？
Would you like to have a SPA with me?

06. 你們有出借毛巾和浴衣嗎？
Do you rent towels and bathrobes?

07. 有的，金額已經包含在票價裡。
Yes, the cost is included in your ticket.

08. 做完 SPA 我感覺太舒服了。
I feel so comfortable after having a SPA.

09. 有專人為我做去角質嗎？
Is there anybody to scrub my body for me?

10. 我想做全身美容保養。
I'd like to have a body treatment.

✎ 關鍵單字／片語

01. **manicure**	手部保養
02. **pedicure**	足部保養
03. **skin care products**	護膚用品
04. **body massage**	全身按摩
05. **maintenance**	保養
06. **facial maintenance**	臉部保養
07. **remove hair**	除毛
08. **body moisturizer**	潤膚保濕
09. **nourish the skin**	滋養皮膚
10. **facial revitalizing**	活顏再生

08 | 戶外活動

許多國外的旅遊勝地，都有不同的戶外活動可以參加。不論是水上活動、登山健行活動或是空中刺激的滑翔翼活動等等，都充滿了驚奇與新鮮感，真是令人期待啊！但要特別提醒，參加這些活動，一定要注意安全，才能讓旅遊行程更加有趣精彩喔！

實境對話

A: Is there any entertainment around here?
這附近可以做一些什麼運動呢？

B: The beach is about 20 minutes from here.
離這裡約 20 分鐘就是海邊。

B: You can do some water sports there.
你可以到那裡做一些海上活動。

A: Could I rent the equipment?
有器具可以租借嗎？

B: Yes, there are jet skis, surfboards and swimming equipment.
有啊！有水上摩托車、衝浪板以及游泳用具。

A: Is there any coach to help me out?
有專人指導嗎？

B: I think so.
我想應該有吧。

A: Great! Are you going with me?
太棒了！你要跟我一起去嗎？

B: No, I got something else to do.
不了，我還有其他事要做。

B: Have a good time!
玩得開心點。

你可以聽懂／口說更多

01. 這附近有高爾夫球場嗎？
Is there any golf course around here?

02. 我可以預約今天下午嗎？
Could I make an appointment for this afternoon?

03. 哪裡可以租借器具呢？
Where can I rent the equipment?

04. 請一位指導老師費用是多少呢？
How much will it cost to hire an instructor?

05. 兩小時多少錢呢？
How much does it cost for two hours?

06. 我想去滑雪，請問哪裡比較好呢？
I want to go skiing. Any good ski resorts?

07. 有沒有適合初學者的課程？
Is there any course for beginners?

08. 在這附近潛水安全嗎？
Is it safe to dive here?

09. 在這裡游泳很危險。
It's dangerous to swim here.

10. 這附近有什麼兜風的好去處嗎？
Is there any place near by that I can go for a ride?

關鍵單字／片語

01. **beginner**	初學者
02. **horse-riding**	騎馬
03. **water skiing**	滑水
04. **surf**	衝浪
05. **float board**	浮板
06. **goggles**	蛙鏡
07. **diving**	潛水
08. **oxygen tank**	氧氣筒
09. **fishing tackle**	釣魚用具
10. **grass ski**	滑草

09 | 照相

如果你到了著名的比薩斜塔，導遊叫你假裝做一個看起來像是能推倒比薩斜塔的動作，是不是很有意思呢？這個時候就要拿出手機或專業數位相機、底片相機，拍下你可愛的樣子，再帶回台灣給親朋好友看，所以「照相」在旅遊當中是一個幫我們留住所有回憶的好方法喔！

實境對話

A: Excuse me, could you take a picture for my girlfriend and me?
不好意思，可以幫我和我女朋友照張相嗎？

B: Sure! Where do you want to pose?
沒問題！你們想在哪裡照呢？

A: We want the sunset and this building in the background, thank you!
我們想以夕陽和這棟建築物為背景，謝謝！

B: Do you want the picture to be portrait or landscape?
要照橫的還是直的？

A: It doesn't matter, as long as you get us and the view in!
都可以，人和背景有在鏡頭內就好了。

B: Ok. Say "cheese"!
好！笑一個！

A: That was very kind of you, thank you!
你真熱心，謝謝你！

B: No problem! Anytime!
哪裡，舉手之勞而已！

👆 你可以聽懂／口說更多

01. 請你替我和米奇照相好嗎？
Could you take a picture for Mickey and me, please?

02. 可以跟我合照嗎？
Could you take a picture with me?

03. 這裡禁止拍照嗎？
Is it prohibited to take pictures here?

04. 我想買一卷底片。
I want to buy a roll of film.

05. 請問有 36 張、400 度的底片嗎？
Do you have a roll of 36 pictures, ISO 400 films?

06. 我要一卷 24 張的彩色底片。
I want a roll of 24 pictures color film.

07. 我想洗這一卷底片。
I want to get this film developed.

08. 洗一卷多少錢呢？
How much is it to develop a roll of film?

09. 多久可以好呢？
How long will it take for the film to be developed?

10. 這台相機有點問題，可以幫我看一下嗎？
There is a problem with this camera. Could you take a look for me?

✍ 關鍵單字／片語

01. **flashlight**	閃光燈
02. **camera shutter**	快門
03. **lens**	鏡頭
04. **a tripod**	三腳架
05. **point and shoot camera**	傻瓜相機
06. **disposable camera**	拋棄式相機
07. **film**	底片
08. **black-and-white film**	黑白底片
09. **digital camera**	數位相機
10. **take a picture**	照相、拍照

10 | 露營

出發去露營前，你可以到專門店購買露營時會用到的東西，讓你能夠好好享受在野外謀生的趣味。找一個銷售員給你點意見，看你還缺什麼東西，出發前可以補齊之前沒有想到會用上的用具，確保露營時可以度過愉快的夜晚。

實境對話

A: Hello, can you tell me how much a one-man tent costs? It's just for myself.
哈囉，請問一個人的帳棚要多少錢呢？我自己要用的。

B: Yes, the price range is from 200 to 700 dollars.
好的，價錢從兩百到七百元都有。

A: How much is that one?
那個要多少錢？

B: That is 400 dollars. And it's on sale this week.
那個是四百元。這個禮拜在特價。

A: Ok, that sounds fine. I would like to buy that one.
好的，聽起來不錯。我想要買這個。

B: Do you need a sleeping bag or other accessories?
你有需要睡袋和其他的用品嗎？

A: Yes, can you suggest anything I might need?
有的，請你給我建議我可能需要什麼？

B: Well, a sleeping bag, a flashlight, a stove and a plastic mattress to put under your sleeping bag as it might get damp during the night.
嗯。睡袋、手電筒、爐子，晚上時可能會變得潮濕，可以墊在你睡袋下的塑膠床墊。

👆 你可以聽懂／口說更多

01. 我們這個週末計畫去露營。
We're planning to go camping this weekend.

02. 這是個露營的好天氣。
This is a great camping weather.

03. 你們打算去哪裡露營？
Where do you plan to go camping?

04. 今晚我們在哪兒露營？
Where shall we camp tonight?

05. 我們需要為露營準備什麼？
What do we need for camping?

06. 這個週末去露營怎麼樣？
How about going camping this weekend?

07. 夏天是露營的最佳季節。
Summer is the best season for camping.

08. 我們能去露營玩個痛快！
We can go camping and enjoy ourselves!

09. 我們檢查一下露營所需物品的清單吧。
Let's check the bring list for the camping.

10. 明天我們是否去露營取決於天氣情況。
Whether we will go camping tomorrow depends on the weather.

✍ 關鍵單字／片語

01. **go camping**	露營
02. **tent**	帳蓬
03. **sleeping bag**	睡袋
04. **flashlight**	手電筒
05. **plastic mattress**	塑膠床墊
06. **damp**	潮溼
07. **stove**	爐子
08. **on the weekend**	週末
09. **depend on**	取決於、信賴
10. **range**	範圍

11 | 騎馬

在能夠駕馭一匹馬之前，你需要知道一些馬術的知識。在你可以上路前，一定要知道如何控制牠的走向和如何讓牠了解你的指令。找個教練指導你駕馭馬的基本知識，讓你可以對馬有基礎的認識與確保安全。

🗨 實境對話

A: Can you tell me the safe way to sit on the horse?
請問如何安全地坐在馬上？

B: Yes, make sure your feet are firmly in the stirrups. Sit upright and hold the reins firmly in your hands.
確定你的雙腳穩穩地踏在馬鐙上，坐直，雙手握緊韁繩。

A: How do I make the horse move forward?
如何讓馬往前走呢？

B: You kick him gently with both heels and you sit up a little higher as you kick.
用你的兩個後腳輕輕踢馬，在你踢牠時坐高一點。

A: And how do I make him turn from right to left?
要如何讓馬從右邊轉到左邊呢？

B: You pull the right rein gently to the right to turn right and the same with the left rein to turn left.
輕輕地把右邊的韁繩往右邊拉讓馬往右邊走，往左邊也是一樣，拉左邊的韁繩往左邊。

A: OK, I understand.
好的。我瞭解了。

A: The horse is moving now.
現在馬在動了。

☝你可以聽懂／口說更多

01. 你會騎馬嗎？
Can you ride a horse?

02. 你在哪兒學的騎馬？
Where did you learn to ride a horse?

03. 現在會騎馬的人很少。
There are few people who can ride a horse now.

04. 騎馬對我來說是小事一件。
Horse riding is just a piece of cake for me.

05. 騎馬並非易事。
It's not an easy job to ride a horse.

06. 附近有專供騎馬用的馬房嗎？
Are there any stables near here?

07. 我們打算這週末去騎馬。
We are going riding this weekend.

08. 你喜歡什麼？騎馬還是射擊？
Which do you prefer, horse riding or shooting?

09. 這是我第一次騎馬。
It's my first time riding.

10. 我最喜歡的運動就是騎馬。你呢？
My favorite sport is horse riding. What about you?

✎ 關鍵單字／片語

01. **horse riding**	騎馬
02. **race-course**	馬場
03. **saddle**	馬鞍
04. **horsewhip**	馬鞭
05. **stirrup**	馬鐙
06. **rein**	韁繩
07. **kick**	踢
08. **move forward**	往前走
09. **a piece of cake**	小事一樁
10. **drink**	飲料

12 | 沙漠旅行

在要往沙漠之前，由於有些沙漠地形險惡或者氣候乾燥，會有些需要預先知道的資訊需要了解。在當地可以詢問清楚未來所要經過的路程再啟程會比較保險。在出發前，還要準備好路上會用到的水和食物，以免走到半路會沒辦法找到需要的支援。

🔊 實境對話

A: Can you tell me the safest route through the desert, please?
請問穿越沙漠最安全的路線是怎麼走？

B: Yes, follow the sign posts carefully, you can't get lost.
如果你仔細地跟著指標走，你就不會迷路了。

A: Can you tell me where I can find water to fill my water bottle?
請問哪裡有水可以裝滿我的水壺？

B: Yes, you will find water on your way. You will see the sign for water.
在你往沙漠的途中，就會看到裝水的指標。

A: Can you tell me if there are any dangerous insects or snakes on this route?
請問這個路線有沒有任何危險的昆蟲或蛇呢？

B: No, it is quite safe but be careful anyway.
沒有，這裡相當安全，但是不管怎樣還是要小心。

B: There is a shuttle service to the train station every hour until 8 p.m..
晚上八點以前，每個小時都會有來回車站的交通服務。

☝你可以聽懂／口說更多

01. 你去沙漠旅行過嗎？
Have you ever traveled in desert?

02. 沙漠裡太乾燥了。
The desert is too dry.

03. 為什麼人們在穿越沙漠的時候要帶上手錶？
Why do people wear watches when they cross the desert?

04. 你可以在沙漠騎駱駝。
You can ride a camel in the desert.

05. 你有沒有想過去沙漠旅行？
Have you ever thought of going traveling in desert?

06. 或許你有機會在沙漠中看到綠洲。
Perhaps you'll have the opportunity to see the oasis in the desert.

07. 沙漠裡的空氣幾乎不含水分。
The desert air contains hardly any moisture.

08. 你可能會在沙漠裡迷路。
You might get lost in desert.

09. 你獨自一人穿越沙漠很危險。
It's very dangerous for you to cross the desert alone.

10. 沙漠風光真是美極了。
The sand scenery is simply gorgeous.

✍ 關鍵單字／片語

01. **desert**	沙漠
02. **oasis**	綠洲
03. **cactus**	仙人掌
04. **ride a camel**	騎駱駝
05. **moisture**	水份
06. **mirage**	沙漠裡的海市蜃樓
07. **opprotunity**	機會
08. **gorgeous**	美極了
09. **dry**	乾燥
10. **scenery**	風景

13 | 划船

在划船前，先找個地方租到船，再租賃其他划船安全器具，
確保划船時，能夠不發生任何意外。划船時，除了觀賞風景
之外，也要小心不要划到太遠的地方，而沒辦法回到租船的
所在。所有東西都準備好時，就可以和好友一起享受自然界
的美景囉！

實境對話

A: Can you tell me how much it costs to hire a boat for the day?
請問租船一天要多少錢呢？

B: It costs 100 dollars per day.
一天要一百塊錢。

A: Do I need any special equipment?
請問我會需要用到任何特殊的器具嗎？

B: Yes, you would need to wear waterproof clothes and boots.
是的，你將會需要穿防水的衣服和靴子。

A: Can I sail to the island and back?
請問可以划船到島上再回來嗎？

B: Yes, most people do that.
可以，大部分的人都這樣做。

A: Where can I borrow a life jacket?
哪裡可以借救生衣呢？

B: Life jackets will be included in boat rental. You can ask the vendor for free life jackets.
救生衣有包含在租船裡面。你可以跟店家詢問免費的救生衣。

👆 你可以聽懂／口說更多

01. 我打算在下星期去划船。
I am planning to go boating next week.

02. 我們一起去划船吧。
Let's go boating together.

03. 我非常擅長划船。
I am very good at rowing a boat.

04. 你想去划船嗎？
Do you feel like going boating?

05. 我們去北海公園划船好嗎？
Shall we go boating in Beihai Park?

06. 我覺得這是一個適合划船的日子。
I think it's a good day to go boating.

07. 明天想不想去划船啊？
Would you like to go boating tomorrow?

08. 你臉色不太好，是不是暈船？
You look pale. Are you seasick?

09. 為什麼不邊划船邊欣賞風景呢？
Why not go boating and enjoy the scenery?

10. 他們正要去划船。你想不想一塊去呢？
They are about to go boating. Would you like to join them?

✍ 關鍵單字／片語

01. **pier**	碼頭
02. **hire a boat**	租船
03. **water proof clothes**	防水衣
04. **life jacket**	救生衣
05. **go boating**	去划船
06. **row a boat**	划船
07. **look**	看起來
08. **pale**	蒼白
09. **be good at**	擅長於……
10. **borrow**	借用

14│衝浪

很多人喜歡衝浪帶來的快感，但是在準備衝浪前要想想哪裡是安全的地方，和氣候是否適宜下水衝浪。在確定一切都安全後，如有盡責的救生員在旁，也可把你衝浪的風險降低。

實境對話

A: Can you tell me what the weather forecast is today? Is it suitable for surfing?
請問今天天氣預報如何，適合衝浪嗎？

B: Yes, it is safe today. But check back with me from time to time and I will let you know of any storm warning.
是的，今天很安全。但是你偶爾要再來跟我確定天氣，我會讓你知道有沒有任何的暴風雨警告。

A: Which part of the beach is the safest place to surf?
請問哪裡是最安全衝浪的地方呢？

B: About 10 minutes walk to your left.
大概往左走十分鐘之後。

A: Is there a lifeguard on duty?
那有救生員值班嗎？

B: Yes, from 8 a.m. to 4 p.m..
有的，從早上八點到下午四點。

A: Have any surfing accidents been reported recently?
最近有沒有任何衝浪事故報導呢？

B: No, it is very safe if you don't go too far.
沒有，如果你不跑太遠的話是很安全的。

👆 你可以聽懂／口說更多

01. 我覺得衝浪挺危險的。
I think it's dangerous to surf.

02. 這兒怎麼看不到有人衝浪？
Why haven't I seen any surfers around here?

03. 你做過風帆衝浪運動嗎？
Have you ever tried windsurfing?

04. 如果浪夠大的話，我們就去衝浪。
We will go surfing if the waves are big enough.

05. 我要到哪裡去租衝浪板？
Where can I rent a surfboard?

06. 在中國玩衝浪的人不是很多。
There aren't many people who surf in China.

07. 衝浪是世界上最受歡迎的水上運動之一。
Surfing is one of the most popular water sports.

08. 我喜歡看衝浪比賽。你呢？
I like watching surfing competitions. What about you?

09. 你們國家是不是很流行衝浪啊？
Is surfing very popular in your country?

10. 想不想跟我去衝浪？
Would you like to go surfing with me?

✍ 關鍵單字／片語

01. **weather forecast**	天氣預報
02. **wave**	浪
03. **go surfing**	去衝浪
04. **warning**	警告
05. **lifesaver**	救生員
06. **on duty**	值班
07. **windsurfing**	風帆衝浪
08. **surfboard**	衝浪板
09. **water sport**	水上運動
10. **accident**	意外事故

15 | 垂釣

遇到釣魚客時，可以交流一些釣魚的心得。有些人的經驗淺，有些人的經驗豐富。在看到別人的漁獲時，心裡也會想要擁有釣到魚的成就感。在開始釣魚之前，先去準備好釣魚的誘餌吧！

實境對話

A: What bait do you use?
你是用什麼釣餌呢？

B: I only use small shrimps. But it depends on what you want to catch.
我只是用小蝦而已，但要看你想釣到什麼魚來用什麼餌。

A: Is it ok with you if I fish here?
請問我也可以在這裡釣魚嗎？

B: Yes, of course. Just give me some space, it might scare the fish.
當然可以，但是請給我一些空間，要不然可能會嚇到魚。

A: My friends invited me to go boat fishing with them next weekend. Are you interested to come along?
我朋友邀請我下週跟他們去船釣，你有興趣一起來嗎？

B: Sounds interesting. Count me in. Hold on, I think the fish is biting.
聽起來蠻好玩的樣子，算我一份吧。等一下，好像有魚上鉤了。

A: Wow! Today is your day!
哇，今天真是你的幸運日耶！

👆你可以聽懂／口說更多

01. 你想不想跟我去釣魚？
Would you like to go fishing with me?

02. 我們去河的下游去釣魚吧。
Let's go fishing by the down-river.

03. 你用什麼作魚餌？
What bait do you use?

04. 這是個釣魚的好地方。
It is a good place for fishing.

05. 你真是個釣魚能手！
What a good angler you are!

06. 我忘記帶魚餌了。
I forgot to bring the bait.

07. 在冰上釣魚是需要技巧的事。
Fishing on ice is a tricky business.

08. 我想把魚重新放生。
I am going to throw the fish back.

09. 我們可以一起釣魚順便交流經驗。
We can go fishing together and exchange our experiences.

10. 天氣晴朗的時候我們經常去釣魚。
We often go fishing on nice days.

✍ 關鍵單字／片語

01. **go fishing**	去釣魚
02. **bait**	魚餌
03. **fly-fishing**	用假繩釣魚
04. **shrimp**	蝦子
05. **crab**	螃蟹
06. **boat fishing**	船釣
07. **come along**	一起來
08. **lucky day**	幸運日
09. **down-river**	下游
10. **angler**	垂釣者

16 | 攀登

想要享受攀岩的樂趣,就要先裝戴好攀岩時需要用到的確保工具。在沒有攀岩的經驗時,最好先在社團裡和社員一起練習攀登的技巧。和團員互相切磋琢磨,讓自己好好了解攀岩的危險性和刺激感。一切都熟悉後,再去利用自然的山面,來實際運用之前所學的技巧。

🦶 實境對話

A: Are there any climbing groups I can join here?
這裡有任何我可參加的攀岩社嗎?

B: Yes, if you apply at the office and fill out the form. You can join a team.
有的,如果你來辦公室申請,填寫表格,你就可以參加一隊。

A: I need to buy some climbing equipment. Can you help me?
我想要買些攀岩用具,你可以幫助我嗎?

B: Yes, there is a complete climbing kit to rent for 100 dollars. And 50 dollars deposit. That's refundable.
好的,這裡完整的登山用品租借是金額一百元,和五十元的押金。押金是可退還的。

A: Ok, I will fill out the form and hire the equipment from you, please.
好的,我會填寫表格,然後再跟你租借用具。

B: Very good. Please fill the form and sign here and here.
很好。請填寫這個表格,然後在這裡和這裡簽名。

🖑 你可以聽懂／口說更多

01. 攀登是一項高危險性的活動。
Climbing is a high-risk activity.

02. 我喜歡室內攀岩。
I like to go indoor climbing.

03. 每個人都必須努力向上攀登。
Everybody mush try to climb up.

04. 我怎樣才能在一小時內登上這座山？
How can I climb the hill in an hour?

05. 向頂峰攀登時身上都熱起來了。
Climbing to the summit gets very warm.

06. 我最喜歡攀登的過程。
The course of climbing is my favorite part.

07. 攀岩運動能考驗人的勇氣和技巧。
Rock-climbing is a test of nerves and skill.

08. 你應該先學一學攀登的技巧。
You should learn some skills before climbing.

09. 攀登能夠考驗人的耐力。
Climbing can test people's stamina.

10. 不是所有人都敢冒著風雨攀登高峰。
Not all people are brave enough to climb the mountains in the rain.

✍ 關鍵單字／片語

01. **go climbing**	去攀登、爬山
02. **apply**	申請
03. **high-risk**	高危險性
04. **indoor climbing**	室內攀岩
05. **summit**	峰頂
06. **rock climbing**	攀岩運動
07. **nerve**	膽量
08. **skill**	技巧
09. **stamina**	忍耐力
10. **climb the mountains**	爬山

17 | 潛水

在你潛水前，可以先去店家租借到潛水專用的器具。在穿戴好潛水用具時，你可能需要一些指導或者了解水性。潛水不同於其他活動，可以有機會觀賞到水裡面的生物和植物。在潛水時，也一定不要忘了該上岸的時間，平安回到安全的陸地上。

實境對話

A: How much air is in the tank?
有多少氣在氧氣罐裡？

B: It contains about 10 minutes breathing time. You must surface after that.
它大概有十分鐘可以讓你呼吸，之後你一定要來到水面。

A: Are there any dangerous fish or sharks around here?
這裡有沒有任何危險的魚或者鯊魚呢？

B: No, it is quite safe. I dive here every day.
沒有，這裡相當安全。我每天都在這裡潛水。

A: Can you assist me on my dive?
你可以幫助我潛水嗎？

B: Yes, but that will cost extra for my time. If you don't want to miss the great view, I would also suggest you to rent an underwater camera.
好的，但是你要多付額外的錢。如果你不想錯過這美景的話，我建議你另外租一台水底相機。

A: Thanks for reminding me. The sea looks calm today, let's go diving!
謝謝你提醒我。海面看來風平浪靜，我們去潛水吧！

👆 你可以聽懂/口說更多

01. 你們是想去爬山還是去潛水？
Do you want to go mountain climbing or sea diving?

02. 你會潛水嗎？
Can you dive?

03. 我覺得潛水是項非常危險的活動。
I think diving is a very dangerous activity.

04. 你們當中誰潛水潛得最深？
Which one of you can dive the deepest?

05. 並不是每個人都會潛水。
Not everybody can dive under the water.

06. 潛水的感覺真爽！
The feeling of diving is so good!

07. 你有聽說過裸潛嗎？
Have you ever heard of skin-diving?

08. 星期天的潛水活動將持續一整天。
The diving activity will last all day on Sunday.

09. 我水性很好，因為我家住在海邊。
I excel at swimming because I live near the sea.

10. 大衛是名非常出色的潛水夫。
David is an excellent diver.

✎ 關鍵單字/片語

01. **go diving**	去潛水
02. **diver**	潛水者
03. **snorkeling equipment**	浮潛用具
04. **tank**	罐子
05. **underwater**	在水面下的
06. **skin-dive**	裸身潛水
07. **feeling**	感覺
08. **under the water**	在水面下
09. **excel at**	擅長
10. **excellent**	超棒

18 海水浴場

到海邊玩時，除了下水游泳之外，有時想要享受一下日光浴，有時又想要動動筋骨，參加一下海灘活動。海邊有些地方可以租到很多器具。讓你除了玩水之外，也可拿本書，好好享受海風吹拂和海邊蔓延著的渡假慵懶氣息。

實境對話

A: Where can I find a beach chair to rent?
請問哪裡可以租到海灘椅呢？

B: There are beach chairs for rent all along the beach.
你沿著海灘都可以租到海灘椅。

A: Are there any activities today?
今天有沒有任何活動呢？

B: Yes, there is a volleyball game starting in 1 hour.
有的，在一小時後就會有一場排球比賽開始。

A: Can anyone join?
每個人都可參加嗎？

B: Yes, it depends on the age group. There is a separate game for adults and children.
是的，依年齡層做區分。大人和小孩子都有分別的比賽可以參加。

A: Sounds exciting. But I'll have to apply some sunscreen first, I definitely don't want to get sun burnt.
聽起來很刺激呢。但我需要先擦些防曬乳，我可不想曬傷。

B: You're right. The sun is strong today. You'd better put on your sunglasses as well.
你說對了。今天的太陽很烈。你最好也把太陽眼鏡戴上。

👆你可以聽懂／口說更多

01. 這是很好的海水浴場。
This is a fine beach.

02. 那個海水浴場每年都舉辦形式多樣的慶祝活動。
The beach holds a variety of celebration activities every year.

03. 我喜歡那裡獨特的藍色海水。
I love the unique blue sea there.

04. 我真的很想去海水浴場。
I'd really like to go to the beach.

05. 我們可以在海灘上舒服地曬太陽。
We can relax on the beach and enjoy the sunshine.

06. 那你應該去有救生員的海水浴場。
You should go to the beach with lifeguards.

07. 我想看白色的沙灘。
I would like to see the white sand beach.

08. 海灘上的景色太美了。
The scenery on the beach is really beautiful.

09. 沿著海灘散步是件多麼愜意的事啊。
Walking along the beach is such a relaxing moment.

10. 我們去海灘上曬太陽吧。
Let's go to the beach to sunbathe.

✍ 關鍵單字／片語

01. **bathing beach**	海水浴場
02. **beach chair**	海灘椅
03. **beach umbrella**	海灘遮陽傘
04. **suncream**	防曬霜
05. **suntan lotion**	助曬乳液
06. **sunburn**	曬傷
07. **sunbathe**	作日光浴
08. **apply sunscreen**	擦防曬霜
09. **sand beach**	沙灘
10. **sunglasses**	太陽眼鏡、墨鏡

19 | 滑雪

在出發到滑雪場之前，要好好了解滑雪的方法。否則到雪場滑雪時，一不小心就會倒栽蔥。在你所在的當地有時候會有練習滑雪的地方，讓你能夠嚐試一下滑雪的訣竅。如果要順順利利的體驗滑雪的刺激，一定要避免快速運動中所帶來的超級危險性喔！

實境對話

A: Shall I take lessons at a local ski resort before I go to the mountain?

在我到山上之前，我是否應該在這附近的滑雪場上一些滑雪課程？

B: Yes, it's a good idea as you will get familiar with the equipment.

是的，這主意不錯。因為你會比較熟悉如何使用滑雪器具。

A: Do I need to make an appointment at my local ski resort?

我需要和這裡的滑雪場預約時間嗎？

B: Yes, you can do a beginner ski program.

是的，你可以上一個短期的滑雪課程。

A: What else can I do besides skiing?

除了滑雪還可以做什麼呢？

B: Don't worry. There are quite many activities you can do. You can go sledding, snowboarding, and I believe there will be plenty of snow for you to make a snowman.

別擔心，還有很多其他活動。你可以去玩雪橇、玩滑雪板，而且我相信一定有足夠的雪讓你堆一個雪人呢！

👆你可以聽懂／口說更多

01. 冬天是滑雪的最佳季節。
Winter is the best season for skiing.

02. 什麼是初學者滑雪道？
What is the beginner trail?

03. 滑雪杆對於保持平衡是很重要的。
Ski poles are important to maintaining your balance.

04. 你都去哪兒滑雪呢？
Where do you go skiing?

05. 我們為什麼不到瑞士去滑雪呢？
We don't we go skiing in Switzerland?

06. 想不想跟我們一起去滑雪？
Would you like to join us on a skiing trip?

07. 我想我會摔斷腿的。
I think I am going to break my leg.

08. 我們可以坐纜車到滑雪場。
We can ride the cable car to get to the ski field.

09. 滑雪是我們國家最流行的運動。
Skiing is the most popular sport in my country.

10. 學會一些基本技巧才能玩得安全。
Learning some basic skills is the safe way to go.

✐ 關鍵單字／片語

01. **go skiing**	去滑雪
02. **basic skill**	基本技巧
03. **ski lift**	滑雪纜車
04. **ski run**	滑雪道
05. **advanced skier**	滑雪高手
06. **bunny hill**	初學者滑雪道（約三十度的坡地）
07. **ski jumping**	跳臺滑雪
08. **ski boots**	滑雪靴
09. **sled**	雪撬
10. **snowboard**	滑雪板

20 | 高空彈跳

在嘗試高空彈跳前，要好好搞清楚如何確保安全。詢問在場的指導員，遵循每一個安全的步驟，再踏上平台上的定點。如果疏忽了任何步驟，很有可能會造成挽救不回來的事故。所以，仔細聆聽指導員的講解，在極限運動中，就可以好好享受高度和高速的快感了。

👊 實境對話

A: Do I need any safety equipment?
我需要配戴任何安全器具嗎？

B: Yes, the body harness will be strapped around you. It is similar to the harness used in mountain climbing.
是的，安全腰帶應該要繫在你的身上。它是類似登山攀岩時所繫的腰帶。

B: Carabiners will be used to connect your body harness to the bungee cord. These are metal, hook-like clips.
鉤環要扣住安全腰帶來結合彈跳繩。它們是像鉤子一樣的金屬夾子。

A: How far would I fall?
我可以降落多遠？

B: Rebound is the first, second, and how ever many it takes, bounce from when the cord reaches the maximum length.
你會彈回來一次至兩次，或者看有多少次，彈到繩子可以延伸的最大限度。

👆 你可以聽懂／口說更多

01. 高空彈跳是一件非常令人激動的極限運動。
Bungee jumping is a very exciting extreme sport.

02. 高空彈跳並不需要專門的身體訓練。
Bungee jumping does not require any special physical training.

03. 在澳門的時候我們去玩了高空彈跳。
We went bungee jumping when we were in Macao.

04. 五百英尺？我可做不到！
500 feet? I would never be able to do that!

05. 我打算週六去玩高空彈跳。
I am planning to do bungee jumping on Saturday.

06. 你玩過高空彈跳嗎？
Have you ever tried bungee jumping?

07. 我昨天去玩高空彈跳了。感覺太刺激了。
I went bungee jumping yesterday. It was so exciting.

08. 北京是我國高空彈跳發展最快最早的城市。
Beijing is the fastest and earliest bungee jumping developing city in China.

09. 它是很嚇人，但是又很讓人興奮。
It is very scary, but very exhilarating.

10. 對人們來説，這既是一種放鬆，又是一項愛好。
For people, it is both a relaxation and a hobby.

✍ 關鍵單字／片語

01. **bungee jumping**	高空彈跳
02. **carabiner**	扣環
03. **harness**	安全帶
04. **bungee cord**	彈跳繩
05. **bounce**	反彈
06. **rebound**	彈回
07. **extreme sport**	極限運動
08. **training**	訓練
09. **exhilarating**	令人振奮的
10. **be able to**	能夠

Chapter

08

打電話篇

Chapter 08 音檔雲端連結

因各家手機系統不同,若無法直接掃描,
仍可以至以下電腦雲端連結下載收聽。
(https://tinyurl.com/2p9brxss)

01 | 打國際電話

TRACK
101

使用公用電話撥打國際電話的計費會比在飯店請櫃檯轉接、直撥外線來得便宜。你可以在國內購買國際電話預付卡，或者到當地機場、商店、便利商店等購買國際電話預付卡。

🗣 實境對話

A: How do I make an international call?
我想打國際電話，請問要怎麼打呢？

B: You can use coins or buy international phone cards.
你可以投幣打公用電話，或者購買國際電話卡。

A: How much is a card?
電話卡一張要多少錢？

B: The cheapest one is 100 dollars.
最便宜的一張 100 元。

A: How long can I talk if I made a phone call to Taiwan?
請問如果打到台灣的話，可以講多久呢？

B: 40 minutes during the day, and about 70 minutes after 9 p.m..
白天的話 40 分鐘，晚上 9 點之後大概可以講 70 分鐘。

A: Excuse me, do you sell international phone cards here?
請問這裡有賣國際電話卡嗎？

A: May I have one?
請給我一張好嗎？

A: Please tell me how to use it.
請告訴我怎麼使用。

👆 你可以聽懂／口說更多

01. 請給我一張國際電話卡。
Please give me an international phone card.

02. 請告訴我公用電話怎麼樣撥打呢？
Could you tell me how to use the public phone?

03. 這電話機是不是故障了？
Is this telephone out of order?

04. 我想打國際電話，可以幫我轉接嗎？
I want to make an international call, could you help me connect through?

05. 我要打到台灣。
I want to make a call to Taiwan.

06. 通話費用是多少？
How much is the rate?

07. 我要打對方付費的電話。
I want to make a collect call.

08. 我要打緊急電話。
I want to make an emergency call.

09. 我要打叫人電話。
I want to make a person-to-person call.

10. 請問我要怎麼撥打國際電話呢？
How do I make an international call?

✏️ 關鍵單字／片語

01. **internation call**	國際電話
02. **international phone card**	國際電話卡
03. **person-to-person call**	叫人電話
04. **collect call**	對方付費電話
05. **emergency call**	緊急電話
06. **telephone booth**	公用電話亭
07. **public phone**	公用電話
08. **out of order**	故障
09. **country code**	國碼
10. **area code**	區碼

02 | 打市內電話

去國外旅遊，如果你有親戚、朋友也在當地，難得去一趟能有機會見面，打個電話問候關心一下，或是約出來喝杯咖啡、找對方當地陪！

實境對話

A: Hello, may I speak to Jenny?
喂？請找珍妮。

B: This is Jenny speaking. Who's calling?
我就是，你哪裡找？

A: It's Wendy! I'm now here in Orange County.
是我，溫蒂！我現在人在橘郡。

B: Wow, Wendy! I'm so surprised. When did you come here?
哇，溫蒂！我好驚訝！你什麼時候來的啊？

A: I just arrived yesterday. We haven't seen each other for a long time. Would you like to hang out and have a cup of coffee?
我昨天才剛到。我們很久沒見面了，要不要出來喝杯咖啡聚一聚？

B: Of course, where are we going to meet?
當然，我們要在哪裡見面呢？

A: I'll be waiting for you at "Friends" café in downtown.
我會在市區的「朋友咖啡廳」等你。

B: I'll be right there.
我馬上到。

🖑 你可以聽懂／口說更多

01. 你們這裡有免費的 Wi-Fi 嗎？
Do you have free Wi-Fi here?

02. 請問比爾在嗎？
Hello, is Bill there?

03. 喂，請問是陳先生的家嗎？
Hello, is this the Chen's residence?

04. 請幫我接 502 號房。
Please connect room 502 for me.

05. 我可以留話給他嗎？
Could I leave him a message?

06. 請轉告她打我的手機，號碼是 090-123456，謝謝！
Please tell her to call my cell phone, the number is 090-123-456, thank you.

07. 我晚一點再打好了。
I will call later.

08. 請問是 1234-5678 嗎？
Is this 1234-5678?

09. 抱歉，打擾你了。
Sorry to bother you.

10. 麻煩你告訴山姆我有來電，請他回電給我，謝謝！
Please tell Sam I called, and have him return my call, thank you.

✐ 關鍵單字／片語

01. **each other**	彼此	
02. **a long time**	一段長時間	
03. **hang out**	好友相聚打發時間	
04. **free**	免費	
05. **mobile phone**	行動電話	
06. **residence**	住處、住家、宅邸	
07. **later**	晚點	
08. **bother**	打擾	
09. **meet**	見面	
10. **local call**	市內電話	

03 | 詢問路線

在不了解如何到某地時，開口問路是最快的捷徑了。給予詢問的人清楚的目標，讓對方能夠掌握，然後指導你到目的地的確切方向。在問路時，最好找熟悉當地的人，他們給予的訊息會比較正確。這樣子就不會走太多冤枉路了。

實境對話

A: Hello, I am now in subway station. Can you tell me how to get to your hotel?
哈囉，現在我人在地鐵站。你可以告訴我要怎麼到你們飯店嗎？

B: Yes, you can take bus number 10 directly to our hotel.
好的，你可以搭 10 號巴士直接到我們飯店。

A: I think I would prefer to walk. Is it very far?
我比較想要走路。路程會很遠嗎？

B: Not too far. It's about 25 minutes walk.
不太遠，大概走路要花 25 分鐘。

A: What direction should I walk?
你可以告訴我要走哪個方向嗎？

B: Turn right from Entrance No. 1 and follow the bus route.
好的。從一號出口右轉，然後沿著巴士路線走。

B: The signs are very clear along the way.
沿路都有很清楚的標示引導。

B: If you can't find your way, ask someone for directions.
如果你找不到路，可以詢問別人怎麼走。

👆 你可以聽懂／口說更多

01. 可不可以告訴我坐幾路車到博物館？
Could you tell me which bus I should take to the museum?

02. 您可以坐 11 路車直達那裡。
You can take No. 11 bus to get there directly.

03. 別著急，您會找到的。
Take it easy, you won't miss it.

04. 恐怕我迷路了。
I am afraid that I lost my way.

05. 請問您能幫我個忙嗎？
Could you please do me a favor?

06. 走過去十分鐘左右就行了。
It will only take about ten minutes to walk there.

07. 請告訴我如何去動物園好嗎？
Would you please tell me the way to the zoo?

08. 可以告訴我您現在的位置嗎？
Could you tell me where you are now?

09. 有捷徑嗎？
Is there any shortcut?

10. 非常感謝您的幫助！
Thank you very much for your help!

✎ 關鍵單字／片語

01. **directly**	直接地
02. **far away**	很遠
03. **landmark**	地標
04. **well sign posted**	標示清楚
05. **opposite side**	對面
06. **take it easy**	放輕鬆、別著急
07. **lose the way**	迷路
08. **do me a favor**	幫我一個忙
09. **shortcut**	捷徑
10. **close**	近

04│詢問旅館空房

詢問旅館的空房，可以在電話中詢問。或者透過旅遊仲介，來詢問更多種旅館空房選擇。在到達目的地之前，通常都要預訂房間。以免到達時，各個旅館房間都被預訂光了。

實境對話

A: Do you have any vacancy?
你們有任何空房嗎？

B: On which date do you require?
你要問哪一天的呢？

A: Do you have any room available on the 2nd and 3rd of May?
你們五月二號和三號有空房嗎？

B: Yes, we have a single and double room on those dates.
有的，我們在這兩天都有一間單人房和雙人房。

A: Is breakfast included and can I see the breakfast menu?
有包含早餐嗎？我可以看早餐菜單嗎？

B: Yes, breakfast is included for all our rooms.
有的，早餐包含在我們所有的住房內。

A: Do you have a special package for bed and breakfast including dinner?
你們有包含早晚餐的住房特別套裝嗎？

B: Yes, we have a special rate including dinner from Monday to Friday.
有的，我們從禮拜一到禮拜五都有包含晚餐的特別優惠。

☝ 你可以聽懂／口說更多

01. 你們有空房間嗎？
Do you have any room available?

02. 那幾天我們還有一間空房。
We still have one room available for those days.

03. 請問你們還有空房嗎？
Do you have any vacancies?

04. 這個禮拜三晚上你們有空房嗎？
Do you have any vacancies this Wednesday night?

05. 你能不能幫我查一查明天是否有空房間？
Can you check for me whether there is any vacant room for tomorrow?

06. 很抱歉，我們全訂滿了。
I am sorry that we are fully booked.

07. 請別掛電話，我來查查有沒有空房。
Hold the line, please. I will check the room availability.

08. 對不起，現在我們沒有空房。
Sorry, we don't have vacancies now.

09. 目前唯一的空房是雙人房。
There's only one double-room available.

10. 恐怕那天沒有單人房了。
I am afraid we have no single room available on that day.

✐ 關鍵單字／片語

01. **vacancy**	空房
02. **pricelist**	價目表
03. **package**	套裝
04. **next week**	下禮拜
05. **tomorrow**	明天
06. **find out**	發現、找到
07. **I am sorry that...**	我很抱歉……
08. **only**	只有
09. **I'm afraid...**	恐怕……
10. **twin room**	雙人房

05 | 電話預約旅館

在預約旅館房間時，通常旅館人員都會要求信用卡資料，確保到時候如果你沒有出現入住的話，他們可以從中取得一些金額，來補償預訂之後又取消的生意損失。有時候可在入住前規定的一段時間取消，就可以免於被扣款的可能了。

🗨 實境對話

A: I want to book a double room for the 2nd and 3rd of May. Are there rooms available?
我想預訂五月二號和三號的一間雙人房。還有空房嗎？

B: Yes, we still have rooms available for these dates.
有的，我們這兩天還有空房。

A: Do I need to pay a deposit or do you accept visa?
我需要付押金或者你們接受信用卡？

B: Yes, we require a deposit to secure your booking and we accept visa.
是的。我們會要求支付押金來確保你的訂房，然後我們接受信用卡。

A: Can I pay by visa now over the phone and then pay the balance of my bill in cash on departure?
我可以現在透過電話付信用卡，然後在我退房時用現金付剩餘的款項嗎？

B: Yes, your visa details are taken just for the deposit, you can pay cash as you prefer when you check out.
可以。你提供的信用卡資料只是用來確保支付了押金。你想要的話，可以在退房的時候支付現金。

👆 你可以聽懂／口說更多

01. 哈囉，可以幫我轉接到訂房組嗎？
Hello. Can you put me through to Room Reservations, please?

02. 您需要什麼樣的房間？
What kind of room would you like?

03. 客房預訂部，能為您效勞嗎？
This is Reservations, what can I do for you?

04. 我能預定一間雙人房嗎？
Can I reserve a double room, please?

05. 一有空房我會打電話給您的。
I will call you as soon as we have a vacancy.

06. 這間雙人房有浴室嗎？
Does the double room have a bathroom?

07. 您那天什麼時間到達？
What time will you arrive on that day?

08. 您是要標準房還是豪華房？
Would you like a standard room or a deluxe room?

09. 我想訂一個房間住兩天。
I want to book a room for two days.

10. 可以幫我保留這間單人房嗎？
Is it possible to reserve the single room for me?

✍ 關鍵單字／片語

01. **confirm**	確認
02. **availability**	有效
03. **require**	要求
04. **What kind of...?**	什麼樣的……？
05. **detail**	細節、詳情
06. **pay cash**	付現
07. **included**	包含
08. **reception**	接待處
09. **bathroom**	浴室
10. **Is it possible to...**	有可能……？

06 | 電話訂票

電話預訂和購票時，要問好時間和場次。可以在網路上先看好座位表，再打電話給票務人員。除了事先匯款的選擇，就是提供信用卡資料扣款。票務人員有時候可以提供一些訊息。讓你可以選擇好位子和比較少人、位置選擇多的場次。

實境對話

A: I would like to book a ticket for a concert.
我想要預訂一張音樂會的票。

B: Yes, what concert would you like to see?
好的。你想要看哪場音樂會呢？

A: I am interested in classical music. Can you suggest a good concert?
我想要聽古典音樂。你可以建議我一個好的音樂會嗎？

B: We have a very good classical concert starting next Friday, running for two nights.
我們有一個從下禮拜五開始，連續兩天的古典音樂會。

A: How much are the tickets?
票價多少呢？

B: The tickets cost $45 for the front rows, and $30 near the back area.
靠近前排的票要 45 元，靠近後面的要 30 元。

A: Is there a booking fee and if I decide to cancel, is there a charge for that?
訂票有收費嗎？如果我決定取消，是不是要收費？

B: There is no booking charge, but there is a cancelation fee.
訂票並沒有收費，但有取消的費用。

👆你可以聽懂／口說更多

01. 非常抱歉，那個航班的機票已訂完。
   I am sorry. We are all booked out for that flight.

02. 你訂票了嗎？
   Have you booked your ticket?

03. 中國航空公司訂票處，需要幫忙嗎？
   Air China Flight Reservations. May I help you?

04. 隨時給我電話好讓我幫你訂票。
   Give me a call so I can book tickets for you.

05. 您要幾張票？
   How many tickets do you want?

06. 我現在可以訂票嗎？
   Shall I book a ticket now?

07. 我想訂頭等艙的機票。
   I'd like to book a first class ticket.

08. 我早上剛用電話訂了票。
   I booked the ticket by phone this morning.

09. 您想訂頭等艙還是經濟艙？
   Would you like first class or economy class?

10. 你想要單程票還是往返票？
   Do you want a one-way or a round-trip ticket?

✍ 關鍵單字／片語

01. **concert**	演唱會
02. **classic music**	古典樂
03. **decide to**	決定
04. **cancel**	取消
05. **cancelation fee**	取消的費用
06. **How much...?**	……多少錢？
07. **What time...?**	什麼時候……？
08. **front row**	前排
09. **visa card**	信用卡
10. **book ticket**	訂票

07 | 接聽電話

接聽電話時，有一些電話禮儀，是固定的。通常只要練習幾次，就可以比較熟悉和了解如何應對。在答覆電話時有一些簡單的句子，可以常常使用應對。在詢問要交談的對象是否有在現場時，也有同樣的模式可以學習用來使用和表達。

👉 實境對話

A: Hello, this is James. Who's calling, please?
哈囉，我是詹姆斯。請問是哪位？

B: Hello, James. This is Mary. Can I speak to your mother?
哈囉，詹姆斯。我是瑪莉。可以跟你媽媽說話嗎？

A: My mother is not here at the moment. Can I take a message?
我媽媽現在不在這裡。你需要留言嗎？

B: No. It's ok, James. I just wanted to have a chat with her.
不用了，沒關係，詹姆斯。我只是想聊聊而已。

A: I Will tell her you called and ask her to call you back.
我要不要告訴她妳有來電，或者要她再打給你？

B: That would be good.
那樣子不錯。

A: Ok, I will give her your message.
好的，我會給她妳的留言。

B: Thank you, James. Bye bye.
嗯，謝謝，詹姆斯。再見。

👆 你可以聽懂／口說更多

01. 請問您找誰？
    Who would you like to speak to?

02. 喂，請問羅伯特先生在嗎？
    Hello. Is Mr. Robert there?

03. 請問您是哪位？
    Who is calling, please?

04. 你覺得她幾點會回來？我有急事找她。
    What time do you expect her to be back? I have something urgent.

05. 您能過會兒再打嗎？
    Would you mind calling back later?

06. 您要找的人來接電話了。
    Your party is on the line.

07. 恐怕他現在不在。
    I am afraid that he is not here now.

08. 可以請李先生聽電話嗎？
    May I speak to Mr. Lee, please?

09. 請稍等，他馬上來。
    Hold on, please. He is coming.

10. 我就是蘇珊。
    This is Susan speaking.

✍ 關鍵單字／片語

01. **speak to sb.**	跟某人講電話
02. **away / out**	不在
03. **call back**	回撥
04. **call / phone / ring**	打電話
05. **available**	有空
06. **unavailable**	沒有空
07. **have a chat with**	和……聊天
08. **answer the phone**	接電話
09. **pick up the phone**	接電話
10. **hang up the phone**	掛斷電話

08 | 電話留言

TRACK
108

找某人講電話但對方不在現場時,可以麻煩接電話的人幫忙
留言或傳話,等到對方回到現場時,接電話者可以通知或要
求對方回覆電話,讓一些疑問或訊息,可以順利轉達或者告
知。

👍 實境對話

A: Hello. Can I speak to John? This is his English teacher, Paul Brady.
哈囉,約翰在嗎?我是他的英文老師,保羅布萊迪。

B: Hello, Mr. Brady, this is his mother, Margaret. John is not here at the moment. Can I take a message?
哈囉,布萊迪先生。我是他的媽媽,我的名字是瑪格麗特。約翰目前不在這裡,有需要幫你留言嗎?

A: Hello, Margaret. John had a class at 2 p.m. today but did not attend.
哈囉,瑪格麗特。約翰下午兩點有課,但他並沒有出席。

A: I need to talk to him to find out why he did not come. Can I leave a message with you?
我需要跟他聊聊,要知道他為何沒有來。可以幫我留言嗎?

B: Yes, I can take your message or you can call back later. I'm sure he will be here soon.
可以。我可以幫你留言,或者你可以等下再打來。我確定他等一下會在這裡。

A: Ok, I will leave a message with you. Ask him to call me as soon as you see him.
好的。請幫我留言。當你一看到他時,請叫他回電給我。

👆 你可以聽懂／口說更多

01. 你需要留言嗎？
May I take a message?

02. 她現在不在。
She is not here at the moment.

03. 我可以留言給她嗎？
Can I leave a message for her?

04. 很樂意轉達您的留言。
I will be glad to give him the message.

05. 請告訴她給我回電話好嗎？
Could you tell her to call me back?

06. 他出去了，要不要留話？
He is out right now. Would you like to leave a message?

07. 他一回來我就把留言給他。
I will give him the message as soon as he comes back.

08. 你有一個電話留言。
There is a telephone message for you.

09. 有電話留言給我嗎？
Is there any telephone message for me?

10. 請告訴他彼得給他打過電話。
Please let him know that Peter called.

✏️ 關鍵單字／片語

01. answering machine	自動答錄機
02. take a message	（幫對方）留言
03. leave a message	留言（給對方）
04. make a phone call	打一通電話
05. as soon as...	立刻……
06. dial	撥打電話
07. This is...	我是……
08. come back	回來
09. right now	現在
10. voicemail	電話留言

09 | 電話轉接

打電話到任何公司或機構時，都會先打到主機。如果不了解
分機號碼多少，都可打到主機，由接電話的人員為你服務。
在電話轉接到正確的分機以前，都要讓轉機人員好好了解你
的需求，以便讓他們能夠幫你轉到正確的人選，提供適合你
的各種資訊和服務。

實境對話

A: Hello, Paul speaking. How can I help you?
哈囉，我是保羅。有什麼要為你服務？

B: Hello. This is Sean. I would like to speak to Peter.
哈囉，保羅。我是尚恩。我想要找彼得。

A: Yes. Can you tell me what extension he is on?
好的，你可以告訴我他的分機嗎？

B: I think it is extension 251, or 521. I'm not really
sure.
好的，我想他的分機是 251 或者 521。我不太確定。

A: Ok, Sean. I will try both and see if I can reach
Peter for you.
好，尚恩。我會試試兩個分機，看是否我可以幫你找到他。

A: I can't seem to locate Peter right now. He must be
away from his desk. Would you like to leave your
number and I will have him call you back?
我現在似乎不能夠聯絡上彼得，他一定是離開他的位子了。
你要不要留下你的號碼，然後我會叫他回電給你？

B: Peter has my number already. Please ask him to
call me back urgently.
彼得已經有我的號碼了。請叫他趕緊回電給我。

👆 你可以聽懂／口說更多

01. 請等一下，為您接通。
Hold on, please. I will connect you.

02. 我將為您轉接史密斯先生。
I will put you through to Mr. Smith.

03. 我給您接 105 分機。
I will connect you to extension 105.

04. 我查一下電話號碼，請稍等。
I will check the number. One minute, please.

05. 我把您的電話接到售票處去了。
I am transferring your call to the ticket office.

06. 請把電話轉到另一條線路上去。
Please have the call transferred to another line.

07. 格林先生打來的，請接二號線。
Mr. Green is on line two.

08. 請凱薩琳小姐聽電話好嗎？
Would you please ask Miss Catherine to answer the phone?

09. 電話線路不好，請別掛。
The line is bad. Do not hang up, please.

10. 我把您的電話轉接過去，請別掛斷。
I will transfer your call. Could you hold the line, please?

✎ 關鍵單字／片語

01. **put you through**	幫你轉接過去
02. **extention number**	分機號碼
03. **urgently**	緊急地
04. **connect**	給……接通電話
05. **on the phone**	電話中
06. **busy line**	忙線
07. **bad connection**	收訊不良
08. **call waiting**	插撥
09. **hold the line**	不要掛斷
10. **call transfer**	電話轉接

10 | 電話報平安

到遠地旅行或者出外到另一個地方，通常打回家報平安都是一種必要的禮貌，讓家裡的人或者掛念你的人可以安心，知道你平安到達目的地。所以通常在經歷過長途旅行，或者到達目的地時，雖然疲累，但是打個電話告知目前狀況，也是個蠻貼心的舉動。

實境對話

A: Hello mom, I arrived safely. Just to let you know, in case you were worried. Are you ok?
哈囉，媽媽。我安全到達。我只是要讓妳知道，要不然妳會擔心。妳還好嗎？

B: Yes, I am fine now that you have called to let me know.
是的。你打給我，讓我知道你到了，我就沒事了。

A: Yes, it was a long journey but I am finally here. Do you miss me?
是的。這是一個很長的旅途，但我終於到了。妳有想我嗎？

B: Yes, we all miss you very much and can't wait until you return.
有的。我們都很想你，然後等不及你回來了。

A: I will call you again as soon as I settled down, please tell everyone I miss them too and I will be back soon.
等我安頓下來時，我會再打給妳。請告訴大家，我也想念他們，然後我會很快回去的。

B: OK, I will. Please be careful and write often.
好的。我會的。請小心，常寫信回來。

你可以聽懂／口說更多

01. 別擔心，我現在很好。
Don't worry. I am very good now.

02. 你為什麼不給你媽媽打個電話報平安呢？
Why don't you call your mom and let her know you are safe now?

03. 我打電話告訴您我已經安全到達了。
I am calling to tell you that I arrived safely.

04. 我非常擔心你。
I am very worried about you.

05. 我是想給您報平安的。
I want to tell you that I arrived safely.

06. 親愛的爸爸，是我啊，我現在已經在倫敦了。
Dear daddy, it's me, I have been in London now.

07. 你現在到家了嗎？
Have you got home now?

08. 旅途非常順利。
It was a very smooth flight.

09. 請放心。我一切都好。
Please don't worry. Everything goes well.

10. 你旅途順利嗎？
Did you have a good flight?

關鍵單字／片語

01. **let me know**	讓我知道
02. **journey**	旅途
03. **miss**	想念
04. **settle down**	安頓下來
05. **don't worry**	別擔心
06. **rest assured**	放心
07. **safety**	安全
08. **wish you...**	祝你……
09. **worried**	擔心的
10. **fine / okay / good**	好的、沒問題的

Chapter

09

銀行金融篇

Chapter 09 音檔雲端連結

因各家手機系統不同，若無法直接掃描，仍可以至以下電腦雲端連結下載收聽。（https://tinyurl.com/yckhufs8）

01 | 兌換貨幣

出國旅遊的時候，最重要的當然是「錢」，很多人都會事先換好美金，再到當地換成當地貨幣，其實這樣一來會損失兩次匯差喔！建議出國前最好先計算一下自己的預算，直接先在台灣換好當地的貨幣，這樣可以避免被收兩次匯差。如果真的錢不夠用了，再去當地銀行辦理兌幣吧！

👍 實境對話

A: How may I help you, sir?
先生，我能為您服務嗎？

B: I want to know what today's exchange rate is for US dollars to Yen.
我想知道今天美元換日幣的匯率是多少。

A: Oh, the Yen dropped today.
喔，今天剛好日幣下跌。

A: You can change 120 Yen for a dollar.
一美元可以換到 120 元日幣。

B: I want to change 300 US dollars to Yen.
那我想把這 300 美元換成日幣。

A: OK, no problem, please wait for a moment.
好，沒問題！請稍等一下。

B: Do I need to pay an extra service charge?
需要另付手續費嗎？

A: No.
不用。

B: And please give me some change.
還請你給我一些零錢。

👆 你可以聽懂／口說更多

01. 我想把這些錢換成歐元，請問在哪一個櫃檯辦理呢？
I want to change the money into Euros, which counter should I go to?

02. 今天的匯率是多少呢？
What is today's exchange rate?

03. 請告訴我今天加幣的匯率。
Please tell me the exchange rate for Canadian dollars today.

04. 我想把這 100 元換成小鈔。
I want to change these 100 dollars to small notes.

05. 我想買台幣 1 萬元的美金。
I want to exchange ten thousand NT dollars into US dollars.

06. 請問 500 元英鎊折合新台幣是多少？
How much is 500 pounds to NT dollars?

07. 會變成多少錢？
How much will it come to?

08. 請給我 3 張一百元，2 張 50 元和 5 個 10 元。
Please give me three hundred bills, two fifties and five tens.

09. 我想把這張大鈔換成小鈔和零錢。
I want to change this big bill into a smaller bill and coins.

10. 請問你們收手續費嗎？
Do you charge service fee?

✍ 關鍵單字／片語

01. **bounced check**	跳票
02. **currency**	貨幣
03. **foreign currency**	外幣
04. **nickel**	5 分錢鎳幣
05. **penny**	1 角硬幣
06. **quarter**	（美、加）25 分硬幣
07. **Euro**	歐元
08. **Yen**	日幣
09. **NT dollar**	新台幣
10. **Renminbi**	人民幣

02 | 兌換旅遊支票

到銀行兌換旅行支票時，要準備一些證明身分的文件來出示給銀行行員看。行員會與旅行支票發行的銀行聯絡，確定是否是真的票券之後就會換成現金給你。你也可以要求兌換成的鈔票是什麼票額，讓你之後消費時可以方便使用。

實境對話

A: I would like to cash a traveler's check, please.
我想要把旅行支票換成現金。

B: Yes, how much is the traveler's check?
好的，旅行支票是多少錢呢？

A: 300 dollars and I would like it in 20 dollar notes.
300 塊錢。我想要換成 20 塊錢的鈔票。

B: Do you have a passport for identification?
你有可以證明身分的護照嗎？

A: Yes, here is my passport and airline ticket.
有的，這是我的護照和機票。

B: Just a moment while we contact your bank, please.
請等一下讓我聯絡你的銀行。

B: It will only take about 5 minutes.
這大概只需要五分鐘。

A: Can you tell me the exchange rate and any other charges?
請問兌換的匯率和其他的收費是多少？

B: Yes, there is a 2% bank charge and this is the exchange rate.
銀行收費是百分之二，然後這個是兌換的匯率。

☝ 你可以聽懂／口說更多

01. 您能幫我把旅行支票換成現金嗎？
Could you cash this traveler's check?

02. 請把這些旅行支票換成現金。
Please cash these traveler's checks.

03. 我需要兌現一張旅行支票。
I need to cash a traveler's check.

04. 您想把所有旅行支票都兌換成歐元嗎？
Do you want to cash all the traveler's checks in Euro?

05. 我能在這兒兌現旅行支票嗎？
May I cash a traveler's check here?

06. 除了紙鈔之外，你可否給我些零錢？
Could you give me some small change besides notes?

07. 機場這裡有沒有兌換貨幣的地方？
Is there a money changer here at the airport?

08. 我遺失了旅行支票。可以申請補發嗎？
I've lost my traveler's checks. Can I have them reissued?

09. 我想要五張面額為二十英鎊的旅行支票。
I would like five traveler's checks of twenty pounds each.

10. 請幫我兌換這些旅行支票好嗎？
Would you cash these traveler's checks for me?

✍ 關鍵單字／片語

01. **traveler's check**	旅行支票
02. **identification**	身分
03. **bank**	銀行
04. **cash**	兌現
05. **just a moment**	稍等一下
06. **contact**	聯絡
07. **take**	花費、佔用
08. **beside**	除了
09. **each**	每一
10. **reissue**	補發

03 | 領錢

領錢時，可以從提款機領取。如金額過高時，提款機會拒絕付款。這時就要走一趟銀行，詢問銀行行員，來幫你作領款的手續。領款時，會需要填寫提款單。有時候行員會要求出示證件和提款卡來證明是否是本人，才會作給款的程序。

🖐 實境對話

A: I would like to withdraw money from my ATM account.
我想要從我的自動提款帳戶裡領錢。

B: How much would you like to withdraw?
你要領多少錢呢？

A: 5,000 dollars, please.
五千塊錢。

B: The limit on our ATM is only 2,000 dollars per day.
我們的自動提款機每天上限只有兩千塊錢。

A: Is it possible I can withdraw from the bank and not the ATM?
我可以從銀行提款而不是提款機提款嗎？

B: Yes, you will need to fill out this form with your bank details and home address.
可以，你將會需要把銀行明細和家裡住址填寫在這個表格。

A: Ok, I will fill out the form and come back to you in a few minutes.
好的，幾分鐘之內我就會填好這個表格，然後再交給你。

B: Very good. I will also need your ATM card.
很好，我也需要你的提款卡。

👆 你可以聽懂／口說更多

01. 您能告訴我自動提款機在哪兒嗎？
   Could you tell me where the ATM is?

02. 請您填寫提款單。
   Fill out a withdrawal form, please.

03. 我可以在什麼地方領錢？
   Where can I withdraw money?

04. 您介意跟我去自動提款機嗎？
   Would you mind coming with me to the ATM?

05. 我想取五百美元。
   I want to withdraw 500 dollars.

06. 為什麼不從銀行領錢呢？
   Why not withdraw money from the bank?

07. 您需要提款卡嗎？
   Will you need an ATM card?

08. 您願意的話可以在那裡領些錢。
   You can withdraw some money there if you like.

09. 我能用這張信用卡領錢嗎？
   Can I withdraw cash with this credit card?

10. 你可以隨時領錢。
   You can withdraw money at any time.

✍ 關鍵單字／片語

01. **withdraw money**	提款、領錢
02. **Automatic Teller Machine**	（＝ATM）自動提款機
03. **ATM card**	提款卡
04. **daily ATM withdrawal limit**	每日提款限額
05. **per day**	每一天
06. **withdrawal form**	提款單
07. **Would you mind...?**	你介意……？
08. **signature**	簽名
09. **seal**	印章
10. **at any time**	隨時

04 | 轉帳

轉帳時，除了提款機轉帳之外，可以在銀行裡請行員幫你作轉帳的服務，給家人、朋友，或者當作貨款，購買物品。行員會請你填寫表格和收取匯款轉帳的手續費用；轉帳到國外時，由於匯率不同和各銀行收取費用不同，轉出的費用到達時會有匯差的狀況。

實境對話

A: I would like to transfer money to my family in my home country.
我想要把錢匯到我的家鄉給我的家人。

B: How much would you like to transfer?
你想要匯多少錢呢？

A: 400 dollars.
四百塊錢。

B: Would you like the money exchanged to your home country currency?
你想要將錢轉換成你家鄉的幣值嗎？

A: No, thank you. Dollars are fine.
不用，美元就可以了。

A: Can you tell me your charge for the money transfer?
可以告訴我匯錢要收費多少嗎？

B: We charge 2% and it also depends on the currency exchange in your country.
我們會收取款項的百分之二，然後會視你家鄉的匯率轉換來收費。

A: Ok, that's fine.
好的，那可以。

👆你可以聽懂／口說更多

01. 我要轉帳。
I would like to transfer from my account.

02. 您可以把錢轉到另外一個帳戶上。
You can transfer money to another account.

03. 轉帳前，請在虛線上簽名。
Before you transfer from your account, sign on the dotted line.

04. 這台自動提款機有轉帳功能嗎？
Does the ATM have a transfer function?

05. 為什麼不把錢轉到另一個帳戶上？
Why not transfer money to another account?

06. 你們收轉帳手續費嗎？
Do you charge for transfer?

07. 請問跨行轉帳的手續費是多少？
How much for the inter-bank transfer?

08. 恐怕這裡不能為您轉帳。
I am afraid that you can not transfer here.

09. 我要怎樣把錢轉到另一個帳戶上？
How can I transfer money to another account?

10. 你們有跨行轉帳的服務嗎？
Do you have an inter-bank transfer service?

✍ 關鍵單字／片語

01. **money transfer**	轉帳
02. **home country**	家鄉
03. **normally**	通常
04. **dotted line**	虛線
05. **account**	戶頭、帳戶
06. **inter-bank transfer**	跨行轉帳
07. **intra-bank transfer**	本行轉帳
08. **non-designated account**	非約定帳戶
09. **designated account**	約定帳戶
10. **password**	密碼

05 | 餘額查詢

查詢銀行帳戶支出，除了可以利用提款機查詢之外，也可以親自到銀行裡問行員詳情。在對於帳戶餘額有疑問時，可以詢問行員款項支出的問題，他們可以釐清我們對於帳戶餘額的疑問。詢問清楚之後，大概就會對自己的支出有概念，花錢時就會多加小心了。

🗨 實境對話

A: I would like to check my bank balance, please.
我想要查我的存款餘額。

B: Yes. Can I have your full name and bank account number?
好的。請給我你的全名和銀行帳戶號碼。

A: Yes, here is my name and this is my bank account number.
好的。這是我的名字和我的銀行帳戶號碼。

B: Your bank account is in debit and this is the amount.
你的銀行帳戶現在有欠款，然後這是金額。

A: It seems there are charges on my account. What are these for?
看起來似乎我的帳戶有被索費。請問是什麼費用？

B: As you are in debit, you are being charged interest.
因為你帳戶有欠款，所以你有被收取利息費用。

A: I would like to bring my balance back up to credit and pay the bank charges.
我想要繳付欠款和被收取的費用。

👆 你可以聽懂／口說更多

01. 你能告訴我餘額還有多少？
Could you tell me my balance?

02. 您在本行的帳戶餘額是一萬元。
Your balance at the bank is 10,000 dollars.

03. 請稍等，我查一下。
Hold on, please. I will check for you.

04. 那我卡裡的餘額是多少呢？
What about the balance on my card?

05. 請幫忙查一下我的帳戶餘額好嗎？
Would you please check my balance?

06. 請出示您的身份證。
Please show me your ID.

07. 可以印一份帳戶明細表讓我自己查看嗎？
May I have a print-out of my bank statement so that I can check it on my own?

08. 請先幫我查一下餘額。
Please check my balance first.

09. 我想查帳戶餘額。
I would like to check my balance.

10. 讓我為您查一下吧。
Let me check it for you.

✍ 關鍵單字／片語

01. **balance**	餘額
02. **bank account number**	銀行帳號
03. **statement**	文件資料
04. **up to date**	最新的
05. **print**	列印
06. **hold on**	等一下
07. **ID card**	身份證
08. **later**	晚點
09. **debit**	把……記入借方
10. **credit**	把……記入貸方

Chapter

10

郵務篇

Chapter 10 音檔雲端連結

因各家手機系統不同，若無法直接掃描，
仍可以至以下電腦雲端連結下載收聽。
（https://tinyurl.com/24353fhm）

01 | 郵費諮詢

寄各種郵件，會有不同的收費。如果要知道郵費如何計算，可以到當地的郵局或上網查詢。有時候可以得到郵局附贈的小冊子，裡面有根據重量和寄往的地點來計算的郵費表。照著郵費表，大致上就可以了解，要攜帶多少錢來付郵費了。

🗣 實境對話

A: Do you have a list of the rates?
你們有郵資費率表嗎？

B: Yes, here is a free booklet of our rates, sending local and worldwide.
有，這是我們免費的郵資費小冊子，寄往當地或全世界的。

A: Ok, thank you. Is tax included on postage in this book?
好的，謝謝你。這本小冊子裡的郵費有含稅嗎？

B: Yes, tax rates are on the last page.
有的，稅率是在最後一頁。

A: Is it better value to buy a book of stamps rather than buy single stamps?
買一整本郵票還是單買一張郵票比較划算？

B: Yes, a book of stamps is better value, you will save 5%.
買一整本郵票會比較划算，你會省 5%。

A: Can I also buy airmail stamps?
我也可以買航空郵票嗎？

B: Yes, but they are not included in the book of stamps.
可以，但那並不包含在整本郵票裡。

👆你可以聽懂／口說更多

01. 請問郵寄印刷品的郵資是多少？
What is the rate for sending printed material?

02. 一封航空信的郵資是五十美分。
The postage for airmail is 50 cents.

03. 這些寄往香港的信的郵資是多少？
What is the postage for these letters to Hong Kong?

04. 明信片的郵資是多少？
What's the postage for a postcard?

05. 請問您有沒有郵資價目表？
Have you got a schedule of postal charges?

06. 寄往倫敦的航空信要多少郵費？
How much is the postage for an airmail letter to London?

07. 這封信的郵費是多少？
What's the postage for this letter?

08. 請把信放在那邊的秤上。
Please put the letter on the scale there.

09. 價格包括郵資在內。
The price includes postage.

10. 郵費也太高了吧！
The postage is too high!

✍️ 關鍵單字／片語

01. **stamp**	郵票
02. **postage**	郵資
03. **post office**	郵局
04. **weight**	重量
05. **send a letter**	寄信
06. **rate**	費用、費率
07. **by sea**	海運
08. **by air**	空運
09. **printed papers**	印刷品
10. **scale**	磅秤

02 | 寄信

有寄信方面的問題，可以到當地的郵局詢問。詳問櫃檯的服務人員，可以知道寫信封、貼郵票的格式，和一些你不了解的郵務問題，在詢問清楚之後，再把信寄出去。格式和郵資都無誤之後，就不用擔心會有被退回來的可能了。

實境對話

A: I need to mail a letter to the United States. Do I need to go to the post office?
我想要寄封信到美國。我需要到郵局寄嗎？

B: You can post a letter from your local mailbox or you can go to the post office too.
你可以投到當地的郵筒。但如果你喜歡，你可以到郵局寄。

A: Will my letter get to the United States faster if I go to the post office?
如果我到郵局寄的話，信會比較快到美國嗎？

B: Yes, because your letter will go directly to the sorting office from the post office.
有的。因為你的信將直接從郵局送到郵件分檢處。

A: Are there different mailboxes for different countries?
寄到不同的國家，是用不同的郵筒嗎？

B: Yes, there is one for local and one for worldwide.
是的。有一個郵筒是寄往本地的，有一個是寄往全世界的。

A: When is the post collected from the mailboxes?
郵差什麼時候會來收郵筒的信？

B: Twice a day. 8 a.m. and 6 p.m..
一天兩次，早上 8 點和下午 6 點。

👆 你可以聽懂／口說更多

01. 你要自己去郵局寄信嗎？
Are you going to post the letter by yourself?

02. 你打算把信寄到哪？
Where are you sending your letter?

03. 我想把這封信寄到臺灣去。
I would like to send this letter to Taiwan.

04. 你給你媽媽寄信了嗎？
Have you sent a letter to your mother?

05. 請在信封上寫上詳細地址。
Please write down the complete address on the envelope.

06. 往紐約寄信需要多長時間？
How long does it take for a letter to get to New York?

07. 寄信最快的方式就是寄限時快遞。
Express mail is the fastest way to send a letter.

08. 別忘了替我把信寄了。
Don't forget to post my letters for me.

09. 我們可以通過郵局寄信。
We can post letters at a post office.

10. 很抱歉忘了給你寄信。
I am sorry I forgot to post your letter.

✍ 關鍵單字／片語

01. **express mail**	限時快遞
02. **registered mail**	掛號信
03. **envelope**	信封
04. **letter**	信
05. **zip code**	郵遞區號
06. **mail carrier**	郵差
07. **surface mail**	平信
08. **air mail**	航空郵件
09. **postmark**	郵戳
10. **worldwide**	遍及全世界的

03 | 寄明信片

寄明信片時，要把收信地址寫清楚。由於明信片都是小小一張，所以很容易把收信地址和寄信地址寫得太靠近，而容易造成退回的可能。用防水的筆寫，如果怕寄信過程明信片沾污，想點辦法保護好明信片，也是個很好的主意。

實境對話

A: Is mailing a postcard the same cost as sending a letter?
寄明信片和寄信是一樣的價錢嗎？

B: Yes, it is the same rate for both.
是的，兩者的郵費是同樣的。

A: Do I need to put the postcard in an envelope as I don't want it to get damaged?
我是不是需要把明信片放在信封裡以免它被破壞？

B: That is your choice, but most postcards arrive undamaged.
那是你的選擇，但是大部分的明信片都是安全到達。

A: Where should I stick the stamp on the postcard?
我應該要把郵票貼在明信片的哪裡？

B: Just above the address on the top right corner.
只要貼在住址上面，右上方的角落。

A: Should I write in pen or marker?
我要用原子筆還是用簽字筆寫呢？

B: Pen is better than marker as it is waterproof.
原子筆比簽字筆好，因為它是防水的。

A: May I borrow your pen?
可以跟你借原子筆嗎？

👆 你可以聽懂／口說更多

01. 你收到我的明信片了嗎？
Have you received my postcard?

02. 你能寄張明信片給我嗎？
Could you send me a postcard?

03. 寄一張明信片到香港要多少錢？
How much would a postcard to Hong Kong cost?

04. 我會時常給你寄張明信片。
I will send you postcards every now and then.

05. 你收到我的明信片了嗎？
Have you received my postcard?

06. 你們有明信片嗎？
Do you have postcards?

07. 無論我在哪都會寄明信片給你。
I will send a postcard to you wherever I am.

08. 為什麼不給你爸爸寄一張明信片呢？
Why don't you send a postcard to your father?

09. 打擾了，請問在哪可以寄明信片？
Excuse me. Where could I send a postcard?

10. 你到東京要給我寄張明信片哦。
Please send me a postcard when you arrive Tokyo.

✍ 關鍵單字／片語

01. **postcard**	明信片
02. **scenery postcard**	風景明信片
03. **postal**	明信片
04. **Postal Service**	郵政業務
05. **mailbox**	郵筒
06. **mail**	寄送
07. **stick**	貼
08. **every now and then**	時常、有時
09. **safely**	安全地
10. **write in pen**	用筆寫

04 | 寄包裹

如果在旅途中，看到當地漂亮的明信片、信紙或是一些精美的紀念品，不妨將它們寄給你的親朋好友吧！

📢 實境對話

A: I want to mail this package.
我想寄這個包裹。

B: Put it on the scale. Where are you mailing to?
請放到磅秤上，要寄到哪裡？

A: Taiwan.
台灣。

B: Do you want to mail it by air or sea?
要寄航空還是海運？

A: What's the difference in price?
請問價錢差多少？

B: 30 dollars by air, 12 dollars by sea.
航空 30 元，海運 12 元。

A: How long will it take by air?
航空的話大概多久會送達？

B: About 10 days.
大概 10 天左右。

A: Then I will send it by air, thank you.
那就航空好了，謝謝！

B: Please fill out this form, and what's in your package? Anything fragile?
請填一下這張表格，你的包裹裡面是什麼？有易碎物品嗎？

A: No, just some souvenirs.
沒有，只是一些紀念品。

👆 你可以聽懂／口說更多

01. 請問這附近有郵局嗎？
   Is there a post office near by?

02. 請問寄這封信到英國要多少錢？
   How much is it to mail this letter to England?

03. 請問幾天會寄達呢？
   How many days will it take?

04. 請給我 3 張 5 分的郵票。
   Please give me three five-cent stamps.

05. 我想買你們的紀念郵票。
   I want to buy your memorial stamps.

06. 每一種給我一套。
   Please give me one of each set.

07. 我想買一份航空郵件。
   I want to buy an airmail envelope.

08. 我要寄掛號。
   I want to send a registered mail.

09. 包裹裡面沒有信件，只是幾本雜誌。
   There are no letters in the package, just some magazines.

10. 請問德克薩斯州的郵遞區號是多少？
   What's Texas's postal code?

✎ 關鍵單字／片語

01. **package**	包裹
02. **express delivery**	限時專送
03. **fragile**	易碎、脆弱的
04. **memorial stamp**	紀念郵票
05. **set**	一套、一組
06. **near by**	附近
07. **magazine**	雜誌
08. **There is / are**	有……
09. **postal code**	郵政編碼
10. **postal order**	郵政匯票

05 | 領取包裹

每個人在期待包裹到來時，總有可能錯失領取包裹的時候，郵差都會留下訊息，表示曾經有來過。如要領取，再約好時間，會再次寄送。錯過了再次寄送的時間，就必須要拿著領取單，到分局或指定郵局領取了。

實境對話

A: I have been expecting a parcel at my home but it did not arrive.
我一直在家等待一個包裹到來，但它還沒有來。

B: The parcel was sent to your home but there was no one to receive it.
包裹之前有送到你家，但那時候並沒有人簽收。

A: So how do I receive my parcel now?
所以我現在要怎麼拿到我的包裹呢？

B: The postman must left a delivery note.
郵差應該有留下一張遞送過的紙條。

A: Yes, here it is. It has a number on it. What does this mean?
有的，在這邊。這邊有個號碼，它是什麼意思？

B: It is the number to track your parcel.
這個是追蹤你包裹的號碼。

A: So how do I collect my parcel?
所以我要如何知道我的包裹現在在哪？

B: You must call the head office, and give them the tracking number to arrange a new delivery time.
你必須打電話給總辦公室，然後給他們追蹤號碼，再來安排一個新的遞送時間。

你可以聽懂／口說更多

01. 我想取從北京寄來的包裹。
I want to pick up my package from Beijing.

02. 我應該從哪裡取包裹？
Where should I get my package?

03. 我是來取包裹的。
I am here to pick up my package.

04. 我是在這裡領包裹嗎？
Do I collect parcels here?

05. 能否告訴我到哪裡領取包裹？
Can you tell me where I can pick up my package?

06. 我們到郵局去取包裹吧。
Let's go pick up the package at the post office.

07. 這是我的包裹單。
Here is my package slip.

08. 這裡是取包裹的地方嗎？
Is this where I get my parcels?

09. 我去取包裹時要帶什麼呢？
What should I bring with me when I collect my parcel?

10. 請出示您的包裹單好嗎？
Would you please show me your package slip?

關鍵單字／片語

01. **expect**	等待	
02. **parcel**	包裹	
03. **receive**	收到	
04. **tracking number**	追蹤號碼	
05. **arrange**	安排	
06. **collect**	領取信件或包裹	
07. **proof**	證明	
08. **locate**	找出……的下落	
09. **postman**	郵差	
10. **note**	紙條	

Chapter

11

緊急狀況篇

Chapter 11 音檔雲端連結

因各家手機系統不同，若無法直接掃描，
仍可以至以下電腦雲端連結下載收聽。
（https://tinyurl.com/2p9e4nhw）

01 | 退稅

如果是在百貨公司或普通商店購買物品，必須在同一間店一次購物達規定的消費金額之後才能退稅，你只要留下店的發票或是收據（領收書）就能辦理退稅手續。另外如果你是到屬於「歐洲聯盟國家」旅行時，不必一國一國申請退稅，等到要離開歐盟國家的最後一站時，再一起申請辦理就好。

🎧 實境對話

A: I am a tourist.
我是觀光客。

A: I have a passport to prove.
我有護照可以證明。

A: I don't have to pay tax when I shop, do I ?
購物不需要付稅金吧？

B: No, you don't.
不，不用付。

A: Is there a tax refund on my new stereo?
我剛剛買的音響可以退稅嗎？

B: Of course.
當然可以。

A: Then please give me a tax rebate form.
那請你給我一張退稅單。

B: Here you are.
給你。

A: Where can I get my tax refund?
請問我可以在哪裡辦退稅呢？

B: You should go to the tax refund counter.
你應該去退稅櫃檯。

👆 你可以聽懂/口說更多

01. 我另外要準備什麼文件呢？
What other documents do I need?

02. 需要蓋章嗎？
Does it need to be stamped?

03. 我該怎麼申請退稅呢？
How do I apply for my tax refund?

04. 請開一張退稅單給我。
Please give me a tax rebate form.

05. 我必須在出境時到機場拿給海關蓋章，然後再寄給你們嗎？
Do I have to have the Customs stamped when I leave, and then mail it back to you?

06. 你是退現金給我還是支票呢？
Do you refund me with cash or check?

07. 我能夠選擇用什麼方式收到稅款嗎？
Can I choose other ways to receive my refund?

08. 你會把支票寄到台灣給我嗎？
Will you mail the check to Taiwan for me?

09. 寄的時間要花多久呢？
How long will the mailing take?

10. 能直接存到我的信用卡帳戶嗎？
Can you deposit it to my credit card account?

✏️ 關鍵單字/片語

01. **tax rebate form**	退稅單
02. **tax refund**	退稅
03. **tax refund counter**	退稅櫃台
04. **tourist**	觀光客
05. **tax free**	免稅
06. **document**	文件
07. **stamp**	蓋章、印章
08. **choose**	選擇
09. **mailing**	郵寄、郵件
10. **How long...?**	多久……？

02 | 遺失物品

如果在國外不小心遺失東西，千萬不要慌張，記得先去警察局或者相關單位辦理登記，那些重要證件、信用卡，也要在第一時間內掛失，不管遺失的東西能不能夠找回來，都要將你的損失降到最低！

實境對話

A: Oh my gosh! Where's my cell phone? It's gone!
噢，天啊！我的手機呢？手機不見了！

B: When did you last see it?
你最後看到它是什麼時候？

A: I think I left it on a bus.
我好像把它忘在公車上了。

A: The bus was No.902.
是 902 號公車。

A: I got off at Second Street around 5:30.
我大約五點半的時候在第二街下車的。

A: I left my bag somewhere in your store. Can you help me look for it?
我把包包放在你們店裡的某個地方。你可以幫我找一下嗎？

B: Sure. What does it look like?
當然，包包是什麼樣子的？

A: It's a red nylon bag.
是一個紅色的尼龍包包。

A: And there's my name tag on it.
上面有我的姓名標籤。

A: My wallet and DC are inside of it.
我的錢包和數位相機都在裡面。

👆 你可以聽懂／口說更多

01. 失物招領處在哪裡？
Where is the "Lost and Found"?

02. 我到處找就是沒有，一定是被偷了。
I have looked everywhere and I can't find it. It must have been stolen.

03. 需要辦什麼手續嗎？
Are there any procedures that I need to go through?

04. 我想申請遺失護照證明給我的保險公司。
I want to apply for a certificate of lost passport for my insurance company.

05. 有沒有人撿到我的相機呢？
Has anyone found my camera?

06. 糟了！我的手錶不見了！
Oh no! I lost my watch!

07. 大家可以幫我找一下嗎？
Can everybody help me look for it?

08. 我的行李不見了，怎麼辦？
My luggage is gone! What should I do?

09. 我剛剛買的東西不是寄放在這裡嗎？
Didn't I put the things I just bought here?

10. 怎麼不見了？
Why are they gone?

✍ 關鍵單字／片語

01. **my gosh / my God**	我的天啊
02. **gone / missing**	不見、遺失
03. **lost and found**	失物招領處
04. **insurance company**	保險公司
05. **Embassy of the R.O.C.(Taiwan)**	台灣駐外大使館
06. **nylon bag**	尼龍包包
07. **inside of**	在……裡面
08. **certificate of lost passport**	護照遺失證明
09. **look for**	尋找
10. **certificate**	證件、證照

03 | 迷路

當迷路時，可以找當地人幫忙指引到你熟悉的路線，讓你可以從有印象的路線，再原路走到你熟悉的路；或者告訴你當地的地標，讓你了解大致上的方位。如果再不能夠了解的話，就請人把你從你迷路的地點，帶到你和朋友可以相遇的地方，叫朋友來接你囉。

實境對話

A: I am new to this area and I think I am lost. Can you help me, please?
我剛來到這個區域，而我想我迷路了。請問可以幫我忙嗎？

B: Yes, what direction did you come from and where do you want to go?
好的，你是從哪個方向過來的？然後你要去哪裡？

A: I just started walking from my home but did not remember where I have been. Do you have a telephone I can use and I can call someone to pick me up?
我只是從我家走出來，但是我並沒有記下來我走到哪裡。你有電話讓我打給人來接我嗎？

B: Yes, we have a telephone in the house. You may call your friend.
有的，我們房子裡有電話。你可以打給你的朋友。

A: Can I have your address so I can tell my friend where to find me?
可以給我你的住址，讓我可以告訴我朋友到哪裡找我嗎？

B: Yes, here are the directions.
有的，這裡是到這的方向。

🖐 你可以聽懂╱口說更多

01. 可不可以告訴我這是哪裡？
Could you tell me where I am?

02. 恐怕我是迷路了。
I am afraid that I've lost my way.

03. 我在這座陌生的城市迷路了。
I got lost in the strange city.

04. 請告訴我怎樣可以找到最近的公車站？
Would you please tell me how to find the nearest bus station?

05. 這是我第一次來這裡。
It's the first time for me to come here.

06. 打擾了，請問這裡是東城區嗎？
Excuse me, is this the East-city District?

07. 要不是遇到你，我可能在山中迷路了。
I might have got lost in the mountains if I didn't meet you.

08. 不，這不是你要找的地方。
No, this is not where you are looking for.

09. 我找不到我住的那家賓館了。
I cannot find the hotel that I am starying.

10. 請告訴我去博物館的路好嗎？
Could you show me the way to the museum?

✎ 關鍵單字╱片語

01. **get lost**	迷路
02. **show me the way**	指引我方向
03. **take notes**	做筆記
04. **pick up**	接送
05. **find the way**	找到路
06. **police station**	警察局
07. **umbrella**	雨傘
08. **return**	歸還
09. **first time**	第一次
10. **area / district**	地區

04 | 汽車拋錨

車子拋錨時，有很多種原因會造成。如果平常沒有注意保養，在路上都有可能會半路停駛，這樣子只能找人求救。尋求修車廠的幫忙，拖吊和修理時都會收費。有時候可能要花上大半天，車子才有可能再度回到你的手中行駛。

🖐 實境對話

A: My car just stopped. What do you think the problem is?
我的車子剛剛停住了，你覺得會是什麼問題呢？

B: There seems to be a fuel problem. Are you sure there is enough gas in the tank?
這些似乎是汽油問題。你確定油箱裡有足夠的汽油嗎？

A: Yes, I filled the tank about 30 minutes before it broke down. Is there anything else it could be?
是的，拋錨前 30 分鐘剛加了油。有可能是其他理由嗎？

B: Yes, it might be your fuel pump or dirt in the fuel line. I will need to tow it back to the garage to take a closer look.
有的，有可能是你的燃油泵或者是污垢卡在油線上。我必須把它拖到汽車修理廠才能夠更進一步的觀察。

A: Is there a charge for towing it back to the garage? And can you give me an estimate before you do anything?
拖車到修理廠要收錢嗎？還有修理前，可以先估價嗎？

B: Yes, there is a towing charge but it is unavoidable, otherwise I can't fix your car.
是的，拖車要收費，這是必要的。否則我不能修理你的車。

👆 你可以聽懂/口說更多

01. 汽車半路拋錨了。
The car's broken halfway.

02. 我的車在回家的路上壞了。
My car broke down on my way home.

03. 由於寒冷的天氣我的車壞了。
My car broke down because of the cold weather.

04. 我們得給修車廠打電話了。
We have to call the garage.

05. 我要把車送到車廠去修理。
I am going to have it repaired in a garage.

06. 我們前面的那部車拋錨了。
The car in front of me broke down.

07. 既然車壞了，我們就換搭公共汽車吧。
Since the car broke down, let's take a bus.

08. 我的車在十字路口拋錨了。
My car broke down at the crossroads.

09. 當汽車拋錨時，我們正行駛了一半的路程。
We were halfway there when the car broke down.

10. 我正在高速公路上駕車的時候，突然車拋錨了。
I was driving along the highway when my car broke down.

✎ 關鍵單字/片語

01. **breakdown**	拋錨
02. **mile**	英里
03. **halfway**	中途
04. **mechanic**	機械工、修理工
05. **engine**	引擎
06. **fuel / gas / gasoline**	汽油
07. **fuel line**	油線
08. **garage**	車庫
09. **repair**	修理
10. **highway**	高速公路

05 | 忘記加油

忘記加油時，上路到一半，車子就會自動停駛。這時候除了趕緊找加油站買油之外，就只能拖車到加油站加油了。趕緊到附近的加油站再買油，把油倒進油箱，車子才會繼續移動！在買油時，通常都要準備裝油的容器裝油，才能夠把油帶到車子，順利加油。

實境對話

A: My motorcycle is running out of gas. Can you direct me to the nearest gas station?
我的機車沒油了。請問可以指引我到最近的加油站嗎？

B: Yes, the nearest gas station is just around the corner.
好的，最近的加油站就在街角附近。

A: Do you know if they have containers to put the gas into as my motorcycle is very heavy to push there?
請問你知道他們有沒有容器可以讓我裝汽油，因為我的機車太重了，沒辦法推到那裡？

B: I'm not really sure as I don't drive so I never have to buy gas.
我不太確定，因為我不開車，所以我從來沒有在加油。

A: Would you mind staying here with my motorcycle and I will walk to the gas station to ask?
你介意和我的機車留在這裡，然後我可以走到加油站詢問？

B: Yes, sure. I can stay here or I can help you push your motorcycle there.
不介意。我可以留在這，或者幫忙你把機車推到那裡。

👆 你可以聽懂／口說更多

01. 我忘記給車加油了。
    I forgot to refuel the car.

02. 恐怕我們走不了了。
    I am afraid that we can't go any further.

03. 我們得找人幫忙了。
    We have to ask somebody for help.

04. 你在家沒有加油嗎？
    Didn't you fill up at home?

05. 我們還能走多遠？
    How long shall we go?

06. 我們去加點油吧。
    Let's go refuel the car.

07. 附近有加油站嗎？
    Is there any gas station nearby?

08. 這下麻煩了，我們沒有備用汽油。
    What a lot of bother. We have no spare oil.

09. 不幸的是，我忘記給車加油了。
    Unfortunately, I've forgotten to fill up the car with fuel.

10. 最近的加油站有多遠？
    How far is the nearest gas station?

✍ 關鍵單字／片語

01. **run out of gas**	沒油
02. **gas station**	加油站
03. **around the corner**	在附近
04. **motorcycle**	摩托車、機車
05. **refuel**	補給燃料
06. **refill**	再裝滿
07. **fill up**	加滿
08. **push**	推
09. **go further**	走更遠
10. **fuel tank**	油箱

06 | 錯過末班車

當沒趕上最後一班車時,除了改搭其他交通工具之外,若沒有其他方法的話,有可能就要留在車站,等待隔天早班車行駛。詢問站務員可否留在當地等待下一班車,他們應該常會遇到類似的情況,會給你大部分人常作的選擇,找個旅館留一夜,或車站長椅躺一下直到天亮。

🗣 實境對話

A: Could you tell me what time the last bus leaves, please?
請問最後一班巴士是幾點離開呢?

B: The last bus has left already. No buses now until the morning.
最後一班巴士已經離開了,到明天早上以前都沒有巴士。

A: Is there any other bus or train service, so I can get to my destination?
是否有其他巴士或者火車服務,讓我到達目的地呢?

B: You will have to walk to the city. There is a 24 hour bus service there.
你必須走到市區裡,在那裡有 24 小時的巴士服務。

A: That seems very far.
那好像是很遠。

A: Is it ok if I rest here in the bus shelter until the office opens?
我是否可以在這邊的巴士休息處休息,直到賣票處營業?

B: Yes, that's fine. Try not to make any noise, and keep the place clean.
嗯,沒關係。試著不要製造噪音,然後保持地方乾淨。

你可以聽懂／口說更多

01. 由於末班車已開走，我只得步行回家。
Since the last bus has gone, I had to walk home.

02. 快點，不然你就趕不上末班車了。
Hurry up, or else you'll miss the last bus.

03. 末班車已經開走了吧？
Has the last train already left?

04. 我們似乎得坐計程車回去了。
It seems we have to go back by taxi.

05. 你還能趕上末班車嗎？
Can you still catch the last bus?

06. 我們錯過了末班車！
We missed the last bus!

07. 末班車半小時前就開走了。
The last bus left half an hour ago.

08. 我忘記了時間，還錯過了最後一班車。
I forgot the time and missed the last bus.

09. 恐怕我已經趕不上回城裡的末班車了。
I am afraid I can't catch the last bus back to downtown.

10. 我錯過了最後一班回家的公車。
I missed the last bus home.

關鍵單字／片語

01. **already**	已經
02. **destination**	目的地
03. **make sure**	確保
04. **bus shelter**	候車亭
05. **make noise**	吵鬧、製造噪音
06. **keep clean**	保持乾淨
07. **hurry up**	趕快
08. **miss the bus**	錯過公車
09. **catch the bus**	趕上公車
10. **or else**	否則、要不然

07 | 搭錯車

搭錯車時，通常都會被建議在下一站下車。下車之後，詢問清楚，或看清楚標示，再搭上正確方向的車別，才能夠到達目的地。有時候你不了解時，可以在車上詢問查票員。他們會給你明智的建議，讓你在趕時間時，順利到達目的地。

🗣 實境對話

A: Is this train heading north? I was late for the train and just jumped on without checking.
這班火車是往北嗎？我趕火車來不及了，所以沒有確定之前就跳上來了。

B: No. This train is heading south. You might need to ask the ticket inspector how to get off this train so you can catch the train going north.
不是，這班火車是往南的。你也許需要跟查票員詢問如何下車，然後再搭往北的火車。

A: Excuse me, I got on the wrong train, I need to go north. Can you help me?
抱歉，我上錯車了。我必須要往北，可以幫我嗎？

C: Yes, you will have to get off this train at the next stop. Go to the ticket office and explain.
好的，你必須在下一站下車。去售票處解釋情況。

A: How far to the next stop? I will need to collect my luggage in the cargo area.
到下一站有多遠？我需要去行李區拿我的行李。

C: The next stop is in 15 minutes, I will meet you at the cargo door then.
下一站是 15 分鐘內到達，我會和你在行李區那裡見面。

你可以聽懂／口說更多

01. 你搭錯車了。
You have got on the wrong bus.

02. 突然間我發現我坐錯車了。
Suddenly, I found that I have taken the wrong bus.

03. 這是開往相反方向的火車。
This is going in the opposite direction.

04. 怎麼了？我搭錯車了嗎？
What's wrong? Am I on the wrong train?

05. 對不起，您上錯車了。
I am sorry, but you got on the wrong bus.

06. 對不起，我們不去美術館。
Sorry. We do not go to the art gallery.

07. 我搭錯車了，該怎麼辦呢？
I took the wrong bus. What should I do?

08. 你應該乘坐相反方向的車。
You should have taken the bus going in the opposite direction.

09. 順便問下，我該搭哪路車呢？
By the way, which bus should I take?

10. 我晚回家是因為搭錯車。
I came home late because I took the wrong bus.

關鍵單字／片語

01. **jump on**	跳上
02. **next stop**	下一站
03. **wrong**	錯誤的
04. **suddenly**	突然地
05. **get on the car**	上車
06. **get out of the car**	下車
07. **ticket inspector**	查票員
08. **fault**	錯誤
09. **find**	發現
10. **opposite direction**	反方向

08 | 找錯錢

TRACK
128

買東西付錢是理所當然的事，但如果老闆粗心或故意找錯錢，那就不應該啦！所以當別人找你錢時，尤其是拿大額面鈔給對方找時，一定要當面點清再離開，才不會造成不必要的損失！

實境對話

A: Here's your change.
這是找你的零錢。

B: Excuse me, Miss. This only costs twenty-eight dollars.
不好意思，小姐，這個東西才 28 元。

B: I gave you a hundred, and you should have given me back seventy-two dollars.
我拿 100 元給你，應該找我 72 元。

B: You shorted me twenty dollars.
你少找我 20 元。

A: Really? Let me check.
真的嗎？讓我確認一下。

A: One hundred minus twenty eight leaves seventy-two.
100 減掉 28 是 72。

A: I only gave you fifty.
我只給你 50 元。

A: Oh, I am sorry for the mistake.
噢！很抱歉我算錯了。

B: It's okay.
沒關係。

👆 你可以聽懂／口說更多

01. 這個東西加了稅金是多少錢？
How much is this after tax?

02. 你能夠算給我聽嗎？
Could you explain it to me?

03. 我已經付給你 30 元了。
I have already given you thirty dollars.

04. 你還沒找我錢！
You haven't given me the change yet.

05. 我買五個的折扣怎麼跟三個的一樣？
How come the discount for buying five is the same as buying three?

06. 你多找錢給我了。
You gave me too much change.

07. 算錯了嗎？
Is the amount wrong?

08. 我覺得你算錯了
I think the amount is wrong.

09. 我再重新算一次。
I will recount it.

10. 你找錯錢了。
You gave me the wrong amount of change.

✍ 關鍵單字／片語

01. **minus**	減	
02. **plus**	加	
03. **after tax**	稅後	
04. **before tax**	稅前	
05. **including tax**	含稅	
06. **excluding tax**	不含稅	
07. **amount**	總數、總額	
08. **change**	零錢	
09. **recount**	重新計算	
10. **count more money**	多找錢	

09 | 遺失小孩

出國旅遊時很可能遇到各種狀況，此時危機處理能力就很重要了。雖然在緊急的時候可能連中文都無法清楚描述狀況，但還是得先練習緊急狀況發生時要求救的英文說法，以備不時之需。

實境對話

A: What's wrong? You look so anxious.
怎麼了？妳看起來很焦急？

B: My son is missing!
我兒子不見了！

A: When and where did you last see him?
你最後是什麼時候在哪裡看到他的？

B: He got lost while we were shopping in the market.
他是在我們在市場裡買東西的時候不見的。

B: What should I do if he got kidnapped? I'm so worried.
如果他被綁架了怎麼辦？我好擔心。

A: Calm down. First of all, you should report to the police.
冷靜一點！首先，你應該去報警。

A: How's your boy look like?
你兒子長什麼樣子？

B: He is a six-year-old Chinese boy, about 3 feet tall.
他是個六歲的華裔男孩，大約三呎高。

B: And he is wearing a Yankee cap, black jacket and jeans.
他戴了一個洋基的棒球帽，穿黑色夾克和牛仔褲。

🖐 你可以聽懂／口說更多

01. 要去警察局報案嗎？
Should I report to the police?

02. 請問最近的警察局在哪裡？
Where is the nearest police station?

03. 他從市區回來的途中不見了。
He went missing on the way home from downtown.

04. 他長什麼樣子？
What does he look like?

05. 還有什麼其他特徵嗎？
Any other details?

06. 我的小孩被綁架了。
My kid is kidnapped.

07. 我的小孩走失了。
My child went missing.

08. 他的眼珠是黑色的，頭髮是咖啡色。
He has black eyes and brown hair.

09. 她穿著一件紅色洋裝，綁馬尾。
She is wearing a red dress with a ponytail.

10. 請冷靜下來。我們幫你會找到他的。
Please calm down. We'll help you find him.

✍ 關鍵單字／片語

01. **missing child**	走失的小孩
02. **police station**	警察局
03. **policeman**	警察
04. **report to the police**	報警
05. **characteristics**	特徵
06. **investigation**	調查
07. **look like**	看起來像……
08. **went missing**	走失
09. **kidnap**	綁架
10. **ponytail**	馬尾

10│信用卡相關問題

信用卡遺失時，立刻向發卡銀行掛失止付，以免遭到盜刷。如果不急著使用，可等到回國之後再申請補發；反之，急需使用的話，就告知發卡銀行你的所在地址，請他們盡速補發寄給你，一般補發天數約要一週，建議行程天數短的人回國再辦補發。

實境對話

A: The total is 2300 dollars.
總共是 2300 元。

B: Can I pay by credit card?
我可以刷卡嗎？

A: Yes, we accept credit card.
可以，我們接受信用卡。

B: Here you are.
給你。

A: Sorry, sir. This credit card is invalid.
先生不好意思，這張卡是無效的。

B: How come?
怎麼會？

A: Sir, your credit card limit has been reached.
先生，你的信用卡超過額度了。

B: Could you call my credit card company for the over limit authorization?
麻煩你幫我向發卡銀行要求超額的授權。

A: I'll do it.
好的。

👆 你可以聽懂／口說更多

01. 我的信用卡不是偽卡。
My credit card is not a fake.

02. 你可以打電話至發卡銀行查證。
You could telephone my credit card company and check.

03. 那我改用現金付款，不要用信用卡。
I will pay in cash instead of credit card.

04. 你的信用卡失效了。
Your credit card is invalid.

05. 你的卡刷不過。
Your credit card has been rejected.

06. 請幫我向發卡銀行要求超額的授權。
Please call my credit card company for the over limit authorization.

07. 你的信用卡卡號是多少？
What's your credit card number?

08. 你的信用卡期限是什麼時候？
What's the expiration date of your credit card?

09. 我刷爆卡了。
I maxed out my credit card.

10. 我要申請補發我的信用卡。
I want to apply for reissuing my credit card.

✍ 關鍵單字／片語

01. **invalid**	無效的、失效
02. **be rejected**	被拒絕
03. **credit card company**	發卡銀行
04. **credit limit**	信用卡額度
05. **authorization**	授權
06. **over limit**	超額
07. **credit card number**	信卡用卡號
08. **fake**	假貨、仿造品
09. **max out**	刷爆
10. **instead of**	代替

11 | 受傷

受傷時到醫院看醫生，常常都要排隊等候。在沒有辦法及時看到醫生時，可以詢問一些減輕症狀的方法。冰敷或者熱敷，在輪到看到醫生時，症狀會有減輕的可能。所以把握黃金時間，作一些小處理，就可以免於患處更嚴重的情況發生。

實境對話

A: I had a fall this morning and I think I hurt my hand. Can I have it examined?
我今天早上摔了一跤，手好像受傷了。可以幫我檢查嗎？

B: Yes. Can you tell me where you think your hand is hurt?
好的。請告訴我你覺得你的手哪裡受傷了？

A: Just below my fingers on my palm, but my fingers hurt too when I move them. Do you think my hand is broken?
大概在我手指頭下方的手掌。但當我動手指時，它們也會痛。你覺得我的手斷了嗎？

B: It is very difficult to tell without an X-ray. It might just be a sprain.
沒有照 X 光很難判定，也許只是扭到而已。

A: Do I have to make an appointment for an X-ray or can I have it done today?
我必須要預約照 X 光嗎？或者我今天就可以照得到呢？

B: You can have it done today but there is a queue. Take a seat, and I will tell you when it's your turn.
你今天可以照得到，但是有很多人排隊等候。你可以坐下來，我到時會跟你說輪到你了。

☝ 你可以聽懂／口說更多

01. 你有沒有受傷？
Have you hurt yourself?

02. 你是怎麼傷到自己的？
How did you hurt yourself?

03. 她的雙腿嚴重受傷。
She suffered serious injuries to the legs.

04. 我從馬上掉下來摔傷了腿。
I fell off the horse and hurt my legs.

05. 快叫救護車！
Call an ambulance right now!

06. 我聽說你受傷了是嗎？
I heard that you got hurt, right?

07. 他受傷了！快救他！
He is seriously injured! Come and help him now!

08. 艾倫多處受傷，其中七處骨折。
Aaron had several injuries, including seven fractures.

09. 我跌倒把腳踝扭傷了。
I fell and twisted my ankles.

10. 在這次事故中很多人受重傷。
Many people were seriously hurt in the accident.

✎ 關鍵單字／片語

01. **get hurt**	受傷
02. **injury**	受傷、損害
03. **harm**	受傷
04. **break a leg**	摔斷腿
05. **break an arm**	摔斷手
06. **fall down**	摔倒
07. **tumble over**	絆倒、摔倒
08. **examine**	檢查
09. **X-ray**	X 光
10. **twist the ankle**	扭傷腳踝

12 身體不舒服

大熱天如果沒有做好防曬，或者在空氣不流動的悶熱地方待著一段時間，之後就會出現中暑的症狀。到時候除了多休息，消暑降溫吹冷氣之外，就是喝大量的水，來把身體的體溫和脫水的情況平衡回來，讓症狀消失，才能夠恢復正常的作息。

實境對話

A: I was at the beach yesterday. It was very hot. I don't feel well today. I wonder if I have sunstroke or heat exhaustion.

我昨天在海邊，天氣很熱。我今天感覺不舒服，我在想我是否中暑了。

B: When did you start feeling sick?

你從什麼時候開始感到不舒服的？

A: Before I went to bed last night.

昨晚我要上床睡覺前，我開始感到不舒服。

B: OK. You must stay indoors away from the sun and drink lots of water.

好的，你必須待在室內，遠離陽光，然後喝很多水。

A: When can I go to the beach again as I love swimming? And can I drink other liquids?

因為我喜歡游泳，我什麼時候可以再到海邊呢？我可以喝其他的飲料嗎？

B: You can go to the beach as soon as you feel better but you must stay in the shade and drink liquids. And water is the best.

在你開始感覺好一點時，你就可以到海邊去。但是你必須待在陰影底下，任何的飲料都可以喝。喝水是最好的了。

👆 你可以聽懂／口說更多

01. 我感覺不舒服。
I am not feeling very well.

02. 我總是頭疼。
I am always having headaches.

03. 我晚上都睡不著。
I can't sleep at night.

04. 我頭痛得很厲害，而且我的鼻涕很多。
I have a bad headache and a running nose.

05. 我今天感覺非常不舒服。
I feel very sick today.

06. 我最近心臟很不舒服。
My heart has been very uncomfortable recently.

07. 你感到不舒服有多久了？
How long have you been sick?

08. 除了喉嚨痛，你有其他不舒服嗎？
Do you have any other discomfort besides sore throat?

09. 你仍感覺身體不舒服嗎？
Are you still feeling under the weather?

10. 我最近感到身體不適。
I feel a bit out of sorts recently.

✎ 關鍵單字／片語

01. **not feeing well**	感覺不舒服
02. **get sunstroke**	中暑
03. **heat exhaustion**	輕度中暑
04. **dehydration**	脱水
05. **sore throat**	喉嚨痛
06. **headache**	頭痛
07. **running nose**	流鼻水
08. **under the weather**	不舒服
09. **discomfort**	不舒服
10. **cough**	咳嗽

13 | 去藥房

在國外，水土不服可能造成你身體的不適，此時如果狀況輕微，可以就近到藥房買藥，只要說出你不舒服的情況，藥局的人就會拿適合的藥給你。如果你的狀況嚴重，就要趕快到醫院做仔細的診察和治療，千萬不要忍耐，以免耽誤病情。

實境對話

A: Hi, may I help you with anything?
嗨，有什麼可以幫你的嗎？

B: I'm not feeling well.
我覺得不舒服。

B: I have sore throat and running nose. I guess I've caught a cold.
我喉嚨痛，還一直流鼻水。我想我是感冒了。

A: Are you allergic to any drugs?
你有對什麼藥過敏嗎？

B: No, I don't think so.
沒有。

A: Okay, these are for the colds. Take two tablets after every meal.
好的，這些是治感冒的藥。三餐飯後吃兩片。

A: Take a good rest and get more sleep.
好好休息、多睡一點。

A: If you still don't feel better tomorrow, I suggest that you should go see a doctor.
如果明天還是沒有比較好，我建議你去看醫生。

B: I see. Thank you.
我知道了，謝謝。

👉 你可以聽懂／口說更多

01. 有沒有解酒藥？
Do you have anything to alleviate a hangover?

02. 我要買胃藥。
I want some pills for my stomachache.

03. 我有點咳嗽，請給我感冒藥。
I am coughing; could you give me some medicine for my cold?

04. 我想買生理期腹部不適的藥。
I want to buy some medicine for period pains.

05. 我要買止痛藥。
I want some painkillers.

06. 有沒有生理食鹽水？
Do you have any saline solution?

07. 我想買維他命 C，請問多少錢？
I want some vitamin C, how much is it?

08. 請問有綜合維他命嗎？
Do you have any multi-vitamin?

09. 我的手被玻璃割到了，可以幫我包紮傷口嗎？
My finger got cut by glass, could you bandage the wound?

10. 我要買眼藥水。
I want to buy eye drops.

✏️ 關鍵單字／片語

01. **cotton stick**	棉花棒
02. **cotton ball**	棉花球
03. **patent medicine**	成藥
04. **lint**	紗布
05. **disposable underwear**	（旅行用）紙內褲
06. **bandage**	繃帶
07. **Hydrogen Peroxide**	雙氧水
08. **iodine**	碘酒
09. **band-aid**	OK 蹦
10. **nail scissors**	指甲剪

14 | 去醫院

初到國外可能會遇上水土不服的問題。但多數人可能不知道，在歐美許多國家非健保身分就醫的話，看個小感冒可能就要七、八千元台幣，就醫門診費用相當可觀，希望出國旅行的各位不會有機會去醫院，但為了以防萬一，除了自行攜帶常用藥品，還是購買當地的醫療保險為佳。

🔊 實境對話

A: What brings you here today?
今天怎麼了？

B: I feel very sick
我覺得很不舒服。

A: Do you have any other symptoms?
有什麼其他症狀嗎？

B: I feel cold, and a running nose.
我覺得很冷，而且一直流鼻水。

A: How long has this been going on?
已經持續多久了？

B: 2 days.
2 天了。

A: You're having a cold.
你感冒了。

A: I'm writing you a prescription.
我開處方箋給你。

A: Are you allergic to any food or medicines?
你對任何食物或是藥物過敏嗎？。

B: No.
沒有。

👆 你可以聽懂／口說更多

01. 請帶我去這裡最近的醫院。
Please take me to the nearest hospital.

02. 我需要會講中文的醫生。
I need a doctor who can speak Chinese.

03. 我的肚子突然好痛，我要掛急診。
My stomach suddenly started to hurt; I need an emergency appointment.

04. 快幫我急救！
Please give me first aid!

05. 我需要住院嗎？
Do I need to stay in the hospital?

06. 我要動手術嗎？
Do I need an operation?

07. 可以告訴我病情嗎？
Could you tell me what's wrong with me?

08. 我鼻塞，喉嚨又痛。
I have a stuffy nose, and my throat hurts.

09. 我鼻水流不停，而且是黃色的。
My nose is running, and the liquid is yellow.

10. 我上吐下瀉。
I vomited and have diarrhea.

✎ 關鍵單字／片語

01. **hospital**	醫院
02. **nurse**	護士
03. **doctor**	醫生
04. **emergency room**	急診室
05. **cramp**	抽筋
06. **first aid**	急救、急救護理
07. **diarrhea**	腹瀉、拉肚子
08. **(surgical) operation**	開刀、手術
09. **surgery**	外科手術
10. **patient**	病人

15 | 車禍

發生車禍,一定要叫警察到現場紀錄、備案,就算要賠償,
只要你有保險,都可以向保險公司申請理賠,不過對於不熟
悉的地方還是要小心駕駛,最好要了解一些基本道路規則之
後再上路。

實境對話

A: Help! I am hurt!
救命!我受傷了。

A: Please take me to the hospital!
請送我去醫院!

B: Are you alright?
你還好嗎?

A: I think my arm has broken.
我的手好像斷了。

B: How can I help you now?
我現在該怎麼做呢?

A: Please don't touch it. Just call an ambulance!
請不要碰它,只要叫救護車就好!

A: I got hit by a car.
我被一輛車撞了。

B: Are you drunk?
你喝醉了嗎?

A: No, I'm not, and I wasn't speeding.
我沒有喝醉也沒有超速。

A: He was speeding and hit me from the back.
是他超速從後面撞上我。

👆 你可以聽懂／口說更多

01. 我發生車禍了，在 1 號高速公路上，請快派人處理。
I had a car accident on No. One high way, please send somebody to help me.

02. 請打這個電話聯絡我的阿姨。
Please call this number and contact my aunty.

03. 後座還有我的兒子，拜託請先救他。
My son is in the back seat, please help him first.

04. 我很痛，請先幫我止血。
I am in a lot of pain, please help me to stop the bleeding first.

05. 我的頭好暈，請讓我躺下。
I feel dizzy, please let me lie down first.

06. 我需要輪椅。
I need a wheel chair.

07. 他因為要超車，所以撞到我了。
He was trying to take over when he hit me.

08. 他闖紅燈，我來不及煞車。
He ran the red light and I didn't have time to stop my car.

09. 我沒注意到有車子過來。
I didn't notice a car was coming.

10. 我只是想走到對面，但這部摩托車卻突然衝向我。
I was crossing to the other side of the road, but this motorcycle suddenly came crashing into me.

✍ 關鍵單字／片語

01. **car accident**	車禍
02. **call an ambulance**	打電話叫救護車
03. **speeding**	超速
04. **run a red light**	闖紅燈
05. **pass**	超車
06. **hit / crash**	撞
07. **wheel chair**	輪椅
08. **brake / stop the car**	煞車
09. **faulty brakes**	煞車不靈
10. **traffic light**	紅綠燈

16 | 搶劫

如果遇到搶劫，最好的方法就是不要激怒歹徒，除非你有把握打得過他，不然最好乖乖地交出他想要的東西，等他逃走以後馬上報警，這樣警察會立刻在附近搜查可疑人物，或許可以馬上抓到，就算沒有抓到，破財事小，正所謂「金錢誠可貴，生命價更高」啊！

實境對話（緊急大聲呼救）

A: Hey! What do you want?
嘿！你要幹嘛？

A: What are you doing?
你在做什麼啊你？

A: No! No! Get away from me!
不要！不要！走開！

A: Help! The guy in red took my purse!
救命！那個穿紅衣服的男人搶了我的皮包！

A: Please catch that man for me!
請幫我抓住那個男人！

A: Get that guy for me!
抓住那個人！

A: Somebody help me!
來人啊！

A: Get the police for me!
叫警察！

A: Somebody robbed me!
搶劫！

A: Don't let him go!
不要讓他跑了！

☞ 你可以聽懂／口說更多

01. 殺人啊！
Someone got killed!

02. 當我掏出皮夾那一刻，他就馬上把它搶走了。
The minute I took out my purse, he robbed it!

03. 我來不及反應，速度實在太快了。
I couldn't react! Everything happened too fast!

04. 他騎車從背後搶走我的皮包。
He was riding a motorcycle and took my bag from the back.

05. 他拿刀威脅我。
He threatened me with a knife.

06. 他向我勒索 1000 元。
He extorted 1000 dollars from me.

07. 他假裝不小心撞到我，就順手拿走了我的錢包。
He pretended to bump into me accidentally, and then took my purse.

08. 公車上很擠，我的護照就是在那個時候被扒走的。
It was very crowded on the bus; my passport was stolen at that time.

09. 大家都是目擊者。
Everybody here is a witness.

10. 我是受害者。
I am a victim.

✍ 關鍵單字／片語

01. **robbery**	搶劫
02. **witness**	目擊者、證人
03. **victim**	受害人
04. **let go**	放開、放走
05. **threaten**	威脅
06. **extort**	敲詐、勒索
07. **strength**	力氣、力量
08. **fight back**	反擊
09. **valuable**	貴重物品、值錢的東西
10. **bump into**	無意中遇到

17 | 火災

如果在國外碰到這樣的天災，實在是很不幸的事，其實在慌亂的情況下，你只要記得說救命，應該就會有幫助，以下的例句如果有時間就看一下，當作學習英文，希望不會用得上才好。

實境對話

A: Help!
救命啊！

A: My room is on fire.
我住的房間著火了！

A: I am a tourist from Taiwan.
我是台灣來的觀光客。

B: Are you okay?
你還好嗎？

A: I am not seriously hurt. I am all right!
我只是輕傷，不要緊。

B: Is anyone still inside?
還有人在裡面嗎？

A: My friend is still in there, go and help him!
我朋友還在裡面，快去救他！

B: This is an emergency. Call the fire department now!
緊急事件，快叫消防隊！

A: My friend is seriously hurt, come and help him!
我朋友受重傷了，快點救他！

B: Call the ambulance now!
快叫救護車！

👆你可以聽懂／口說更多

01. 救命啊，失火了！
Help! Fire!

02. 小心！
Be careful!

03. 快按火災警報器！
Press the fire alarm now!

04. 快找人幫忙！
Find somebody to help him!

05. 這個人停止呼吸了，快急救！
This guy has stopped breathing! Come help!

06. 我被困在電梯裡，快來救救我！
I am stuck in the elevator, come and help me!

07. 我被這扇鐵門壓著，無法移動，快點移開它！
I am under this iron door. I can't move, move it quickly.

08. 門變形了，我打不開，快把門鋸開！
The door has deformed, I can't open it. Please saw it open!

09. 我在這裡，快點救我！
I am here! Come and save me!

10. 我身上著火了！快拿滅火器救我！
I caught on fire! Get the fire extinguisher and help me!

✍ 關鍵單字／片語

01. **fire alarm**	火災警報器
02. **fire extinguisher**	滅火器
03. **catch on fire**	著火
04. **fire company / department**	消防隊
05. **be stuck in**	被困在……
06. **fire hydrant**	消防栓、消防龍頭
07. **fire engine / truck**	消防車
08. **fire escape**	（室外的）逃生梯
09. **ladder truck**	雲梯車
10. **firefighter**	消防人員

18 | 水災

水災來臨前，就要做好準備，把沙包放在家門口擋水，或者把家人遷到安全的地方免於可能發生的危險，都是防止水災災禍降臨的方法。在大水還沒來臨之前，就要想好應對措施。詢問之前有經驗的人，也許可以得到一些想法，讓抗災時能夠有效和及時。

實境對話

A: It has been raining for many days. I wonder if the river is going to flood our town.
已經下了很多天的雨，我在想說河水是否會淹沒我們的小鎮。

B: Yes, the river level is very high. I think there will be a flood.
是的，河水水位很高，我想應該會淹水。

A: Do you think we should prepare sandbags outside our houses?
你想我們應該準備沙包放在房子外面嗎？

B: Yes, that would be a good idea as you never know when the flood will come.
是的，這是不錯的想法。因為你完全不會知道什麼時候水會淹過來。

A: Has the river overflowed before? I am new to this town.
之前河水有氾濫過嗎？我是新來這個小鎮的人。

B: Yes, many times. But there has been more rainfall this year than before.
有的，很多次。但是今年比往年有更多的降雨量。

👆 你可以聽懂／口說更多

01. 這樣大的洪水真是前所未有。
A flood of this sort is really unprecedented.

02. 我家的房子被洪水沖走了。
My house was washed away by the flood.

03. 萬一發生了水災，我們該怎麼辦呢？
If there were a flood, what should we do?

04. 你們沒有任何排水設施嗎？
Don't you have any drainage?

05. 今年過量的雨水已經造成了嚴重的水災。
Excessive rain this year has caused severe floods.

06. 聽說你那兒洪水氾濫呢！大家都沒有事吧？
I heard about the flood there. Is everybody okay?

07. 我們為災區捐款吧。
Let's donate money to the disaster area.

08. 這場洪水造成了很大的損失。
The flood caused a lot of damage.

09. 我很同情那些無家可歸的人。
I have much sympathy for those homeless people.

10. 水災使很多人無家可歸。
The flood makes many people homeless.

✍ 關鍵單字／片語

01. **flood**	水災
02. **heavy rain**	豪雨
03. **rainstorm / tempest**	暴風雨
04. **sandbag**	沙包
05. **rain cats and dogs**	下傾盆大雨
06. **rainfull**	降雨（量）
07. **river level**	河川水位
08. **unprecedented**	空前未有、史無前例
09. **wash away**	沖走
10. **drainage**	排水系統、下水道

19│地震

地震來時，除非是睡得很安穩，或者正在行走。大部分時，如果震度強，平常人都會感覺得到。在老舊的房子裡，有可能會有倒塌的現象，造成傷亡和損失。平常作好防震的準備，了解地震的特性和逃生的方向，就可以免於災禍降臨。

🔊 實境對話

A: I woke up this morning and the ground was shaking.
我今天早上醒來，地在搖晃。

B: There was an earthquake about 8 a.m. this morning.
今天早上八點時有地震。

A: Was there any damage or any casualties?
有任何損失和任何人受傷嗎？

B: No, the earthquake was at the southwest of the island. It's about a 100 miles from here so nothing to worry about.
沒有，地震是在島的西南方。大概離這裡一百英里遠，所以不需要擔心。

A: I just heard it on the radio, no one got hurt. Do you think the earthquake has finished or could there be another one?
我剛從廣播聽到沒有人受傷。你覺得地震已經結束了嗎？或者會有另外一次地震呢？

B: It's very difficult to tell. There might be aftershocks.
這很難說，可能會有餘震吧。

👆 你可以聽懂／口說更多

01. 我從未見過如此強大的地震，太可怕了。
   I have never seen such a powerful earthquake. It's scary.

02. 好幾萬人喪生了。
   Tens of thousands of people died.

03. 自然的力量真的是無窮大啊！
   What a giant act of God!

04. 經歷地震真是一件可怕的事。
   It is a horrible thing to experience an earthquake.

05. 這一地區經常發生地震。
   Earthquakes take place frequently in this area.

06. 這場地震造成了極大的損失。
   The earthquake caused great damage.

07. 你經歷過這樣厲害的地震嗎？
   Have you ever experienced such a serious earthquake?

08. 牆壁因地震而傾斜了。
   The wall fell because of the earthquake.

09. 地震發生的時候，你不能躲在桌子底下。
   You can't hide under the desk when an earthquake happens.

10. 幸運地是，這些房子在地震中沒有倒塌。
   Fortunately, these houses stayed up in the quake.

✍️ 關鍵單字／片語

01. **earthquake / quake**	地震
02. **magnitude**	震級、地震強度
03. **epicenter**	震央
04. **damage**	損害
05. **Pacific seismic zones**	環太平洋地震帶
06. **shake**	搖晃
07. **casualty**	傷亡
08. **destroy**	毀壞、破壞
09. **aftershock**	餘震
10. **sensible earthquake**	有感地震

20 | 風災

TRACK
140

當有颱風或颶風發生之前,最好注意家裡房子哪裡老舊或脆弱。在來得及前,把它們修補好。在風大的時候,可以擋得住風的強大力量,使住家的人和物都可以安全度過風災。如果沒有辦法住在家裡,就要趕緊搬往安全的地方,等待風災過去,再回到家裡整理家園。

實境對話

A: There was a hurricane announcement on TV. Is there anything to worry about?
電視上有颶風的通知,有必要擔心嗎?

B: Yes, you should prepare for the worst as hurricanes can change directions.
有的。你應該有最壞的打算,因為颶風會轉向。

A: I don't think my windows are safe. The force of the hurricane might break the windows. What should I do?
我覺得我的窗戶不太安全,颶風的力量可能會打破窗戶。我應該做什麼呢?

B: You can buy shutters at the local hardware shop. Take the measurements and they can give you the correct size.
你可以在五金行裡買到遮蔽物。把尺寸給他們,然後他們就會給你正確的尺寸。

A: It was said on the news the hurricane is very near here. I think there's not enough time.
新聞說颶風離這裡很近。我想我應該沒有時間了。

👆 你可以聽懂／口說更多

01. 好大的風啊！
The wind is so strong!

02. 外面正刮著大風呢。
There is a gale outside.

03. 狂風吹倒了許多莊稼。
The fierce wind blew down many crops.

04. 對臺灣危害最大的災害是風災。
Wind damage is the main disaster in Taiwan area.

05. 氣象預報員說明天要刮大風。
The weatherman said that there would be a strong wind tomorrow.

06. 大風橫掃全國。
Strong wind swept the whole country.

07. 我們應該同心協力抵禦風災。
We should stick together to keep out the wind damage.

08. 你明天最好不要外出了。
You'd better not go out tomorrow.

09. 防風林可以阻止風把泥土刮走。
Windbreak can stop the wind from blowing soil away.

10. 強風已經吹倒了好幾棵樹了。
The strong wind has blown down a number of trees.

✍ 關鍵單字／片語

01. **hurricane**	颶風
02. **super tornado**	超級龍捲風
03. **typhoon**	颱風
04. **mudslide / mudflows**	土石流
05. **torrential rain**	豪雨
06. **sea typhoon alert**	海上颱風警報
07. **land typhoon alert**	陸上颱風警報
08. **Central Weather Bureau**	中央氣象局
09. **announce**	發佈
10. **windbread**	防風林

語研力 E074

世界好好玩，旅遊英語帶著走：

最能滿足你一顆迫不及待準備出遊的心，帶著它，就出發！

作　　者	曾婷郁
顧　　問	曾文旭
出版總監	陳逸祺、耿文國
主　　編	陳蕙芳
文字校對	翁芯琍
封面設計	陳逸祺
內文排版	李依靜
法律顧問	北辰著作權事務所

印　　製	世和印製企業有限公司
初　　版	2022 年 11 月
初版二刷	2023 年 12 月
出　　版	凱信企業集團 - 凱信企業管理顧問有限公司
電　　話	（02）2773-6566
傳　　真	（02）2778-1033
地　　址	106 台北市大安區忠孝東路四段 218 之 4 號 12 樓
信　　箱	kaihsinbooks@gmail.com

定　　價	新台幣 349 元／港幣 116 元
產品內容	1 書

總 經 銷	采舍國際有限公司
地　　址	235 新北市中和區中山路二段 366 巷 10 號 3 樓
電　　話	（02）8245-8786
傳　　真	（02）8245-8718

國家圖書館出版品預行編目資料

世界好好玩，旅遊英語帶著走／曾婷郁著. -- 初
版. -- 臺北市：凱信企業集團凱信企業管理顧問
有限公司, 2022.11
　面；　公分
ISBN 978-626-7097-49-6(平裝)
1.CST: 英語 2.CST: 旅遊 3.CST: 會話

805.188　　　　　　　　　　　　　111016680

凱信企管

用對的方法充實自己，
讓人生變得更美好！

凱信企管

用對的方法充實自己，
讓人生變得更美好！

凱信企管

用對的方法充實自己，
讓人生變得更美好！

凱信企管

**用對的方法充實自己，
讓人生變得更美好！**